thumbprint

Based on the novella by

JOE
HILL

Written by Jason Ciaramella

Art by Vic Malhotra

Series Edits by Chris Ryall

Letters by Neil Uyetake and Robbie Robbins

Cover by Vic Malhotra

Collection Edits by Justin Eisinger and Alonzo Simón

Collection Design by Robbie Robbins

Special thanks to Mickey Choate.

IDW founded by Ted Adams, Alex Garner, Kris Oprisko, and Robbie Robbins

ISBN: 978-1-61377-748-0

16 15 14 13   1 2 3 4

Ted Adams, CEO & Publisher
Greg Goldstein, President & COO
Robbie Robbins, EVP/Sr. Graphic Artist
Chris Ryall, Chief Creative Officer/Editor-in-Chief
Matthew Ruzicka, CPA, Chief Financial Officer
Alan Payne, VP of Sales
Dirk Wood, VP of Marketing
Lorelei Bunjes, VP of Digital Services

Become our fan on Facebook **facebook.com/idwpublishing**
Follow us on Twitter **@idwpublishing**
Check us out on YouTube **youtube.com/idwpublishing**
www.IDWPUBLISHING.com

Originally published as THUMBPRINT issues #1–3 and KODIAK.

Based on the novella by

JOE HILL

For Katy and Dominic Ciaramella. Thanks for having me.
—Jason Ciaramella

To my wife, for putting up with me while I learned to draw
each and every panel in this book.
—Vic Malhotra

Chapter 1

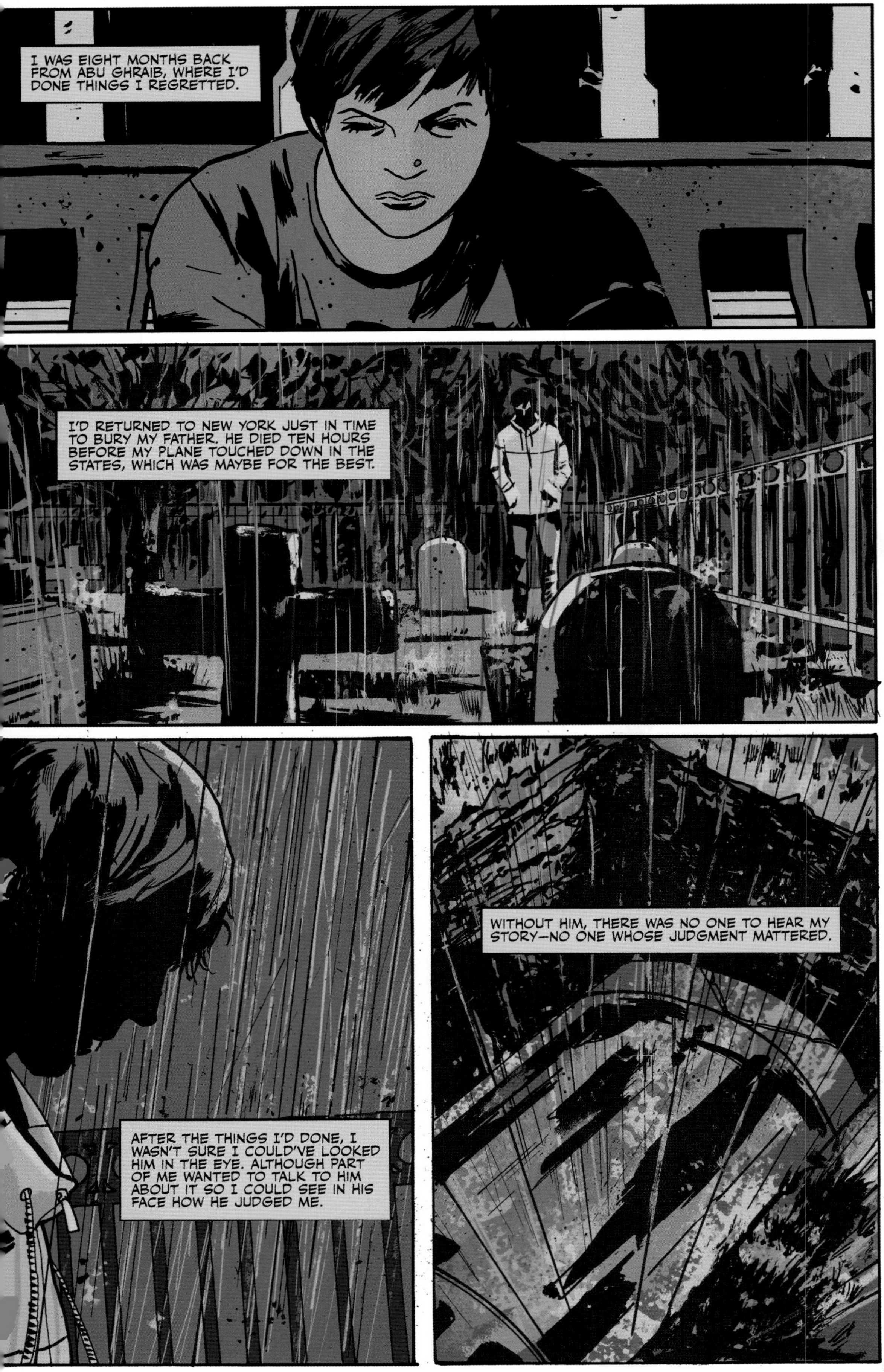
I WAS EIGHT MONTHS BACK FROM ABU GHRAIB, WHERE I'D DONE THINGS I REGRETTED.
I'D RETURNED TO NEW YORK JUST IN TIME TO BURY MY FATHER. HE DIED TEN HOURS BEFORE MY PLANE TOUCHED DOWN IN THE STATES, WHICH WAS MAYBE FOR THE BEST.
AFTER THE THINGS I'D DONE, I WASN'T SURE I COULD'VE LOOKED HIM IN THE EYE. ALTHOUGH PART OF ME WANTED TO TALK TO HIM ABOUT IT SO I COULD SEE IN HIS FACE HOW HE JUDGED ME.
WITHOUT HIM, THERE WAS NO ONE TO HEAR MY STORY—NO ONE WHOSE JUDGMENT MATTERED.

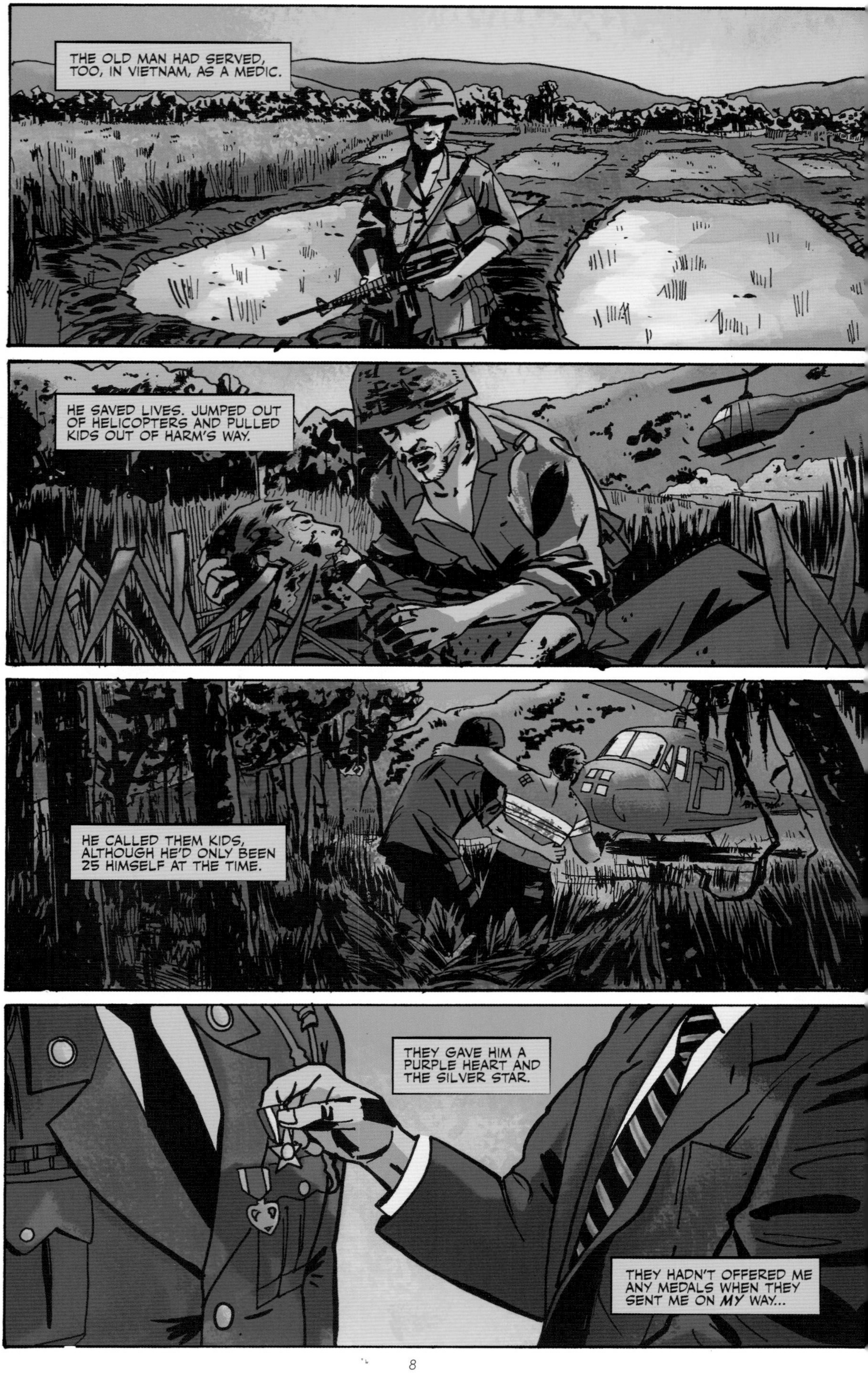
THE OLD MAN HAD SERVED, TOO, IN VIETNAM, AS A MEDIC.
HE SAVED LIVES. JUMPED OUT OF HELICOPTERS AND PULLED KIDS OUT OF HARM'S WAY.
HE CALLED THEM KIDS, ALTHOUGH HE'D ONLY BEEN 25 HIMSELF AT THE TIME.
THEY GAVE HIM A PURPLE HEART AND THE SILVER STAR.
THEY HADN'T OFFERED ME ANY MEDALS WHEN THEY SENT ME ON *MY* WAY...

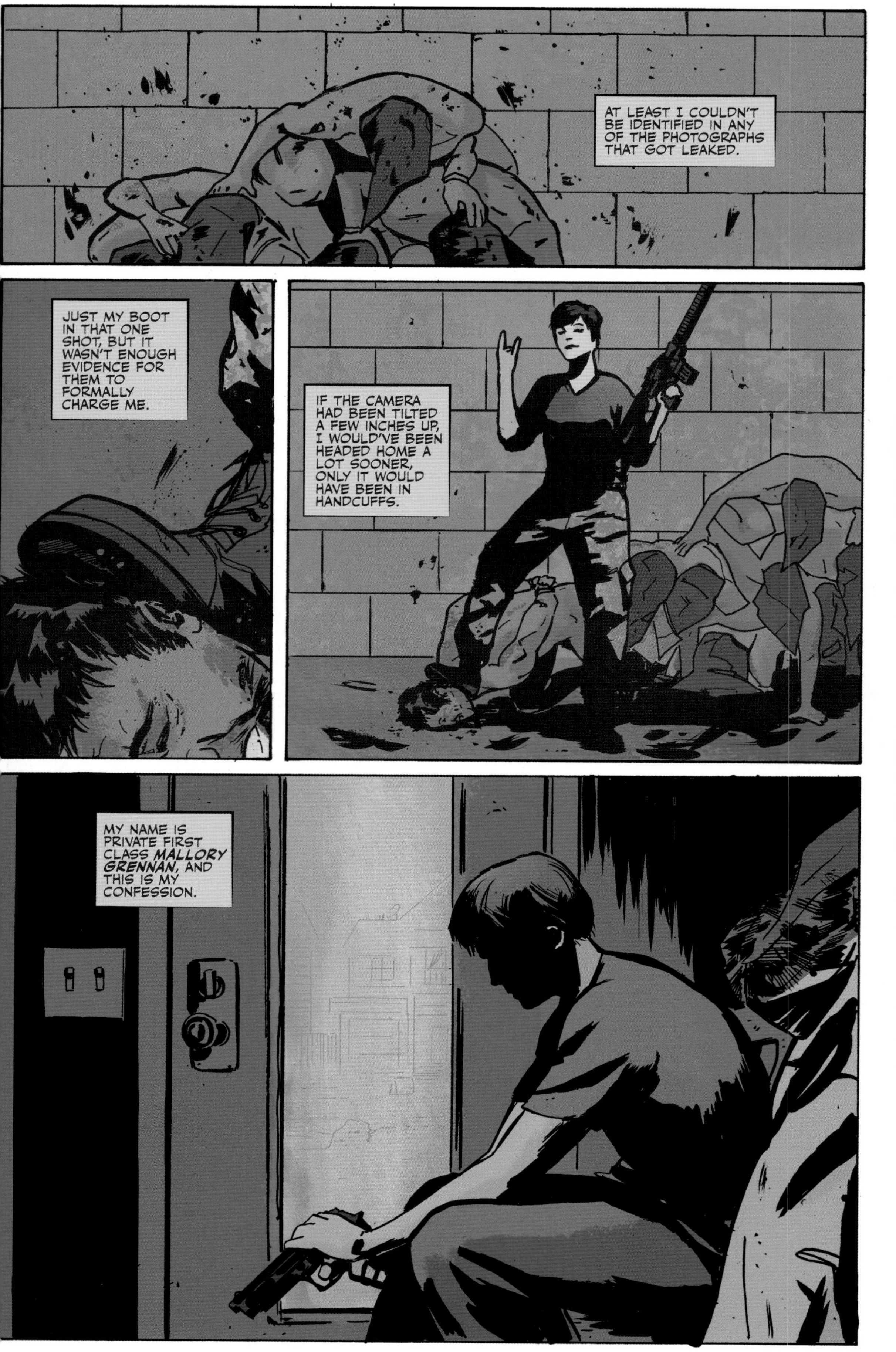
AT LEAST I COULDN'T BE IDENTIFIED IN ANY OF THE PHOTOGRAPHS THAT GOT LEAKED.
JUST MY BOOT IN THAT ONE SHOT, BUT IT WASN'T ENOUGH EVIDENCE FOR THEM TO FORMALLY CHARGE ME.
IF THE CAMERA HAD BEEN TILTED A FEW INCHES UP, I WOULD'VE BEEN HEADED HOME A LOT SOONER, ONLY IT WOULD HAVE BEEN IN HANDCUFFS.
MY NAME IS PRIVATE FIRST CLASS *MALLORY GRENNAN*, AND THIS IS MY CONFESSION.

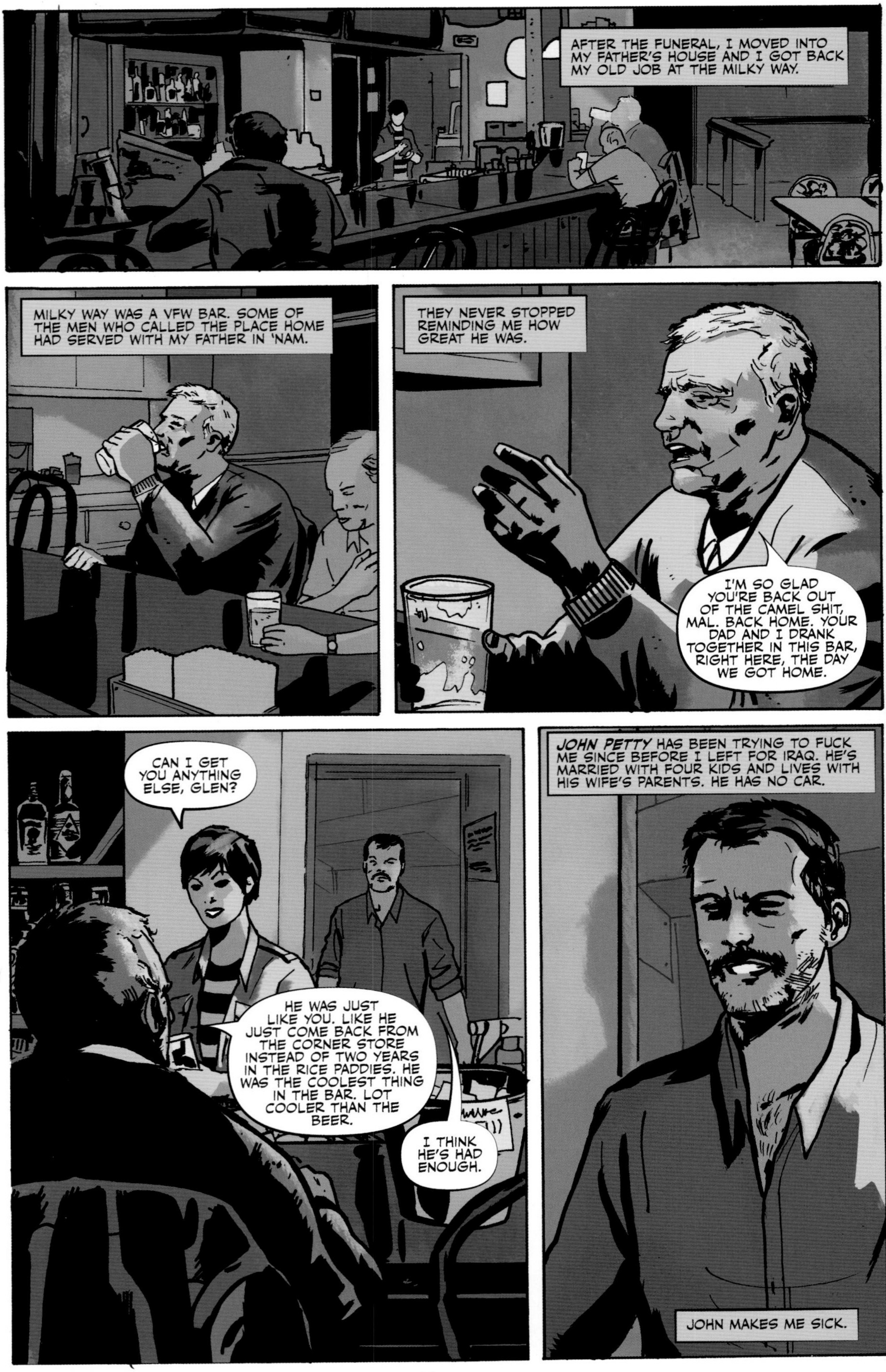
AFTER THE FUNERAL, I MOVED INTO MY FATHER'S HOUSE AND I GOT BACK MY OLD JOB AT THE MILKY WAY.
MILKY WAY WAS A VFW BAR. SOME OF THE MEN WHO CALLED THE PLACE HOME HAD SERVED WITH MY FATHER IN 'NAM.
THEY NEVER STOPPED REMINDING ME HOW GREAT HE WAS.
I'M SO GLAD YOU'RE BACK OUT OF THE CAMEL SHIT, MAL. BACK HOME. YOUR DAD AND I DRANK TOGETHER IN THIS BAR, RIGHT HERE, THE DAY WE GOT HOME.
CAN I GET YOU ANYTHING ELSE, GLEN?
HE WAS JUST LIKE YOU. LIKE HE JUST COME BACK FROM THE CORNER STORE INSTEAD OF TWO YEARS IN THE RICE PADDIES. HE WAS THE COOLEST THING IN THE BAR. LOT COOLER THAN THE BEER.
I THINK HE'S HAD ENOUGH.
JOHN PETTY HAS BEEN TRYING TO FUCK ME SINCE BEFORE I LEFT FOR IRAQ. HE'S MARRIED WITH FOUR KIDS AND LIVES WITH HIS WIFE'S PARENTS. HE HAS NO CAR.
JOHN MAKES ME SICK.

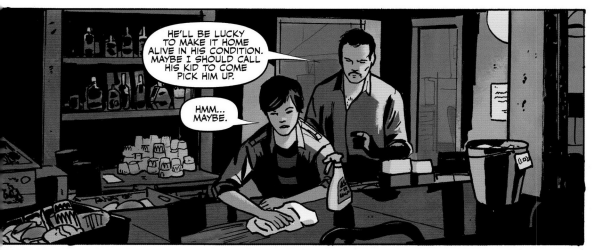

HE'LL BE LUCKY TO MAKE IT HOME ALIVE IN HIS CONDITION. MAYBE I SHOULD CALL HIS KID TO COME PICK HIM UP.

HMM... MAYBE.

SPEAKING OF RIDES, YOU THINK YOU CAN SWING ME HOME AFTER WORK? IT'S JUST UP THE ROAD.

CAN'T YOU WALK?

SURE I COULD...

...BUT I'D RATHER HAVE SOME TIME ALONE WITH YOU TO CATCH UP.

FINE. JUST HELP ME PUT AWAY THE REST OF THE GLASSES AND WIPE DOWN THE TABLES.

WELL, ALL RIGHT.

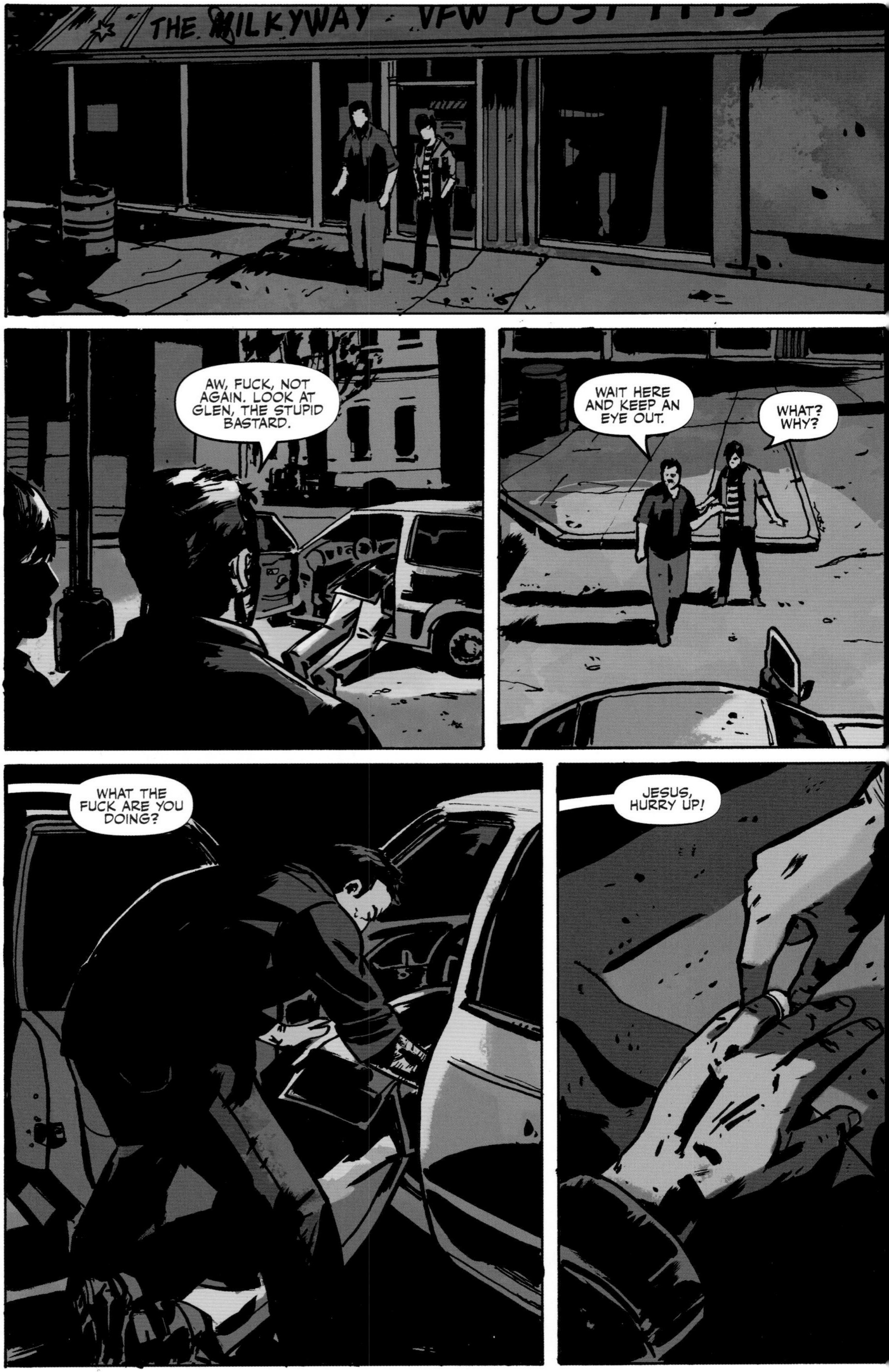
THE MILKYWAY · VFW POST
AW, FUCK, NOT AGAIN. LOOK AT GLEN, THE STUPID BASTARD.
WAIT HERE AND KEEP AN EYE OUT.
WHAT? WHY?
WHAT THE FUCK ARE YOU DOING?
JESUS, HURRY UP!

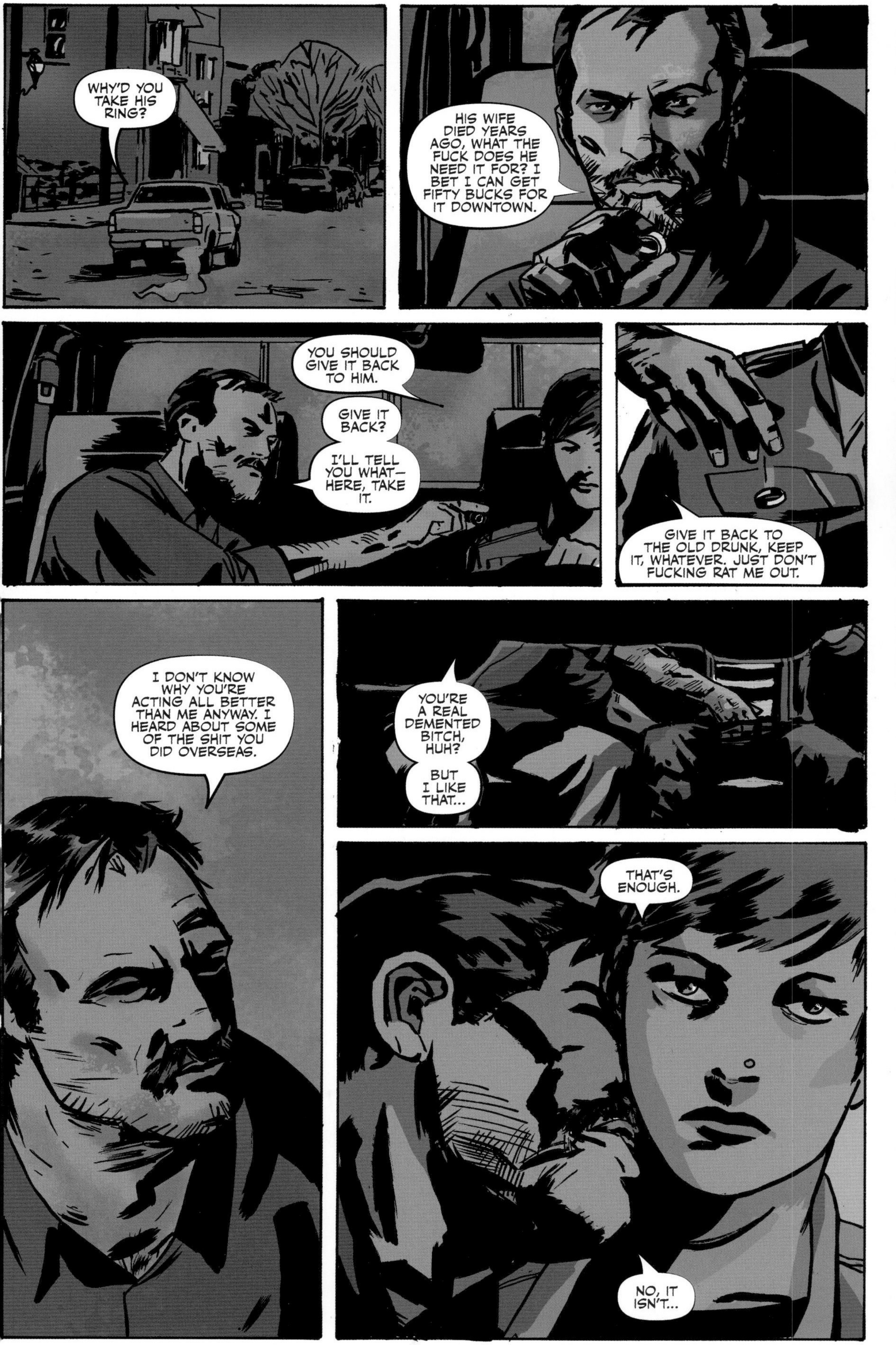
WHY'D YOU TAKE HIS RING?
HIS WIFE DIED YEARS AGO, WHAT THE FUCK DOES HE NEED IT FOR? I BET I CAN GET FIFTY BUCKS FOR IT DOWNTOWN.
YOU SHOULD GIVE IT BACK TO HIM.
GIVE IT BACK?
I'LL TELL YOU WHAT— HERE, TAKE IT.
GIVE IT BACK TO THE OLD DRUNK, KEEP IT, WHATEVER. JUST DON'T FUCKING RAT ME OUT.
I DON'T KNOW WHY YOU'RE ACTING ALL BETTER THAN ME ANYWAY. I HEARD ABOUT SOME OF THE SHIT YOU DID OVERSEAS.
YOU'RE A REAL DEMENTED BITCH, HUH?
BUT I LIKE THAT...
THAT'S ENOUGH.
NO, IT ISN'T...

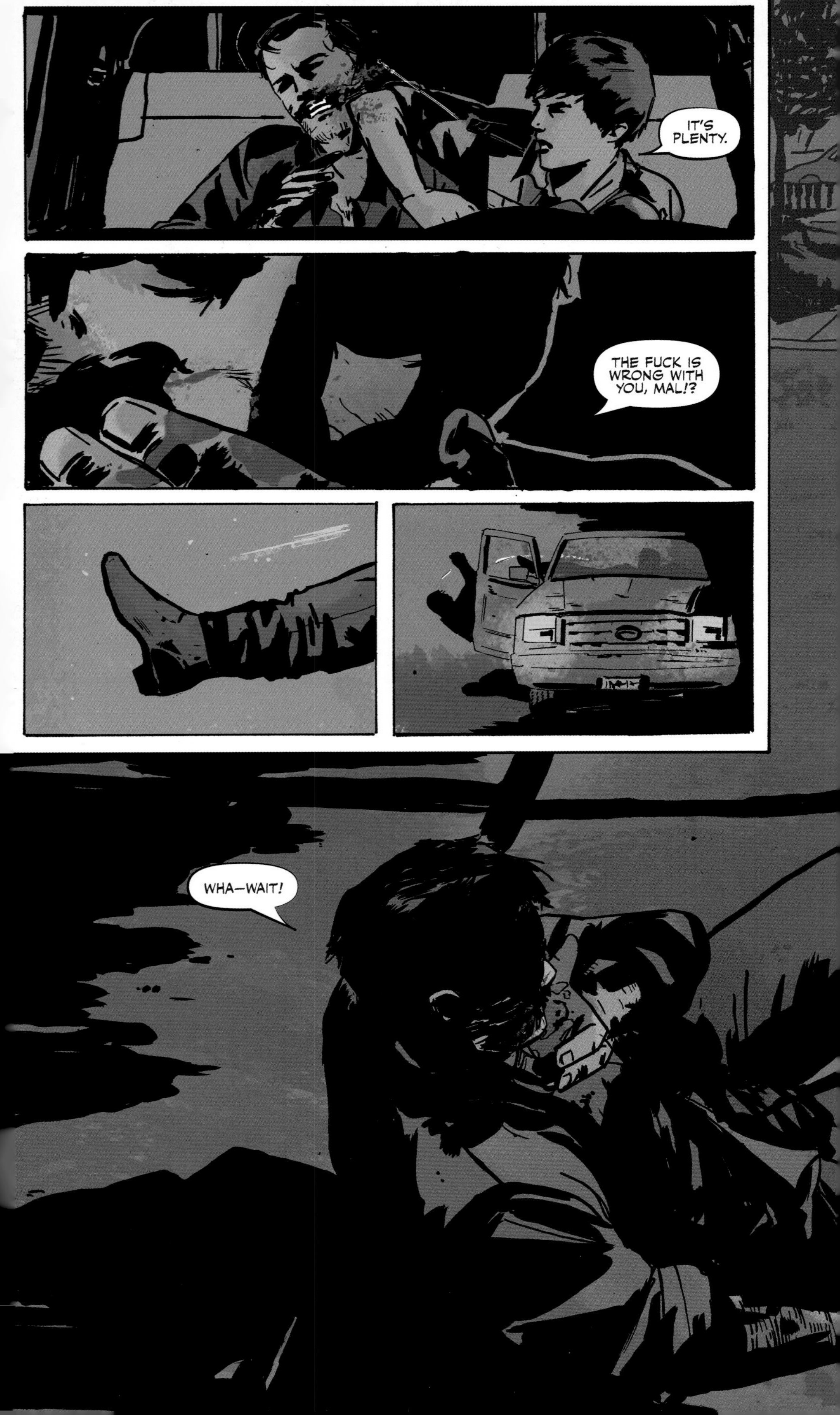
IT'S PLENTY.
THE FUCK IS WRONG WITH YOU, MAL!?
WHA—WAIT!

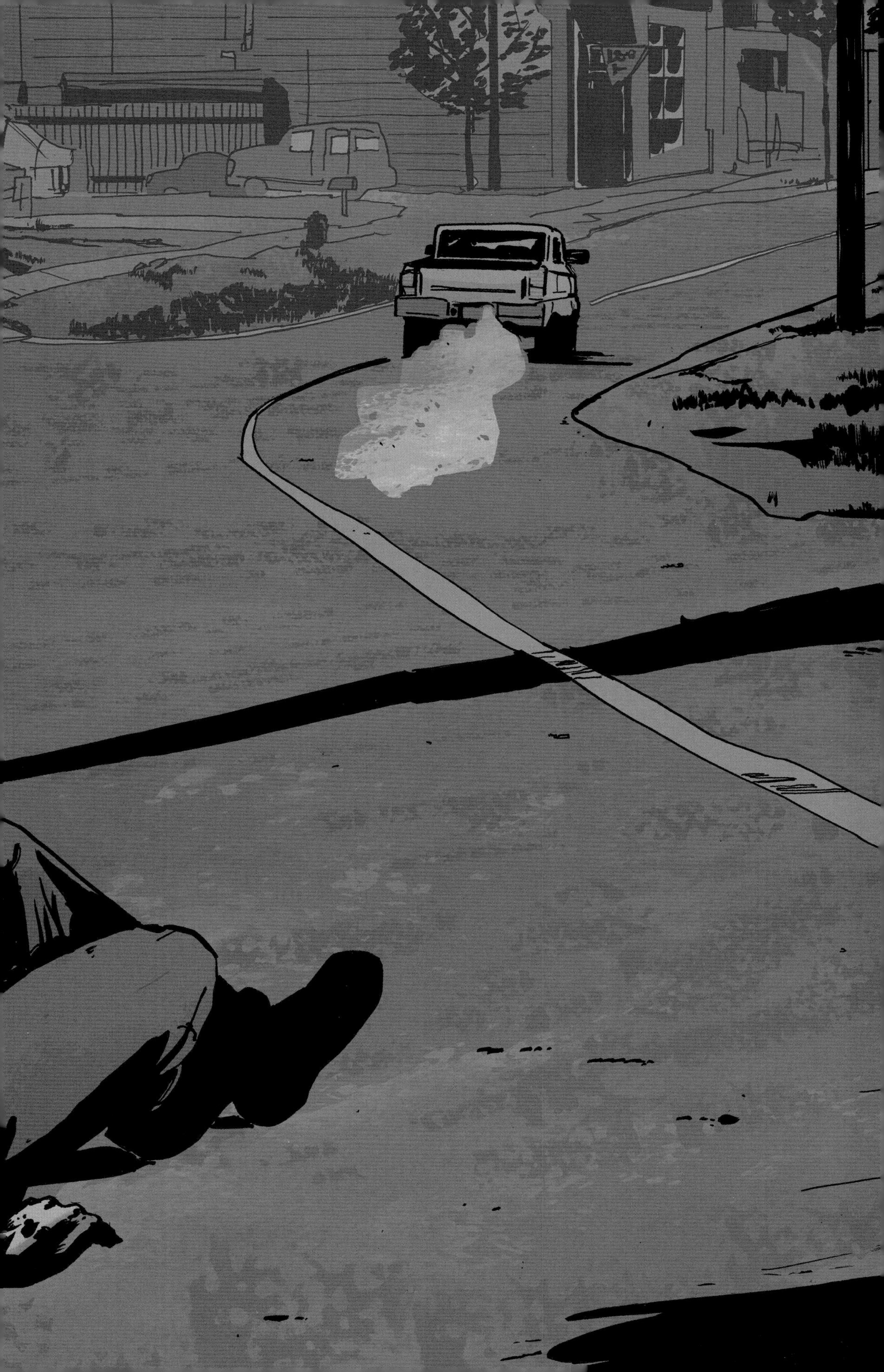

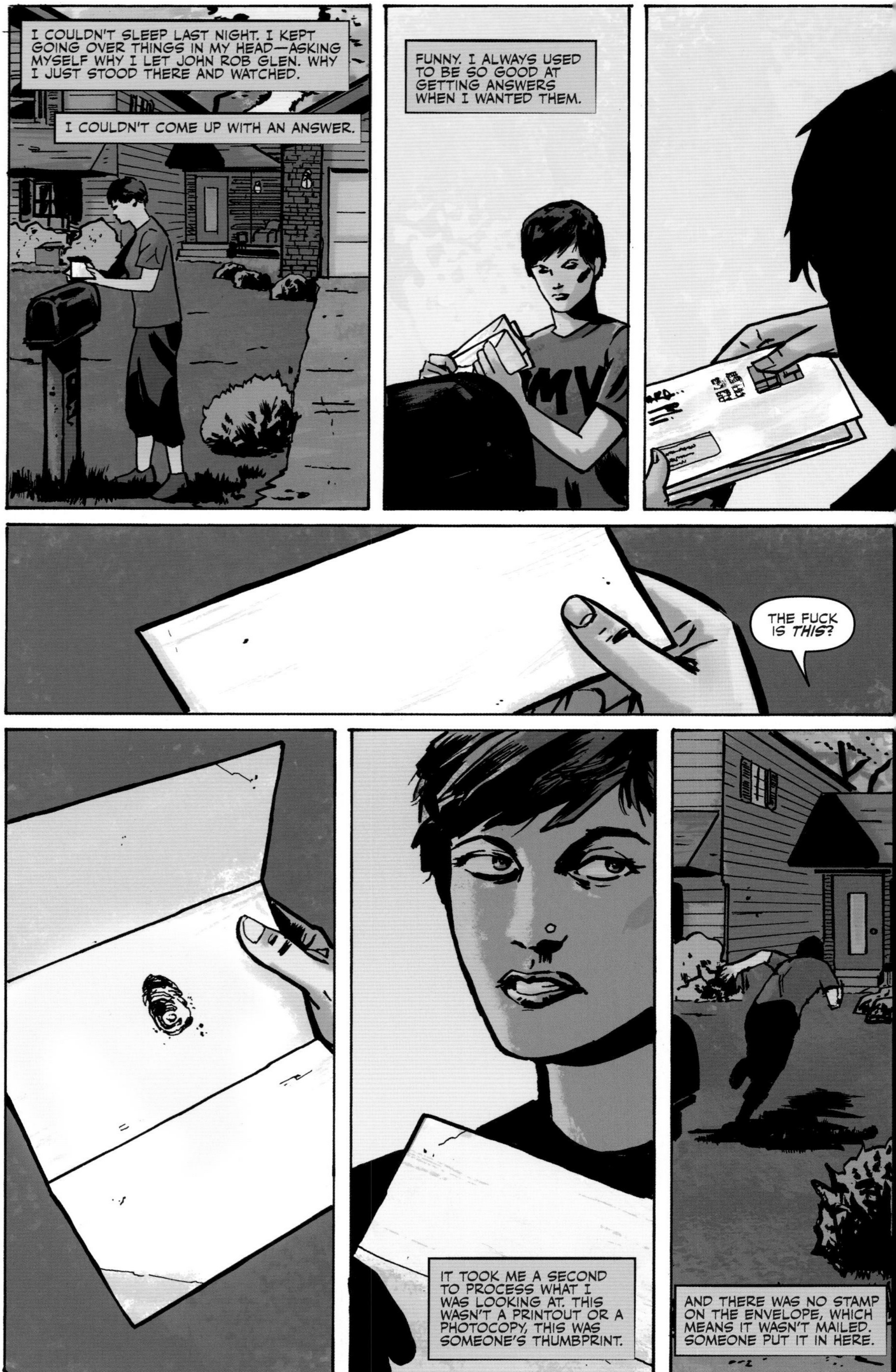
I COULDN'T SLEEP LAST NIGHT. I KEPT GOING OVER THINGS IN MY HEAD—ASKING MYSELF WHY I LET JOHN ROB GLEN. WHY I JUST STOOD THERE AND WATCHED.
I COULDN'T COME UP WITH AN ANSWER.
FUNNY. I ALWAYS USED TO BE SO GOOD AT GETTING ANSWERS WHEN I WANTED THEM.
THE FUCK IS *THIS*?
IT TOOK ME A SECOND TO PROCESS WHAT I WAS LOOKING AT. THIS WASN'T A PRINTOUT OR A PHOTOCOPY, THIS WAS SOMEONE'S THUMBPRINT.
AND THERE WAS NO STAMP ON THE ENVELOPE, WHICH MEANS IT WASN'T MAILED. SOMEONE PUT IT IN HERE.

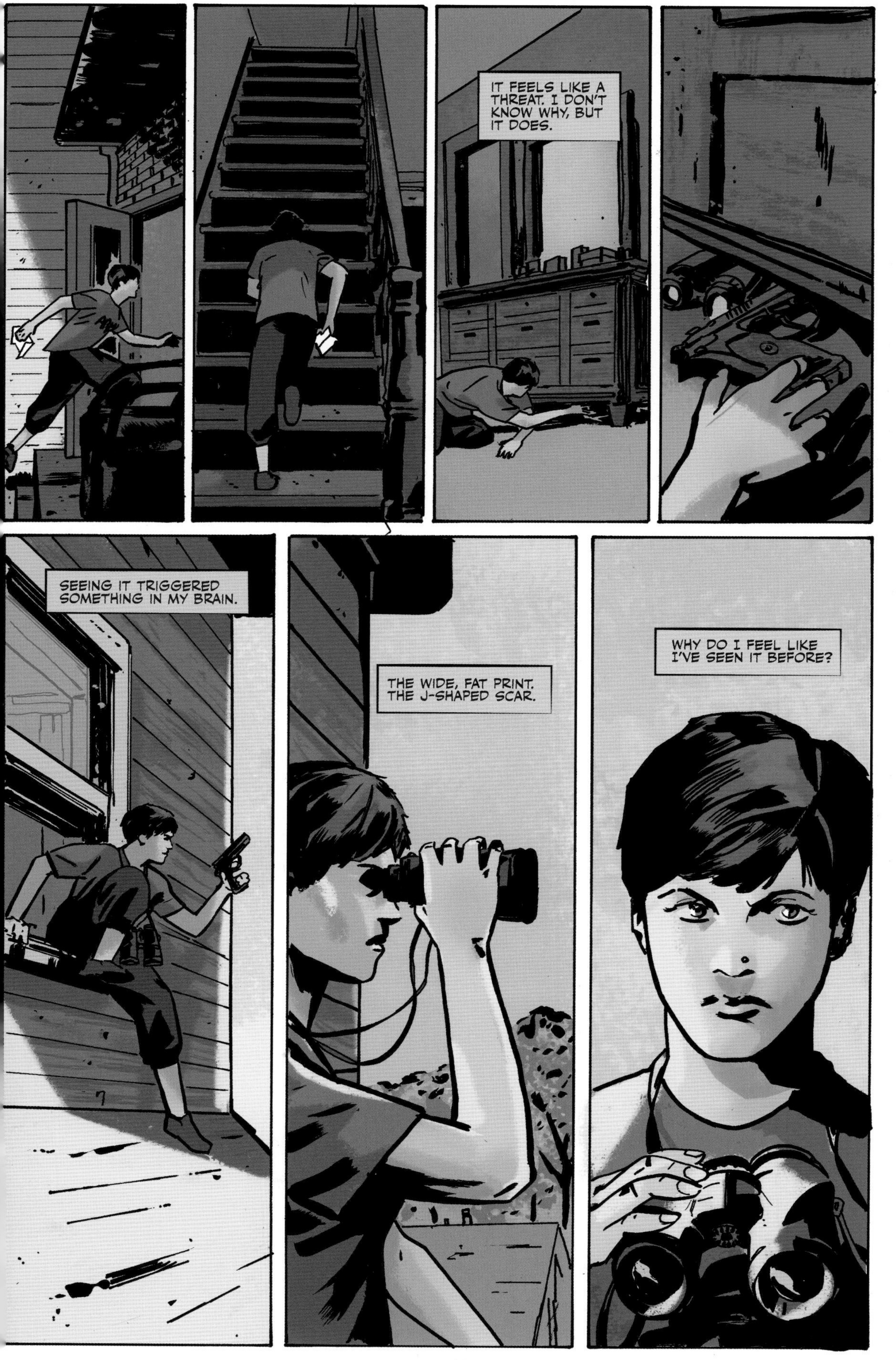
IT FEELS LIKE A THREAT. I DON'T KNOW WHY, BUT IT DOES.
SEEING IT TRIGGERED SOMETHING IN MY BRAIN.
THE WIDE, FAT PRINT. THE J-SHAPED SCAR.
WHY DO I FEEL LIKE I'VE SEEN IT BEFORE?

ABU GHRAIB, IRAQ.

I WAS WORKING ON BLOCK 1A WITH ANOTHER TRANSLATOR NAMED ANSHAW—A NEWBIE JUST A FEW MONTHS OUT OF BASIC— WHEN I GOT THE CALL TO BRING "THE PROFESSOR" TO CI.

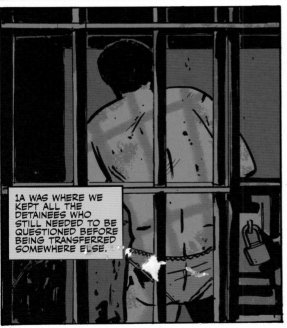

1A WAS WHERE WE KEPT ALL THE DETAINEES WHO STILL NEEDED TO BE QUESTIONED BEFORE BEING TRANSFERRED SOMEWHERE ELSE.

MOST OF THESE GUYS WILL SPEND THE REST OF THEIR LIVES IN PLACES JUST LIKE THIS...

...OTHERS AREN'T SO LUCKY.

⟨LET'S GO, BITCH.⟩

18

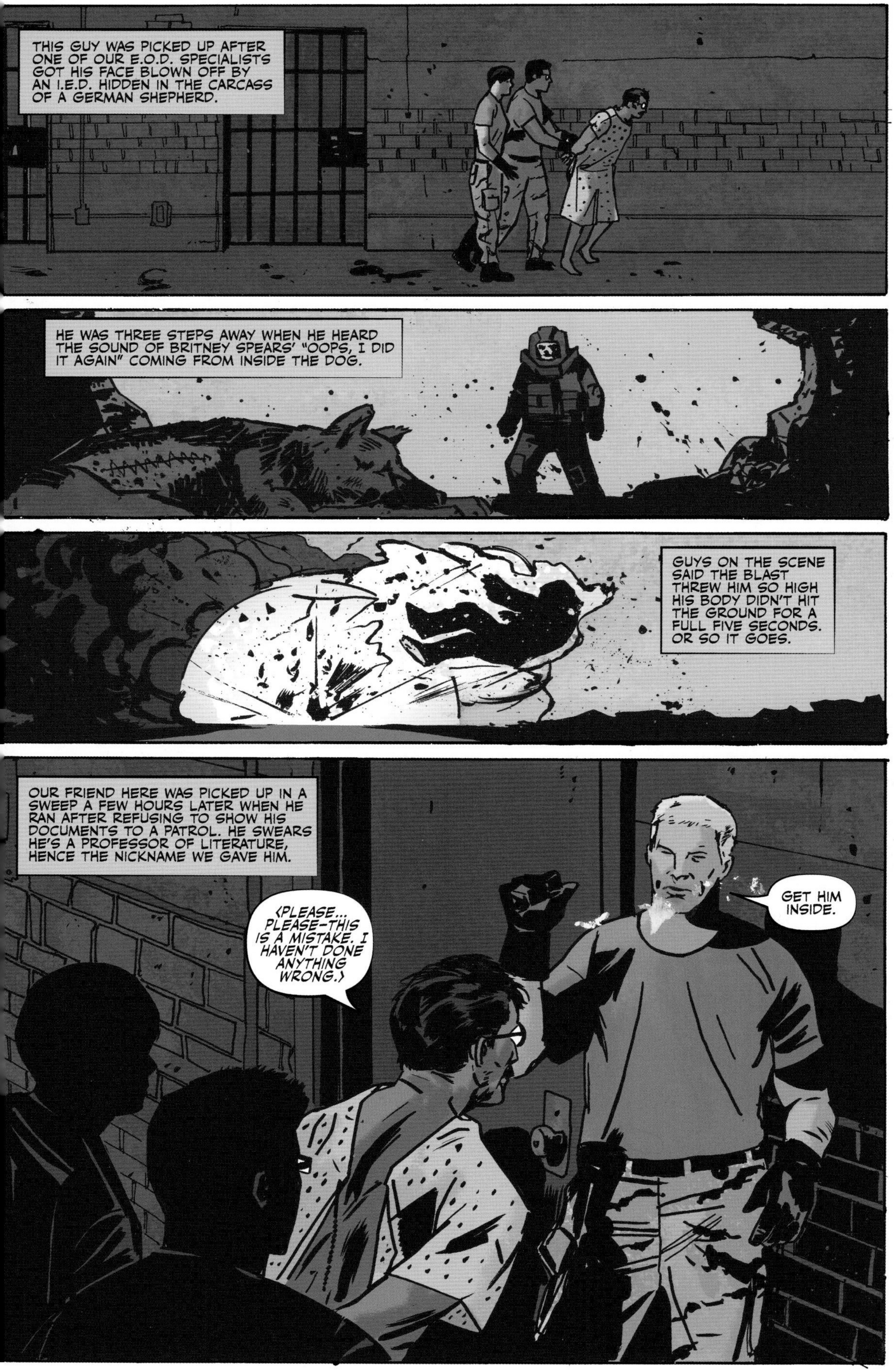
THIS GUY WAS PICKED UP AFTER ONE OF OUR E.O.D. SPECIALISTS GOT HIS FACE BLOWN OFF BY AN I.E.D. HIDDEN IN THE CARCASS OF A GERMAN SHEPHERD.
HE WAS THREE STEPS AWAY WHEN HE HEARD THE SOUND OF BRITNEY SPEARS' "OOPS, I DID IT AGAIN" COMING FROM INSIDE THE DOG.
GUYS ON THE SCENE SAID THE BLAST THREW HIM SO HIGH HIS BODY DIDN'T HIT THE GROUND FOR A FULL FIVE SECONDS. OR SO IT GOES.
OUR FRIEND HERE WAS PICKED UP IN A SWEEP A FEW HOURS LATER WHEN HE RAN AFTER REFUSING TO SHOW HIS DOCUMENTS TO A PATROL. HE SWEARS HE'S A PROFESSOR OF LITERATURE, HENCE THE NICKNAME WE GAVE HIM.
<PLEASE... PLEASE--THIS IS A MISTAKE. I HAVEN'T DONE ANYTHING WRONG.>
GET HIM INSIDE.

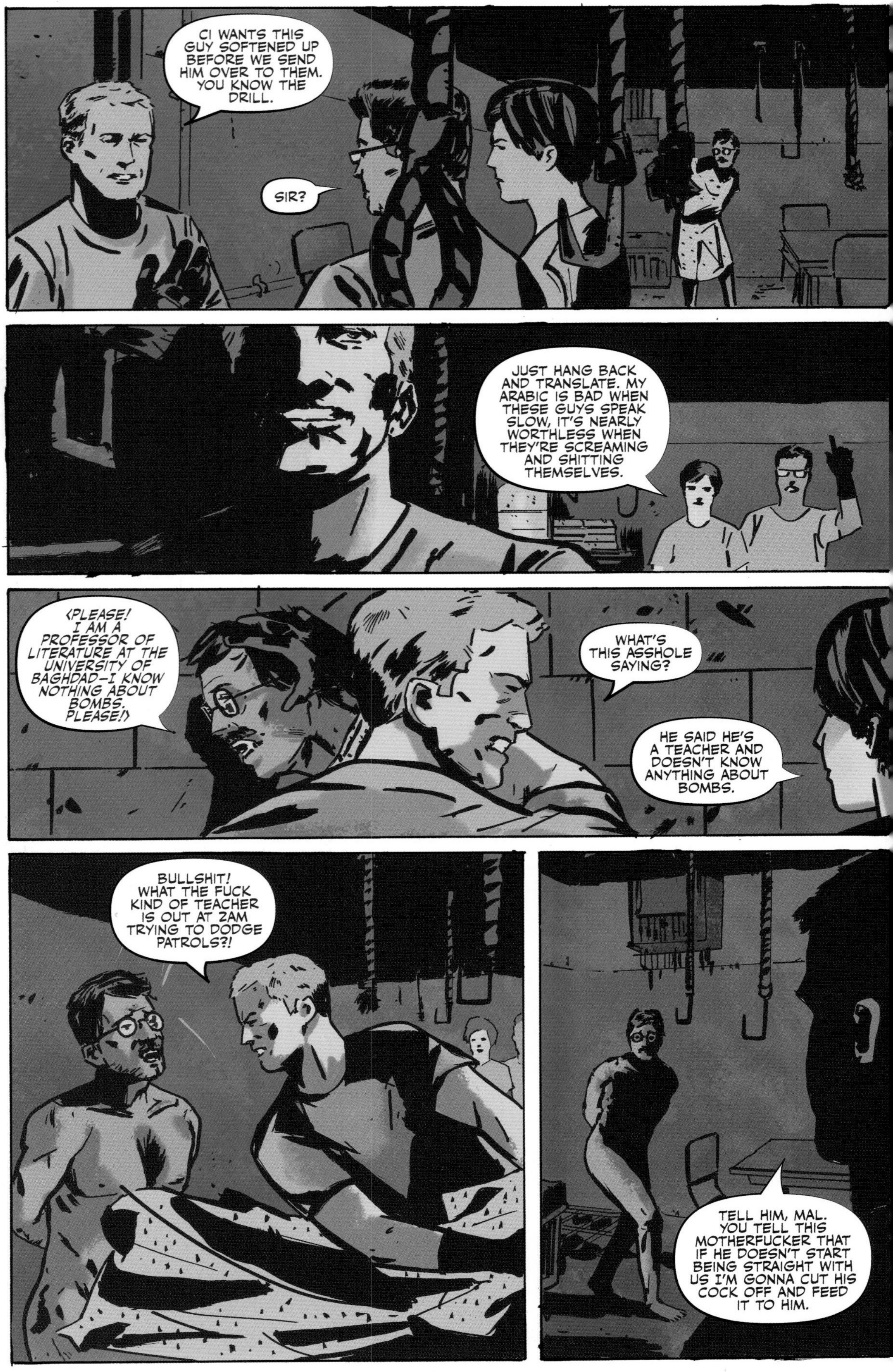

CI WANTS THIS GUY SOFTENED UP BEFORE WE SEND HIM OVER TO THEM. YOU KNOW THE DRILL.
SIR?
JUST HANG BACK AND TRANSLATE. MY ARABIC IS BAD WHEN THESE GUYS SPEAK SLOW, IT'S NEARLY WORTHLESS WHEN THEY'RE SCREAMING AND SHITTING THEMSELVES.
<PLEASE! I AM A PROFESSOR OF LITERATURE AT THE UNIVERSITY OF BAGHDAD–I KNOW NOTHING ABOUT BOMBS. PLEASE!>
WHAT'S THIS ASSHOLE SAYING?
HE SAID HE'S A TEACHER AND DOESN'T KNOW ANYTHING ABOUT BOMBS.
BULLSHIT! WHAT THE FUCK KIND OF TEACHER IS OUT AT ZAM TRYING TO DODGE PATROLS?!
TELL HIM, MAL. YOU TELL THIS MOTHERFUCKER THAT IF HE DOESN'T START BEING STRAIGHT WITH US I'M GONNA CUT HIS COCK OFF AND FEED IT TO HIM.

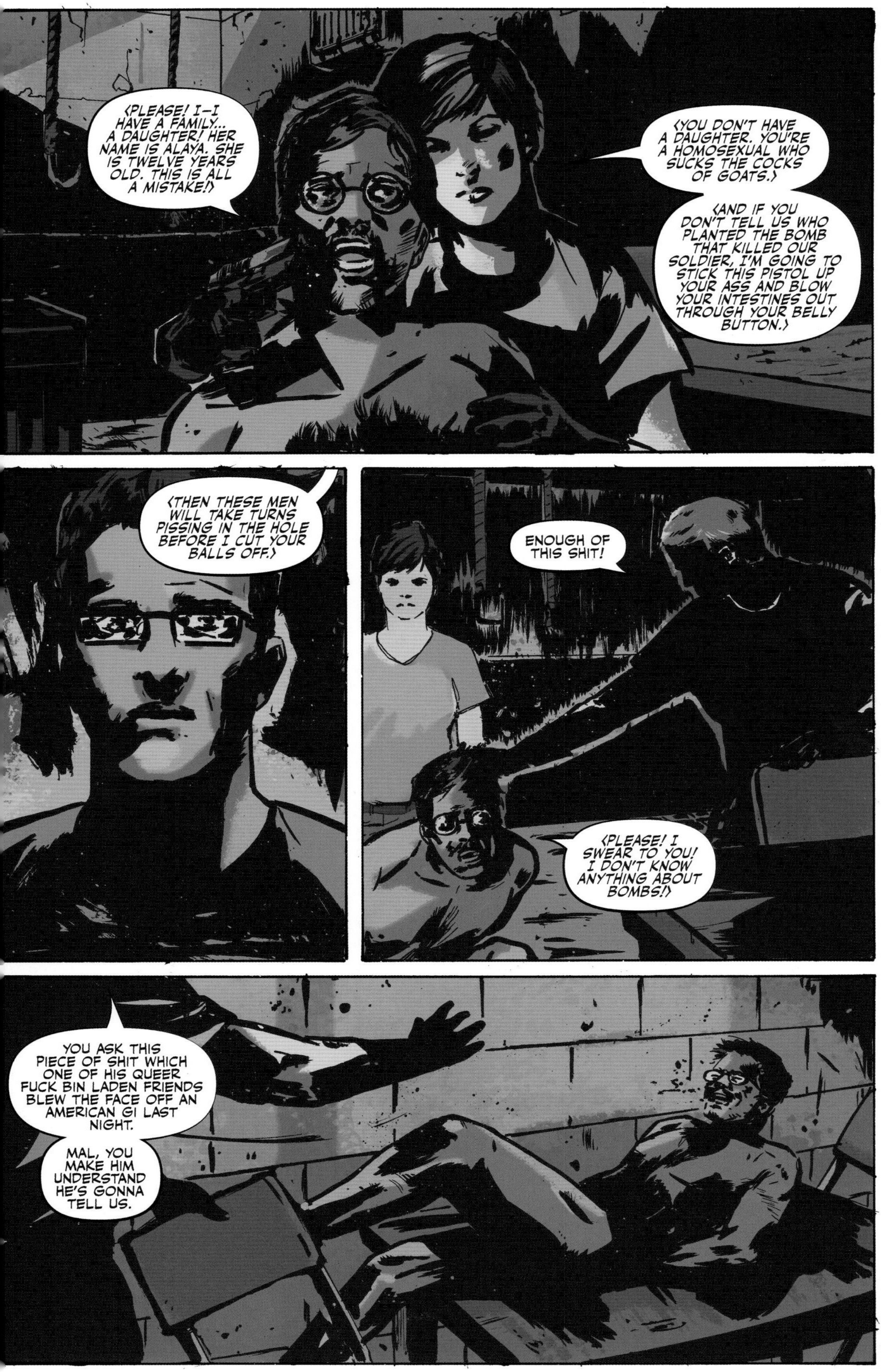
‹PLEASE! I–I HAVE A FAMILY... A DAUGHTER! HER NAME IS ALAYA. SHE IS TWELVE YEARS OLD. THIS IS ALL A MISTAKE!›
‹YOU DON'T HAVE A DAUGHTER. YOU'RE A HOMOSEXUAL WHO SUCKS THE COCKS OF GOATS.›
‹AND IF YOU DON'T TELL US WHO PLANTED THE BOMB THAT KILLED OUR SOLDIER, I'M GOING TO STICK THIS PISTOL UP YOUR ASS AND BLOW YOUR INTESTINES OUT THROUGH YOUR BELLY BUTTON.›
‹THEN THESE MEN WILL TAKE TURNS PISSING IN THE HOLE BEFORE I CUT YOUR BALLS OFF.›
ENOUGH OF THIS SHIT!
‹PLEASE! I SWEAR TO YOU! I DON'T KNOW ANYTHING ABOUT BOMBS!›
YOU ASK THIS PIECE OF SHIT WHICH ONE OF HIS QUEER FUCK BIN LADEN FRIENDS BLEW THE FACE OFF AN AMERICAN GI LAST NIGHT.
MAL, YOU MAKE HIM UNDERSTAND HE'S GONNA TELL US.

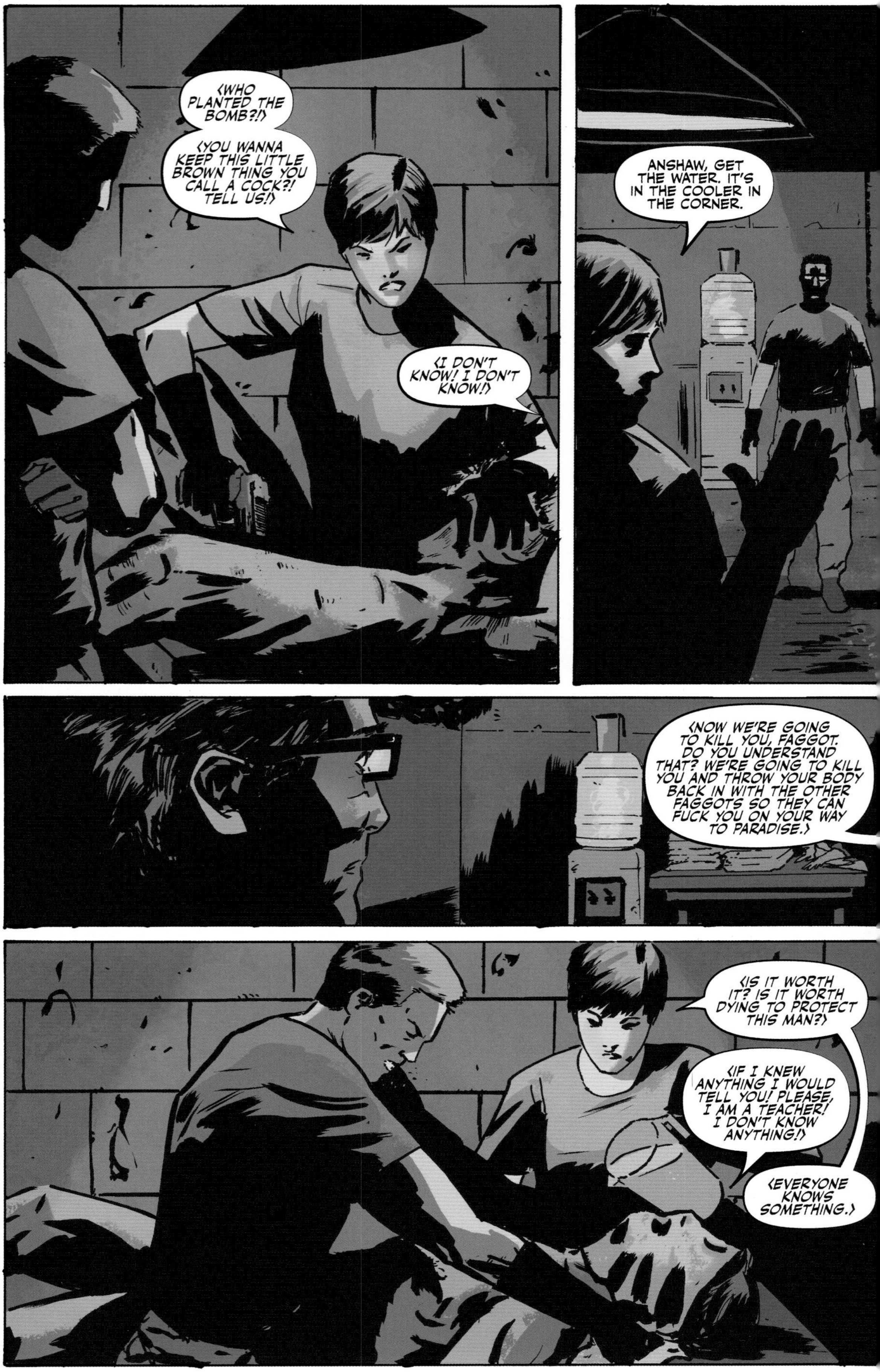
‹WHO PLANTED THE BOMB?!›
‹YOU WANNA KEEP THIS LITTLE BROWN THING YOU CALL A COCK?! TELL US!›
‹I DON'T KNOW! I DON'T KNOW!›
ANSHAW, GET THE WATER. IT'S IN THE COOLER IN THE CORNER.
‹NOW WE'RE GOING TO KILL YOU, FAGGOT. DO YOU UNDERSTAND THAT? WE'RE GOING TO KILL YOU AND THROW YOUR BODY BACK IN WITH THE OTHER FAGGOTS SO THEY CAN FUCK YOU ON YOUR WAY TO PARADISE.›
‹IS IT WORTH IT? IS IT WORTH DYING TO PROTECT THIS MAN?›
‹IF I KNEW ANYTHING I WOULD TELL YOU! PLEASE, I AM A TEACHER! I DON'T KNOW ANYTHING!›
‹EVERYONE KNOWS SOMETHING.›

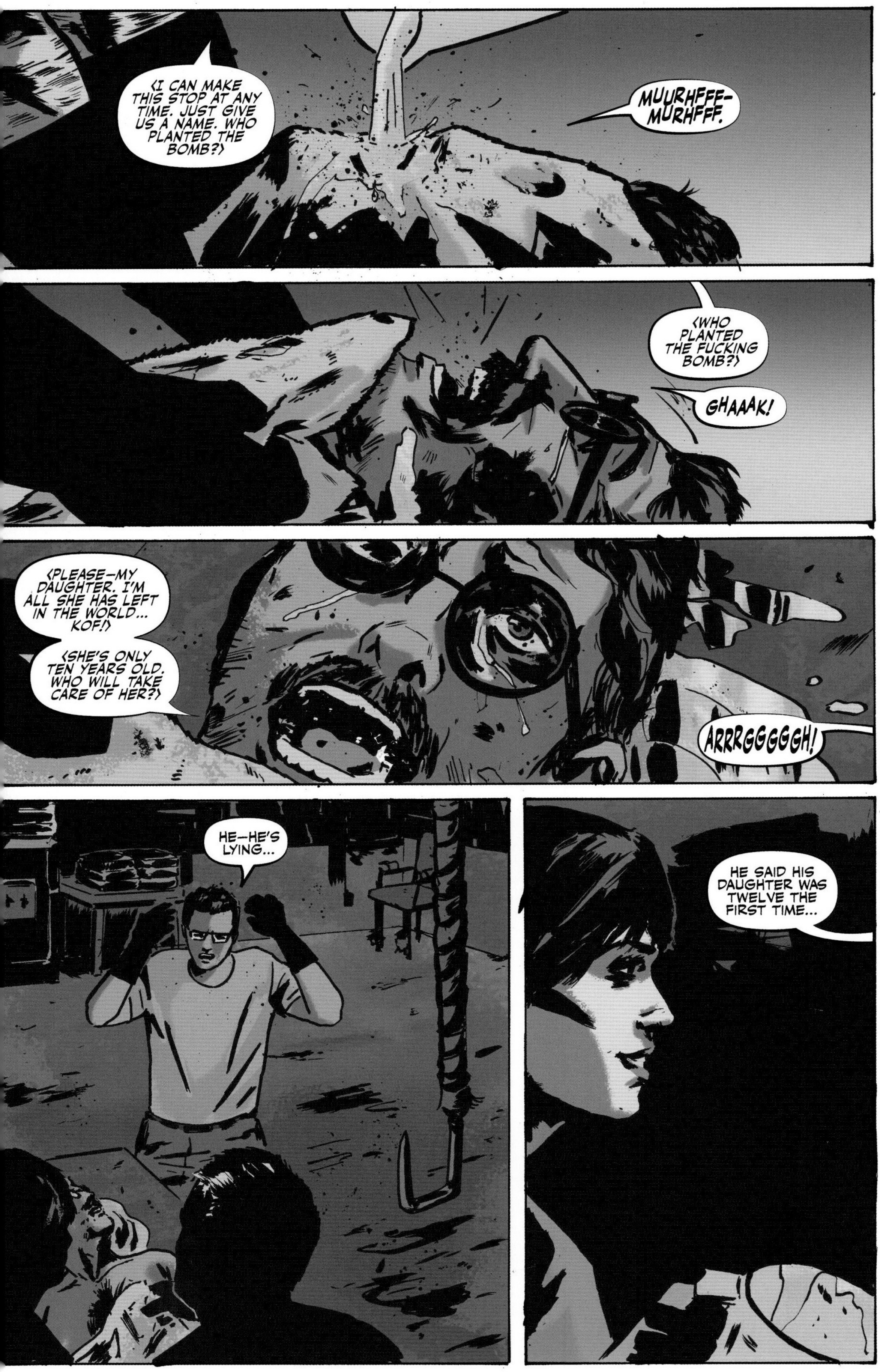
<I CAN MAKE THIS STOP AT ANY TIME. JUST GIVE US A NAME. WHO PLANTED THE BOMB?>
MUURHFFF-MURHFFF.
<WHO PLANTED THE FUCKING BOMB?>
GHAAAK!
<PLEASE--MY DAUGHTER. I'M ALL SHE HAS LEFT IN THE WORLD... KOF!>
<SHE'S ONLY TEN YEARS OLD. WHO WILL TAKE CARE OF HER?>
ARRRGGGGGH!
HE--HE'S LYING...
HE SAID HIS DAUGHTER WAS TWELVE THE FIRST TIME...

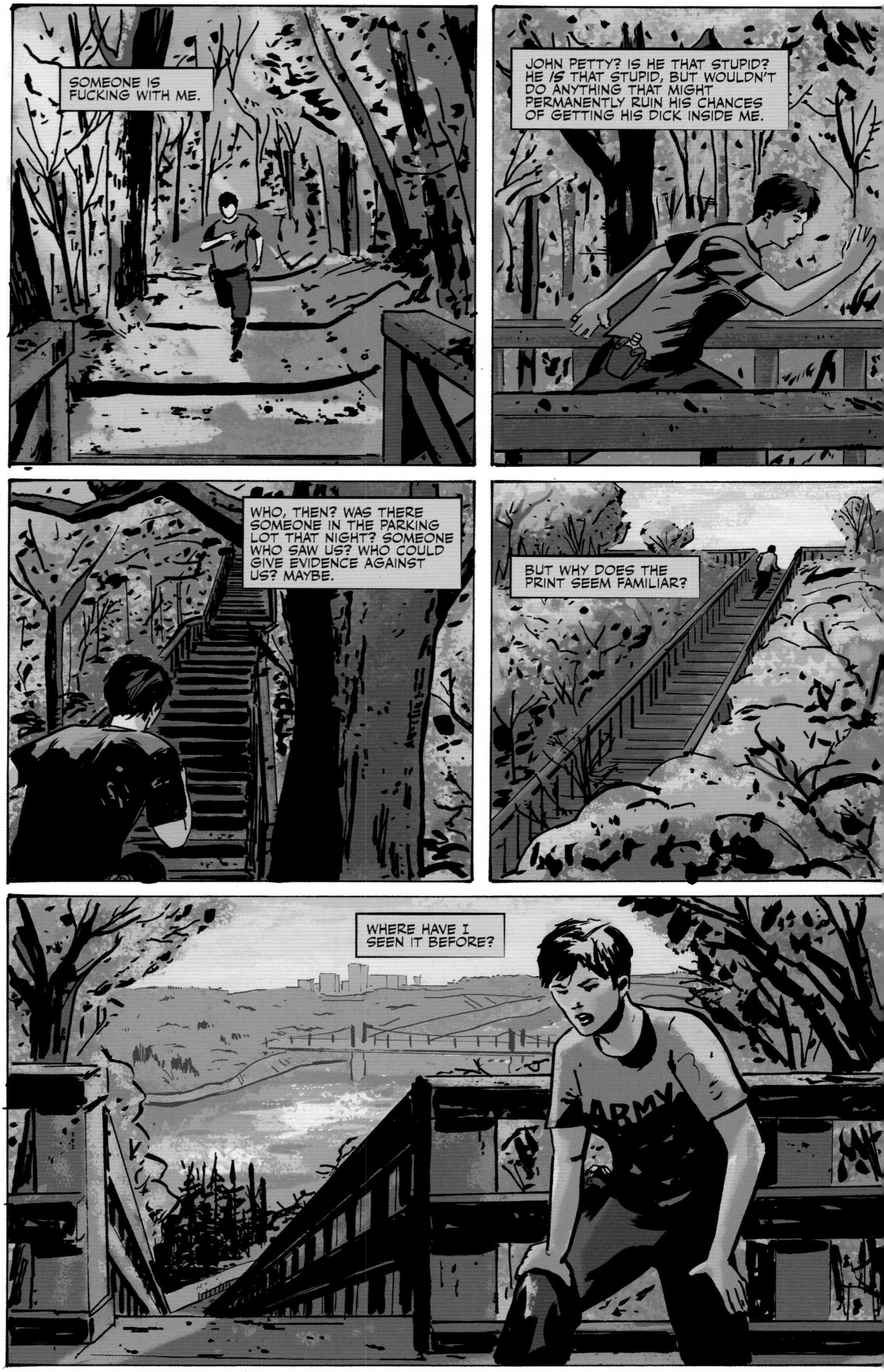
SOMEONE IS FUCKING WITH ME.
JOHN PETTY? IS HE THAT STUPID? HE *IS* THAT STUPID, BUT WOULDN'T DO ANYTHING THAT MIGHT PERMANENTLY RUIN HIS CHANCES OF GETTING HIS DICK INSIDE ME.
WHO, THEN? WAS THERE SOMEONE IN THE PARKING LOT THAT NIGHT? SOMEONE WHO SAW US? WHO COULD GIVE EVIDENCE AGAINST US? MAYBE.
BUT WHY DOES THE PRINT SEEM FAMILIAR?
WHERE HAVE I SEEN IT BEFORE?
ARMY

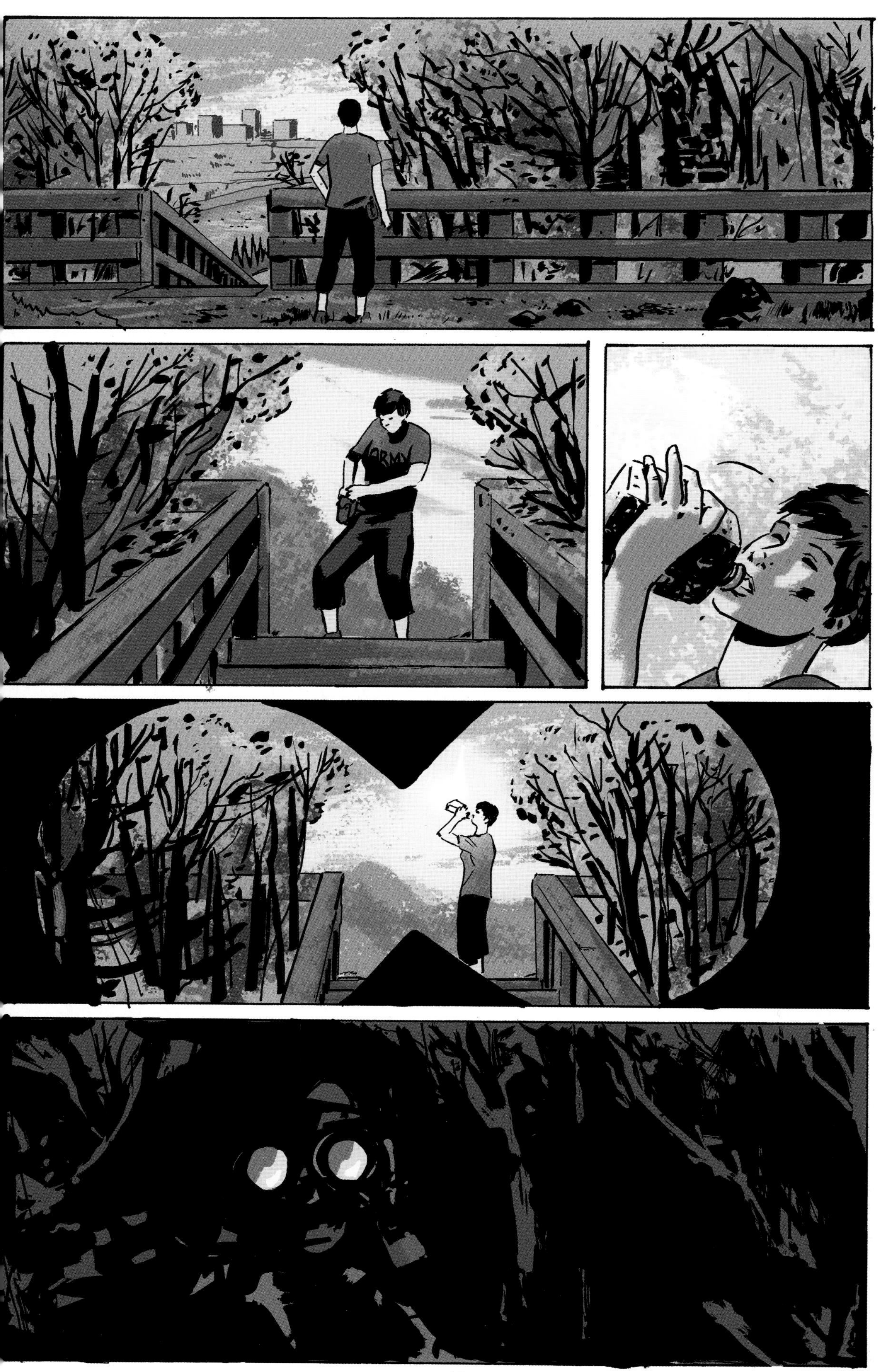
ARMY

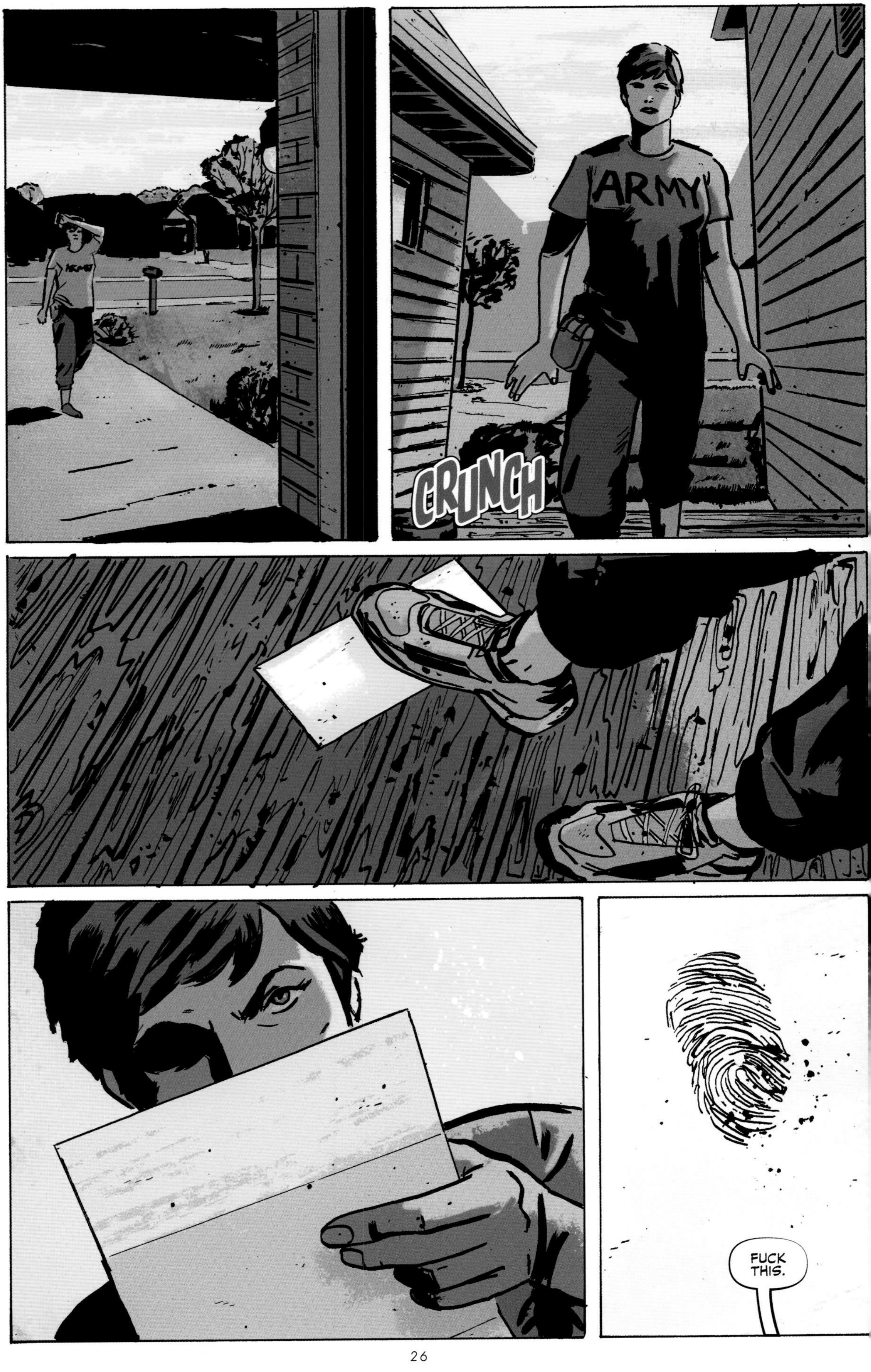

ARMY
CRUNCH
FUCK THIS.

COME ON MOTHERFUCKER! YOU THINK THIS SHIT SCARES ME?! YOU THINK YOU CAN FUCK WITH ME?!

YOU DON'T KNOW WHO YOU'RE FUCKING WITH, PAL—I WILL HURT YOU LIKE YOU'VE NEVER BEEN HURT BEFORE!

YOU CAN TAKE THIS BULLSHIT AND SHOVE IT UP YOUR ASS, YOU HEAR ME?

YOU HEAR ME?!

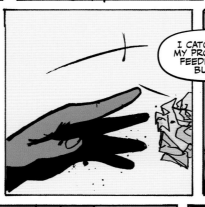

I CATCH YOU ON MY PROPERTY I'M FEEDING YOU A BULLET...

...I DON'T GIVE A FUCK WHO YOU ARE.

SLAM

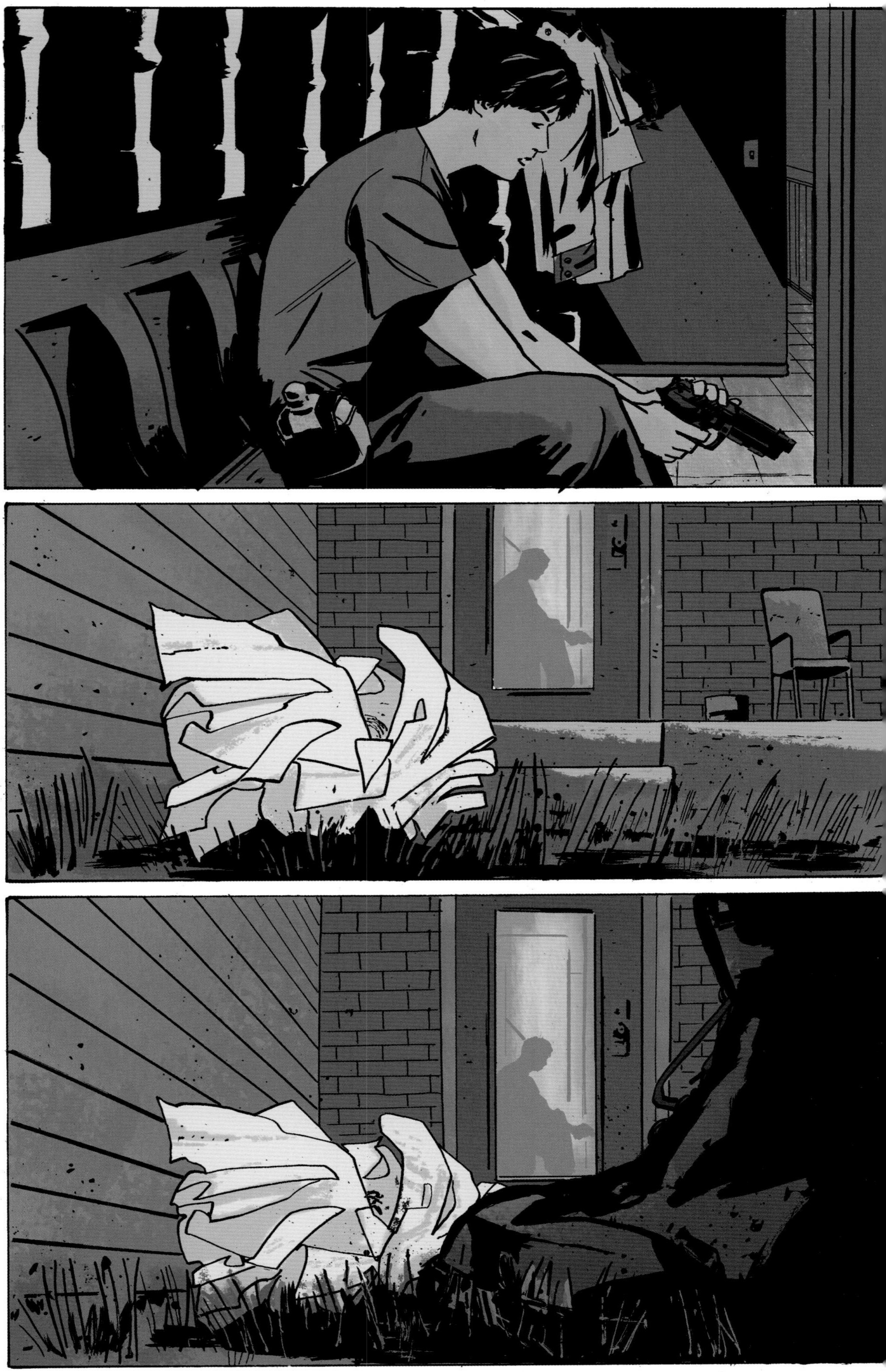

Chapter 2

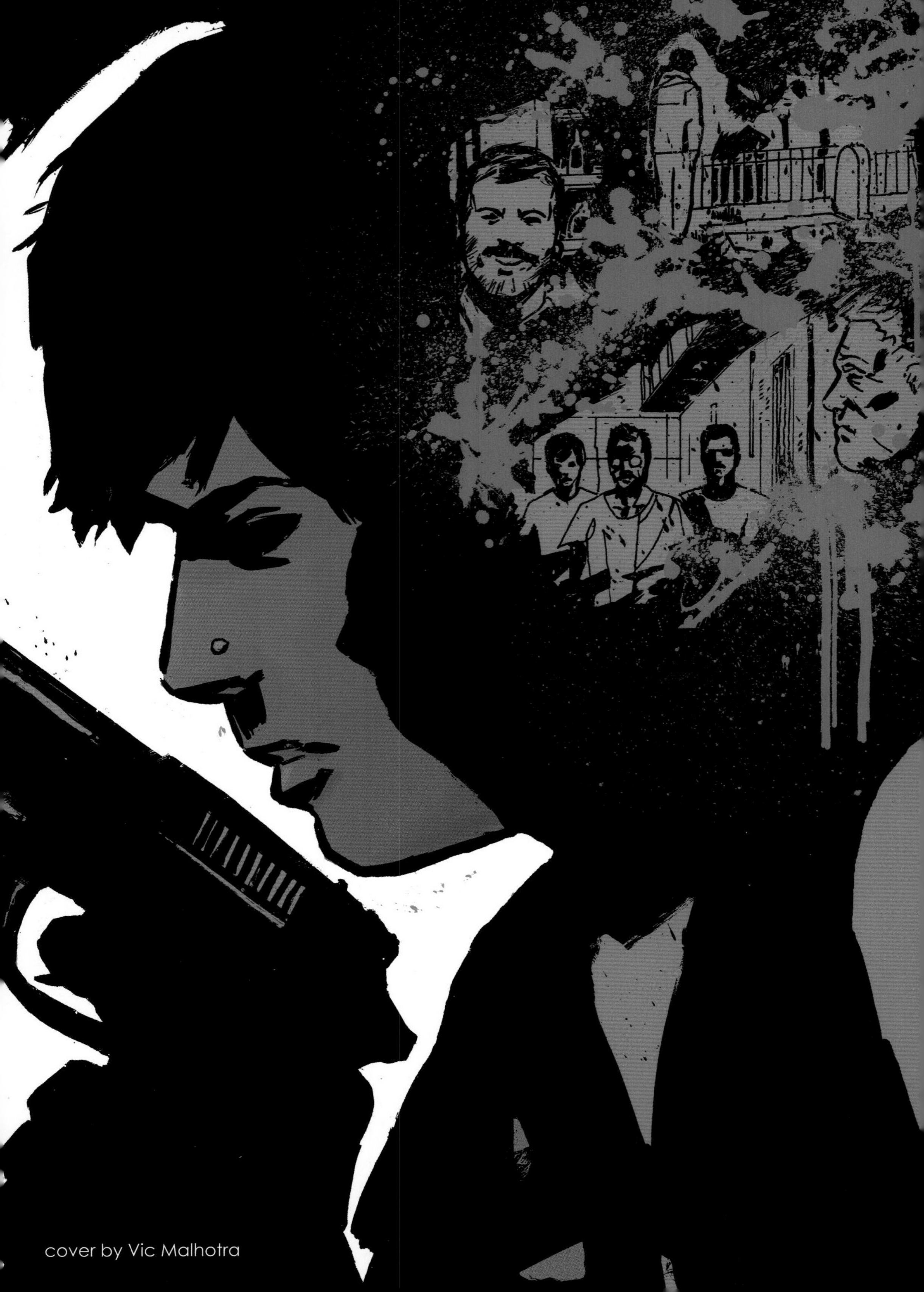

cover by Vic Malhotra

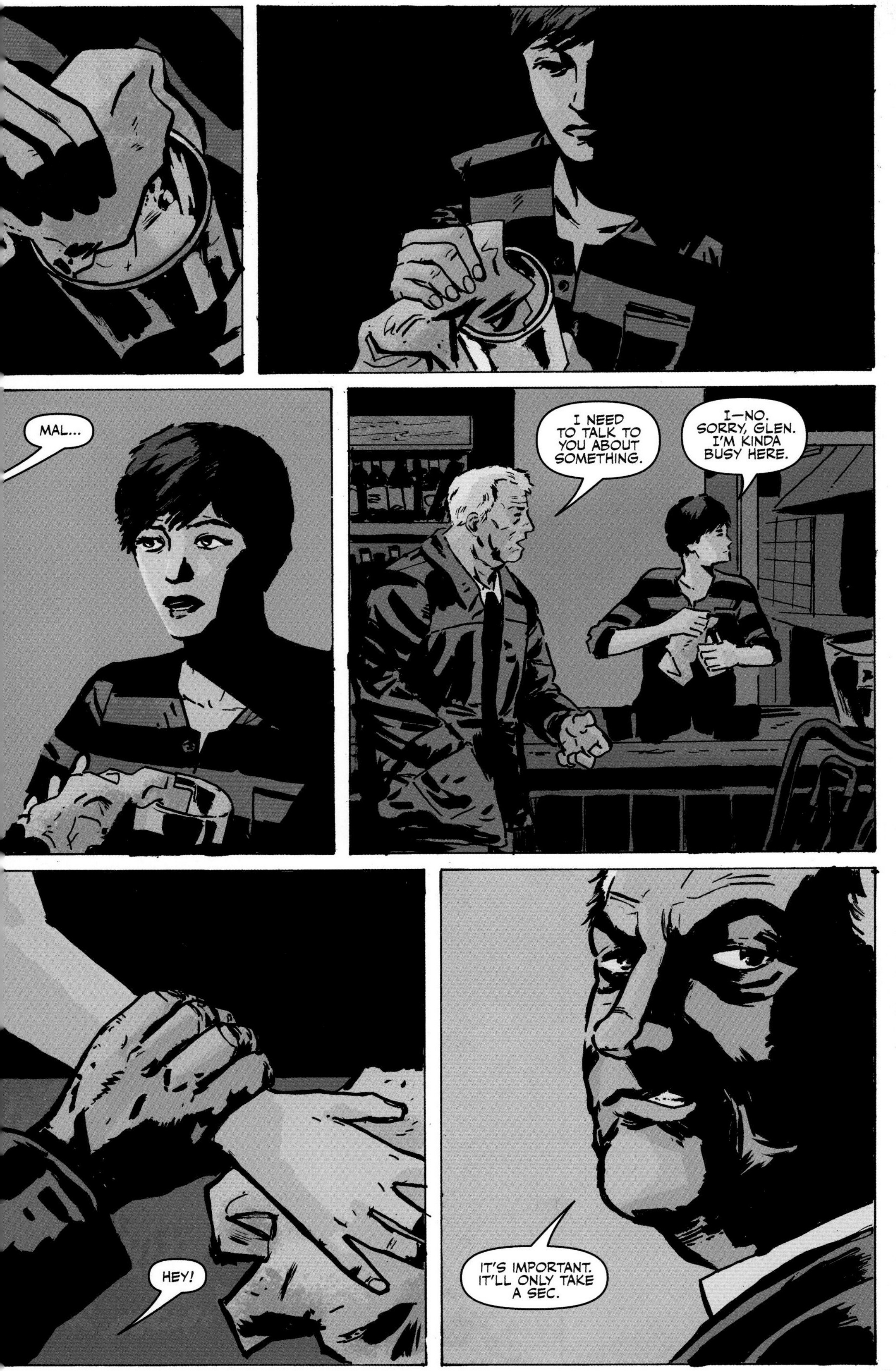
MAL...
I NEED TO TALK TO YOU ABOUT SOMETHING.
I—NO. SORRY, GLEN. I'M KINDA BUSY HERE.
HEY!
IT'S IMPORTANT. IT'LL ONLY TAKE A SEC.

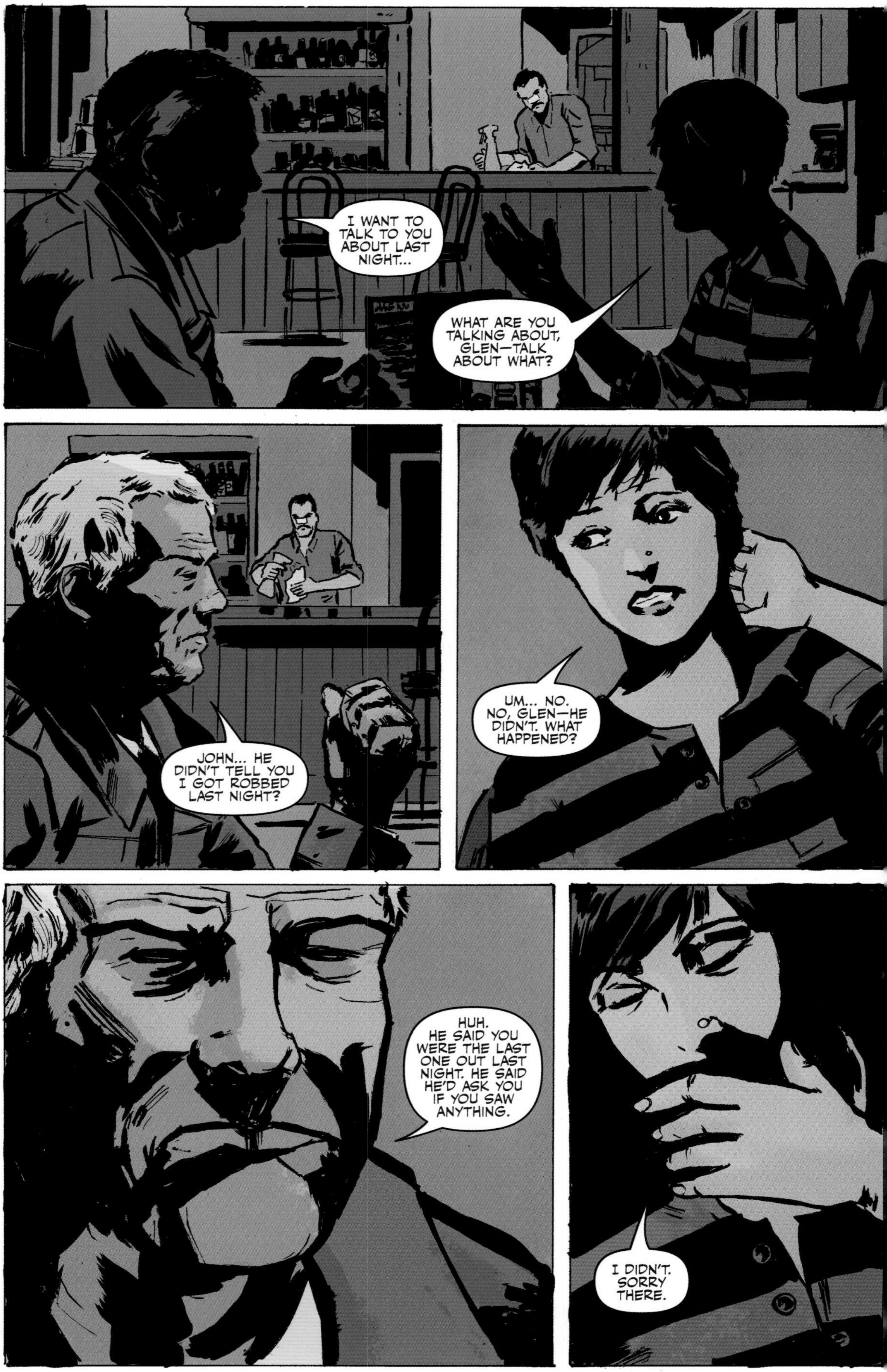
I WANT TO TALK TO YOU ABOUT LAST NIGHT...
WHAT ARE YOU TALKING ABOUT, GLEN—TALK ABOUT WHAT?
JOHN... HE DIDN'T TELL YOU I GOT ROBBED LAST NIGHT?
UM... NO. NO, GLEN—HE DIDN'T. WHAT HAPPENED?
HUH. HE SAID YOU WERE THE LAST ONE OUT LAST NIGHT. HE SAID HE'D ASK YOU IF YOU SAW ANYTHING.
I DIDN'T. SORRY THERE.

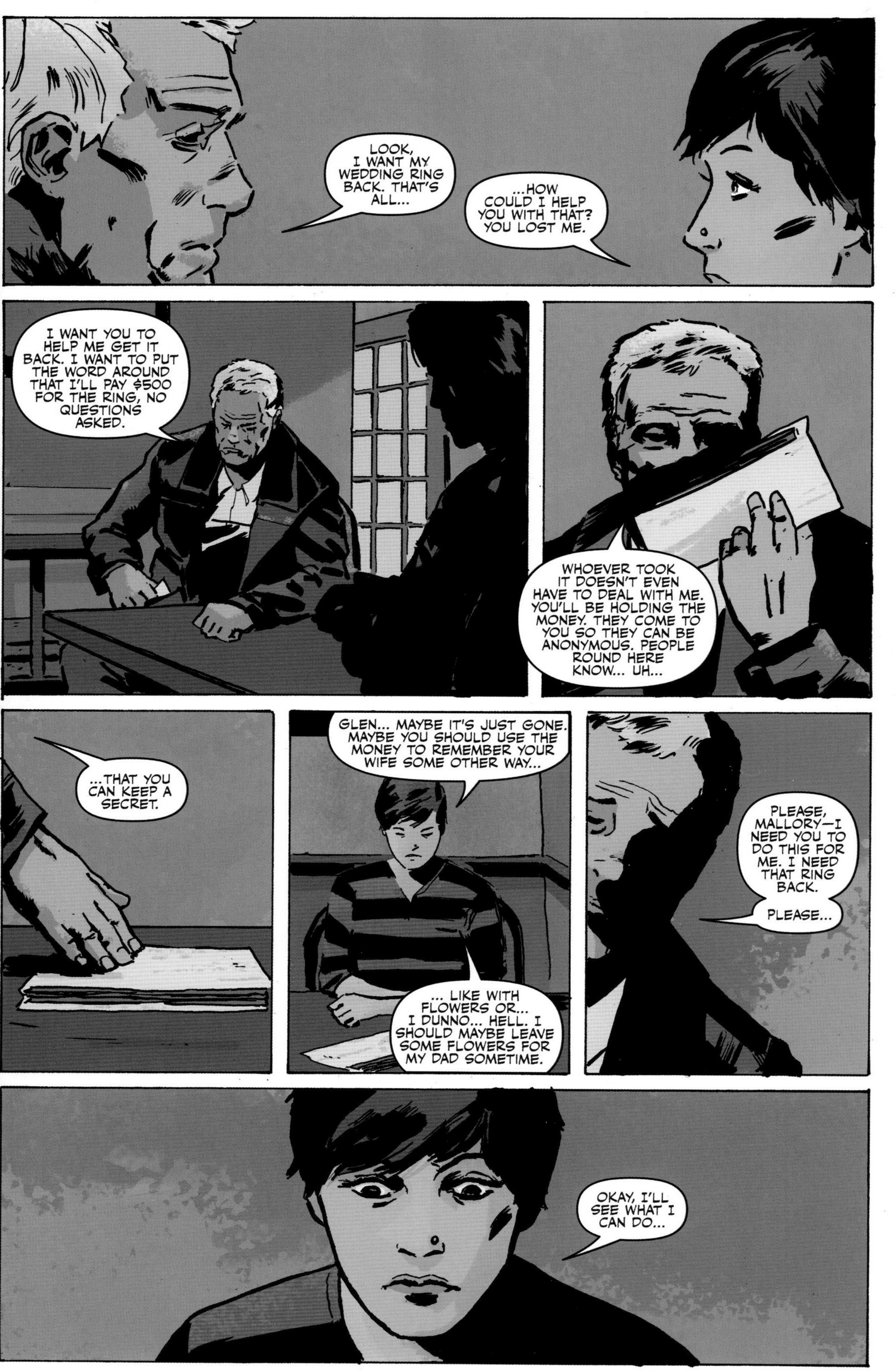
LOOK, I WANT MY WEDDING RING BACK. THAT'S ALL...
...HOW COULD I HELP YOU WITH THAT? YOU LOST ME.
I WANT YOU TO HELP ME GET IT BACK. I WANT TO PUT THE WORD AROUND THAT I'LL PAY $500 FOR THE RING, NO QUESTIONS ASKED.
WHOEVER TOOK IT DOESN'T EVEN HAVE TO DEAL WITH ME. YOU'LL BE HOLDING THE MONEY. THEY COME TO YOU SO THEY CAN BE ANONYMOUS. PEOPLE ROUND HERE KNOW... UH...
...THAT YOU CAN KEEP A SECRET.
GLEN... MAYBE IT'S JUST GONE. MAYBE YOU SHOULD USE THE MONEY TO REMEMBER YOUR WIFE SOME OTHER WAY...
... LIKE WITH FLOWERS OR... I DUNNO... HELL. I SHOULD MAYBE LEAVE SOME FLOWERS FOR MY DAD SOMETIME.
PLEASE, MALLORY—I NEED YOU TO DO THIS FOR ME. I NEED THAT RING BACK.
PLEASE...
OKAY, I'LL SEE WHAT I CAN DO...

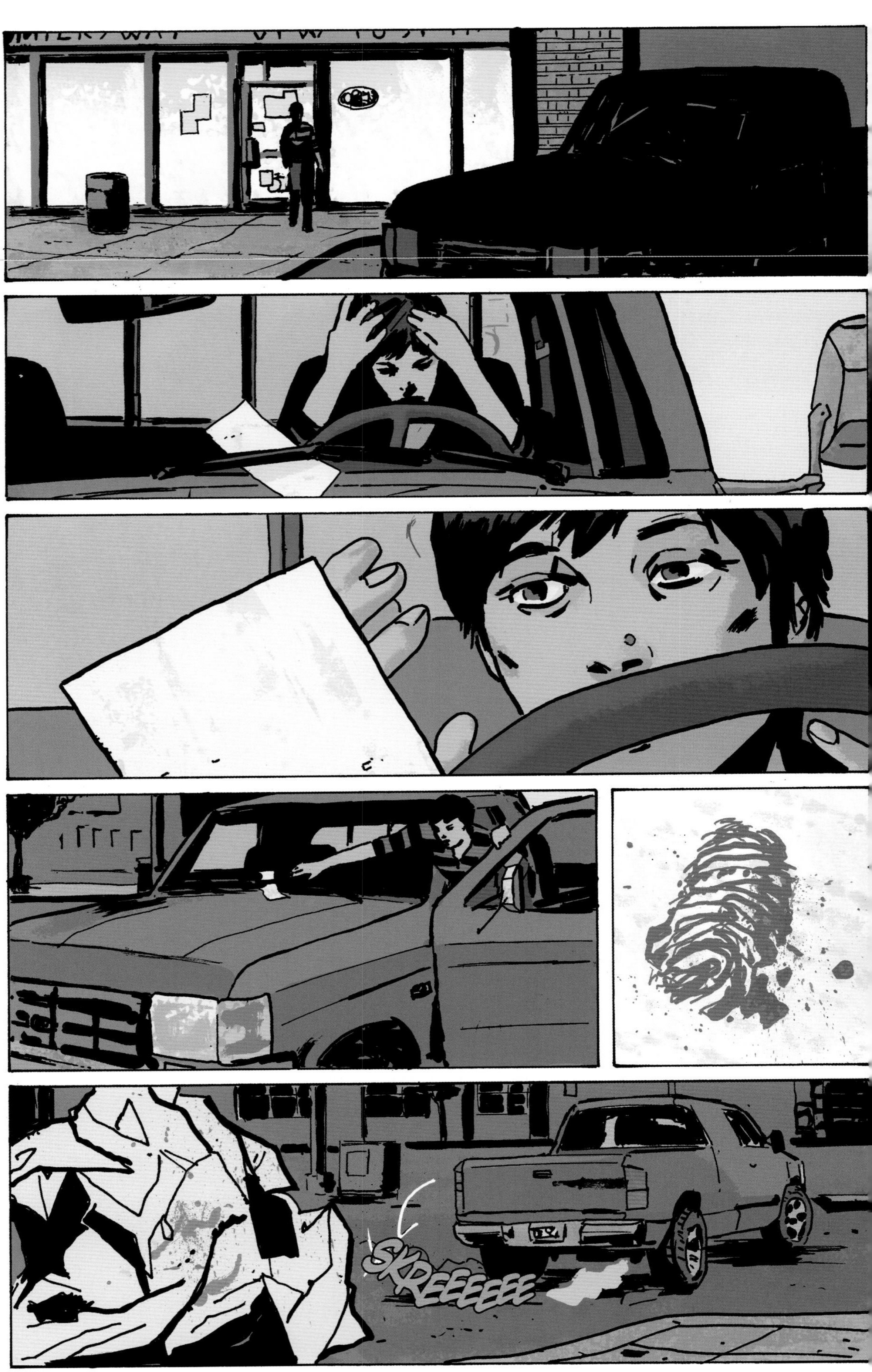
SKREEEEEEE

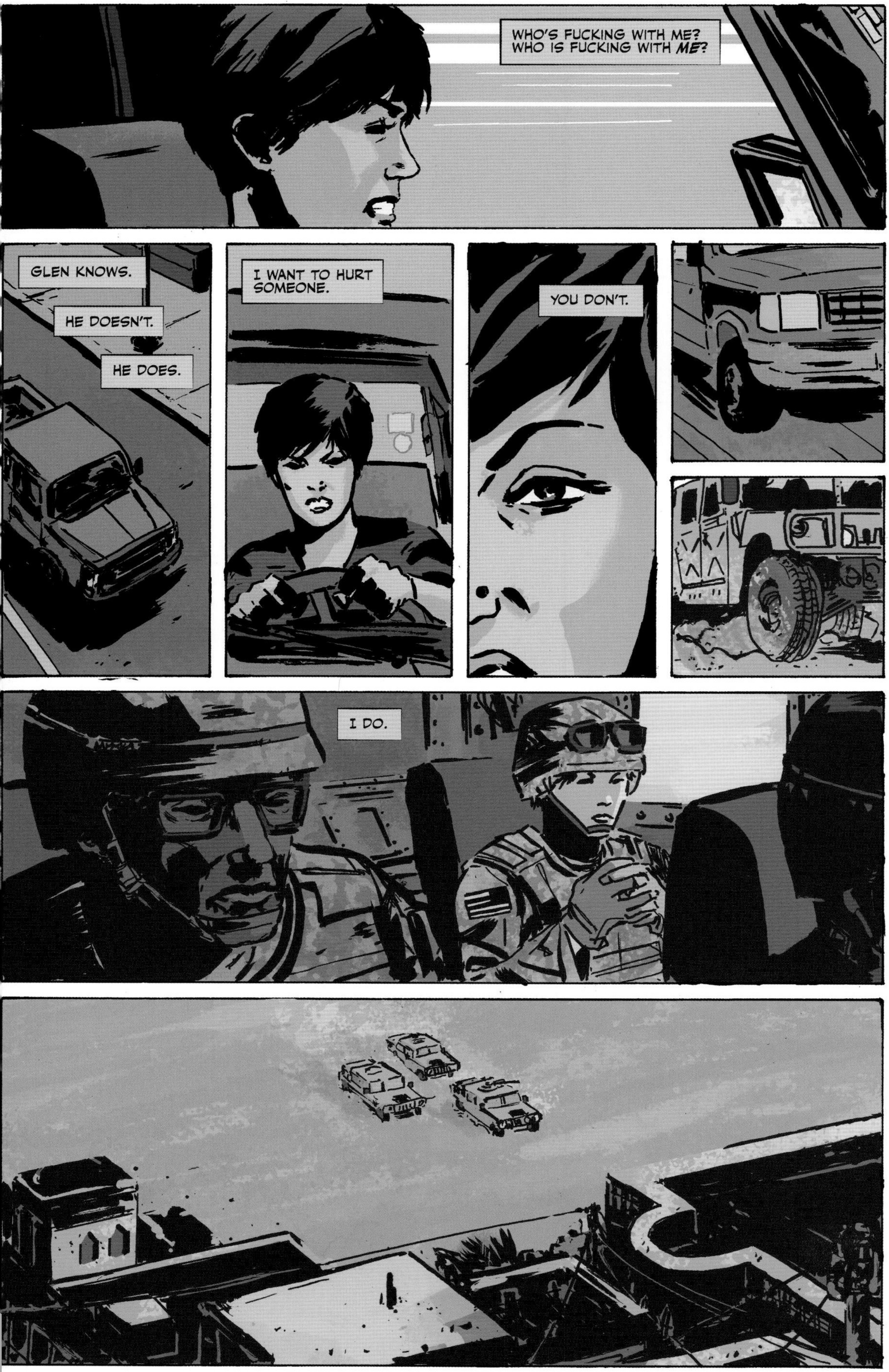
WHO'S FUCKING WITH ME?
WHO IS FUCKING WITH ***ME***?
GLEN KNOWS.
HE DOESN'T.
HE DOES.
I WANT TO HURT SOMEONE.
YOU DON'T.
I DO.

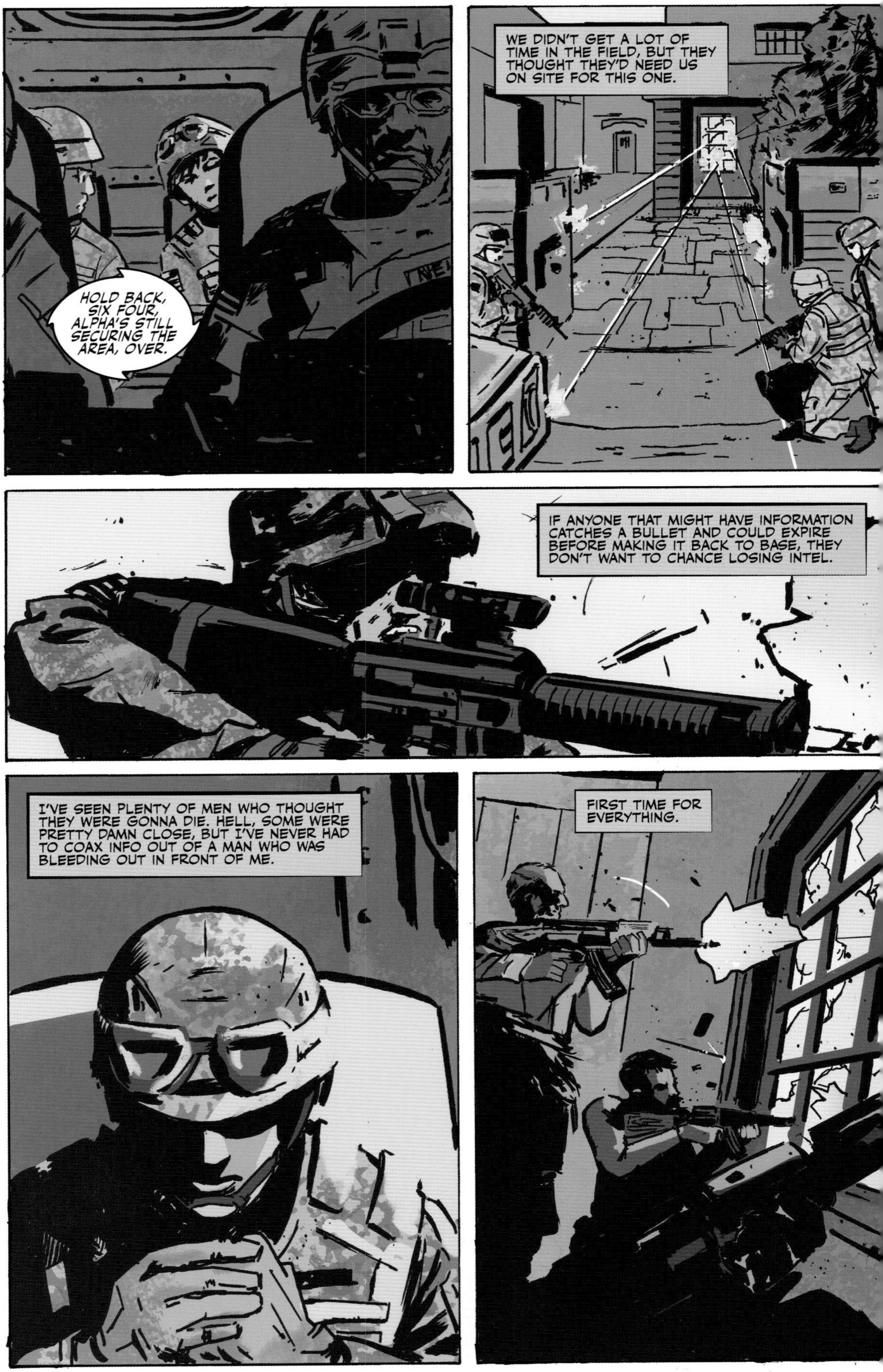
HOLD BACK, SIX FOUR, ALPHA'S STILL SECURING THE AREA, OVER.
WE DIDN'T GET A LOT OF TIME IN THE FIELD, BUT THEY THOUGHT THEY'D NEED US ON SITE FOR THIS ONE.
IF ANYONE THAT MIGHT HAVE INFORMATION CATCHES A BULLET AND COULD EXPIRE BEFORE MAKING IT BACK TO BASE, THEY DON'T WANT TO CHANCE LOSING INTEL.
I'VE SEEN PLENTY OF MEN WHO THOUGHT THEY WERE GONNA DIE. HELL, SOME WERE PRETTY DAMN CLOSE, BUT I'VE NEVER HAD TO COAX INFO OUT OF A MAN WHO WAS BLEEDING OUT IN FRONT OF ME.
FIRST TIME FOR EVERYTHING.

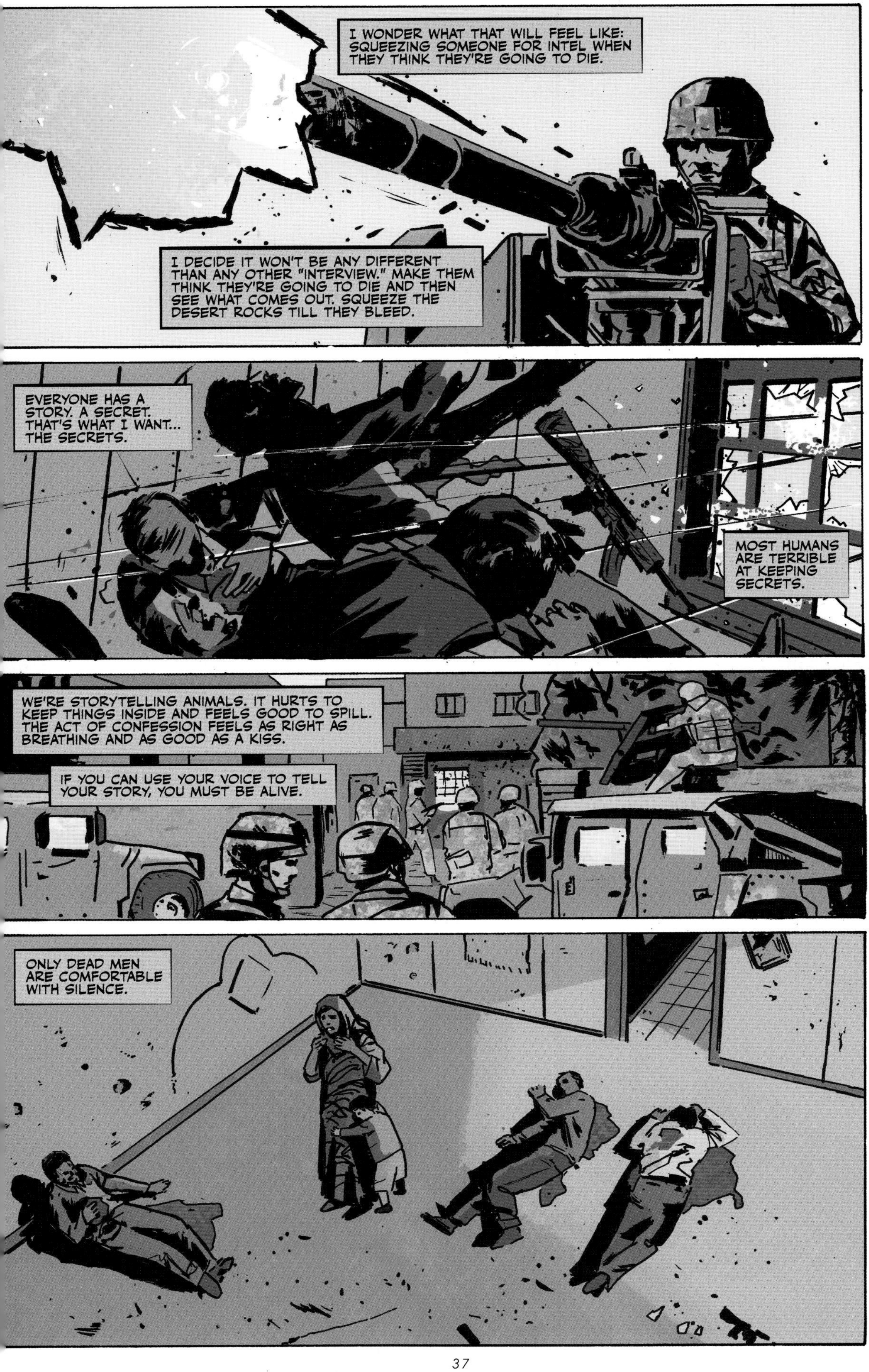
I WONDER WHAT THAT WILL FEEL LIKE: SQUEEZING SOMEONE FOR INTEL WHEN THEY THINK THEY'RE GOING TO DIE.
I DECIDE IT WON'T BE ANY DIFFERENT THAN ANY OTHER "INTERVIEW." MAKE THEM THINK THEY'RE GOING TO DIE AND THEN SEE WHAT COMES OUT. SQUEEZE THE DESERT ROCKS TILL THEY BLEED.
EVERYONE HAS A STORY. A SECRET. THAT'S WHAT I WANT... THE SECRETS.
MOST HUMANS ARE TERRIBLE AT KEEPING SECRETS.
WE'RE STORYTELLING ANIMALS. IT HURTS TO KEEP THINGS INSIDE AND FEELS GOOD TO SPILL. THE ACT OF CONFESSION FEELS AS RIGHT AS BREATHING AND AS GOOD AS A KISS.
IF YOU CAN USE YOUR VOICE TO TELL YOUR STORY, YOU MUST BE ALIVE.
ONLY DEAD MEN ARE COMFORTABLE WITH SILENCE.

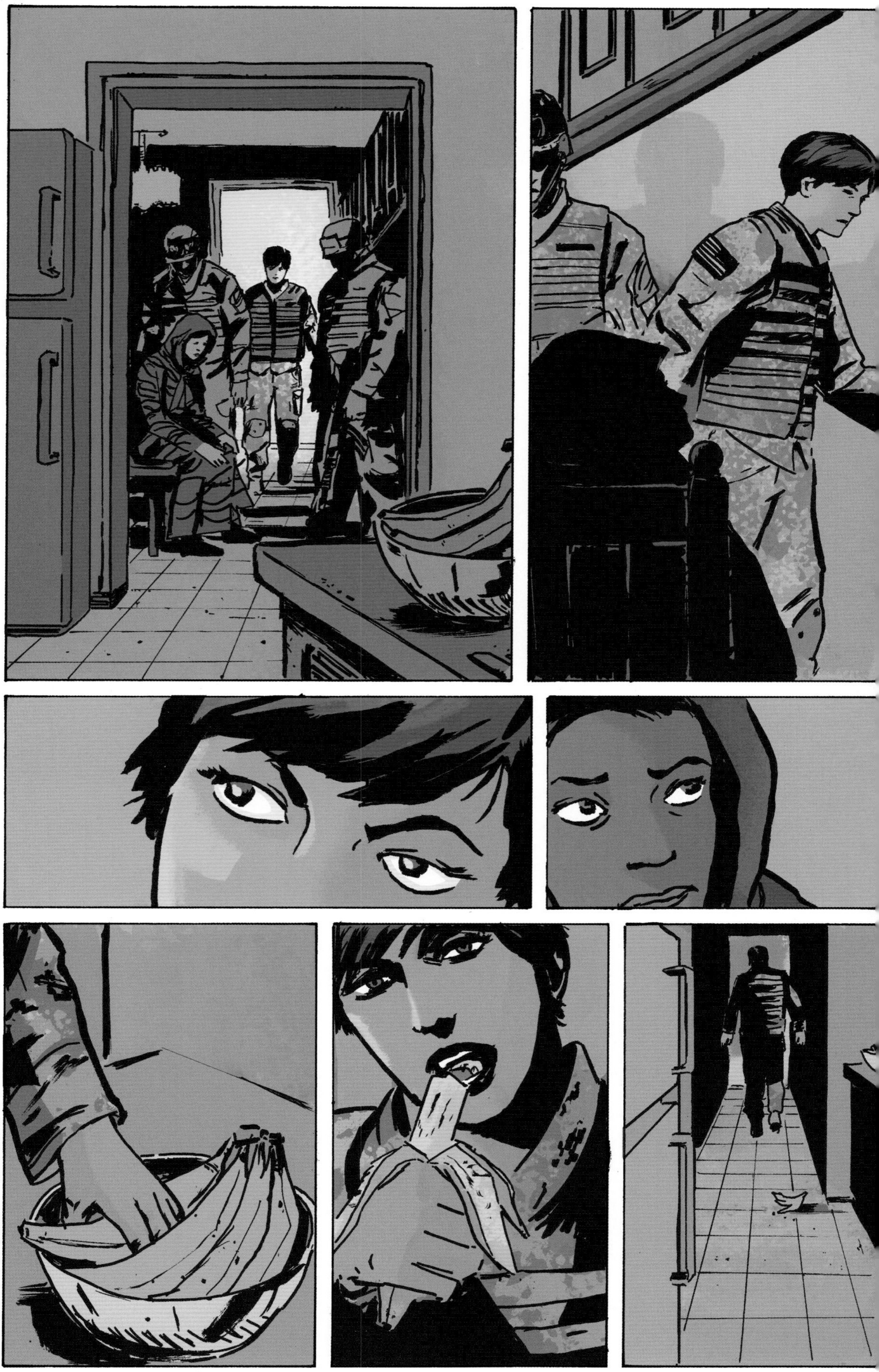

⟨HEL...
HEL...⟩

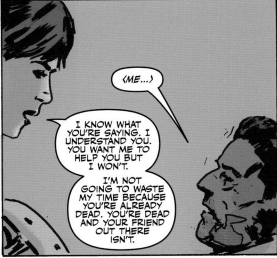

⟨ME...⟩

I KNOW WHAT
YOU'RE SAYING. I
UNDERSTAND YOU.
YOU WANT ME TO
HELP YOU BUT
I WON'T.

I'M NOT
GOING TO WASTE
MY TIME BECAUSE
YOU'RE ALREADY
DEAD. YOU'RE DEAD
AND YOUR FRIEND
OUT THERE
ISN'T.

YOUR
FRIEND IS THE
ONE WHO HAS
THE SECRETS...

HHHHAAAAAAAA...

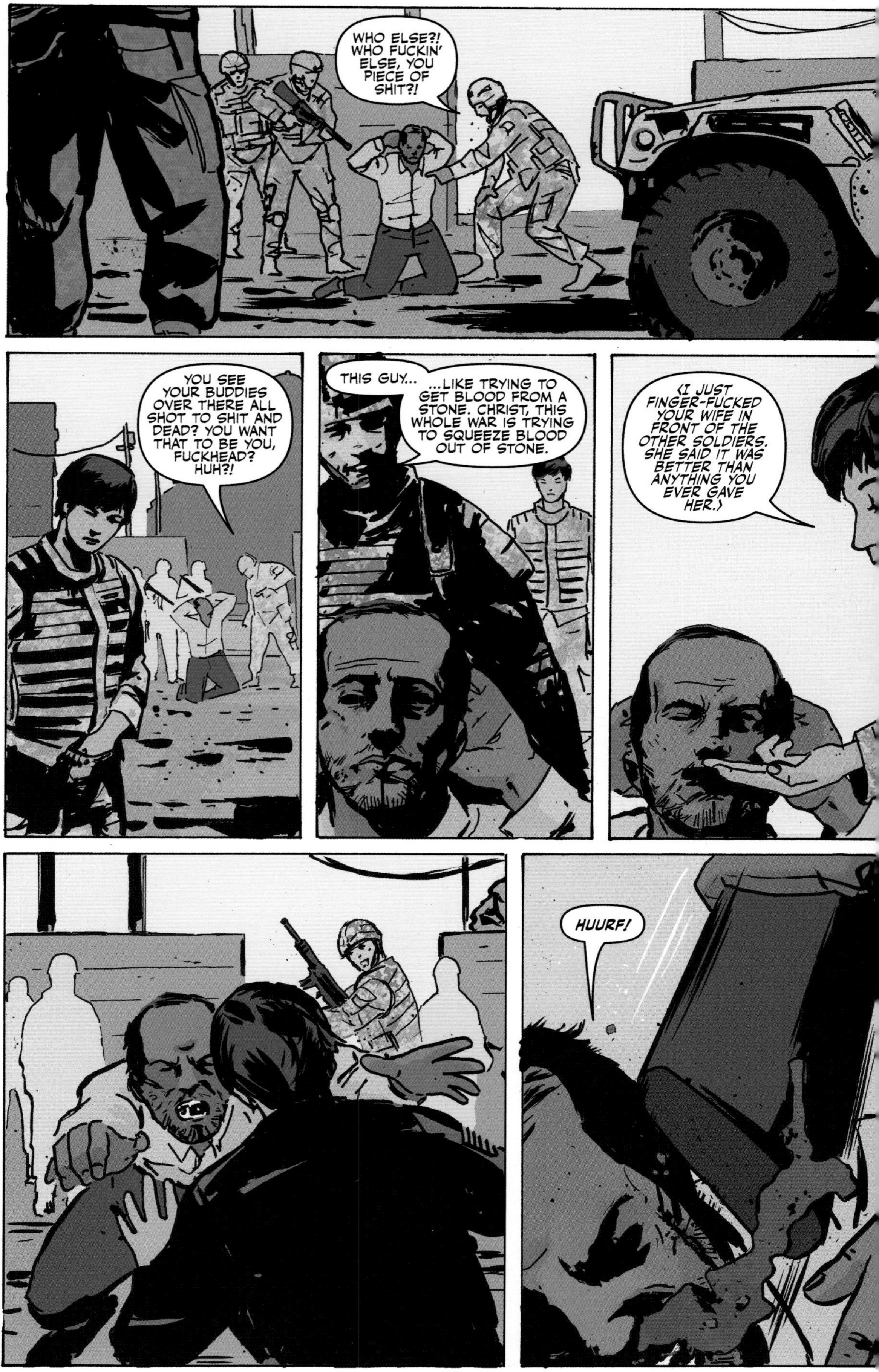
WHO ELSE?! WHO FUCKIN' ELSE, YOU PIECE OF SHIT?!
YOU SEE YOUR BUDDIES OVER THERE ALL SHOT TO SHIT AND DEAD? YOU WANT THAT TO BE YOU, FUCKHEAD? HUH?!
THIS GUY...
...LIKE TRYING TO GET BLOOD FROM A STONE. CHRIST, THIS WHOLE WAR IS TRYING TO SQUEEZE BLOOD OUT OF STONE.
<I JUST FINGER-FUCKED YOUR WIFE IN FRONT OF THE OTHER SOLDIERS. SHE SAID IT WAS BETTER THAN ANYTHING YOU EVER GAVE HER.>
HUURF!

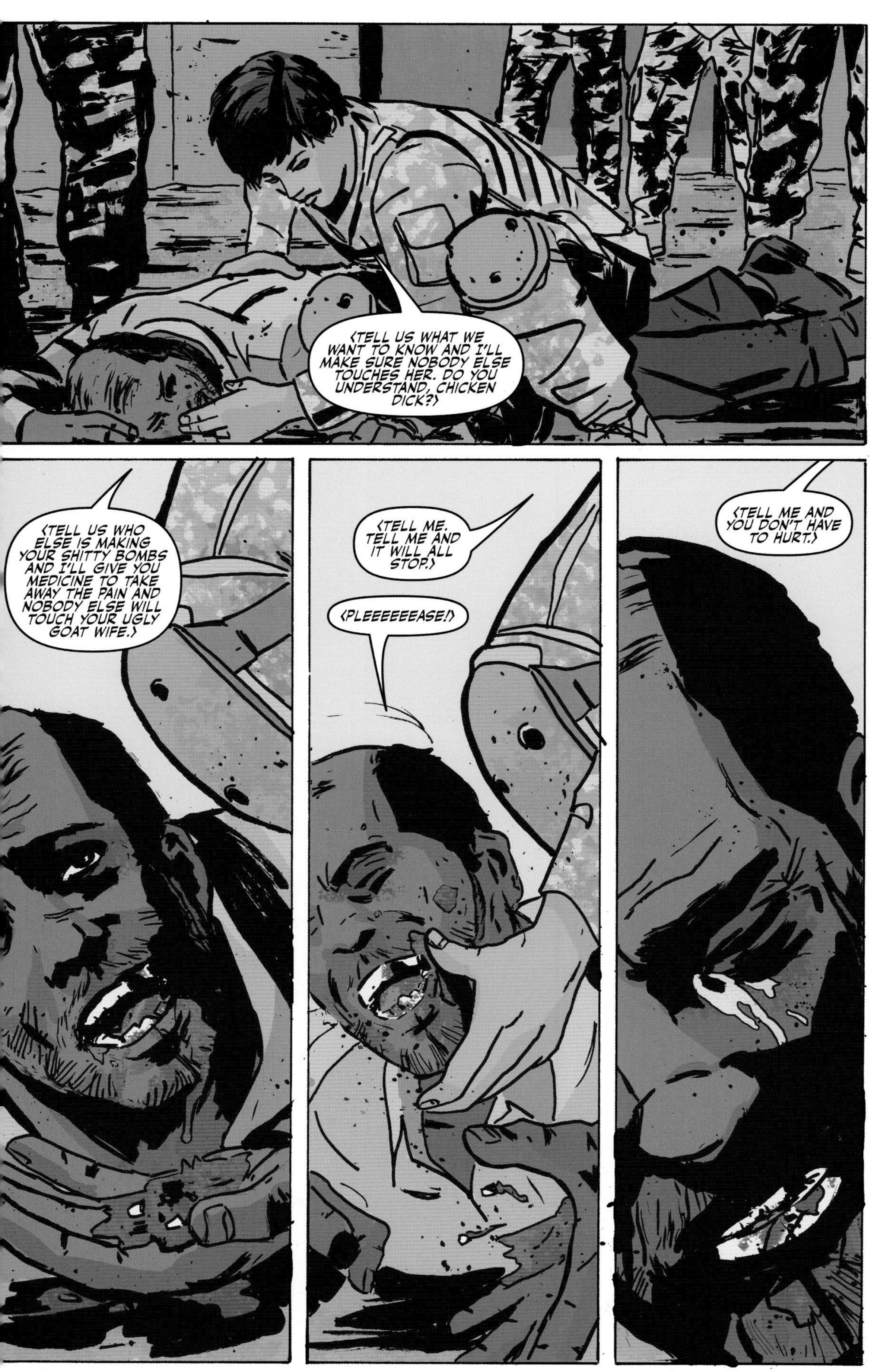
‹TELL US WHAT WE WANT TO KNOW AND I'LL MAKE SURE NOBODY ELSE TOUCHES HER. DO YOU UNDERSTAND, CHICKEN DICK?›
‹TELL US WHO ELSE IS MAKING YOUR SHITTY BOMBS AND I'LL GIVE YOU MEDICINE TO TAKE AWAY THE PAIN AND NOBODY ELSE WILL TOUCH YOUR UGLY GOAT WIFE.›
‹TELL ME. TELL ME AND IT WILL ALL STOP.›
‹PLEEEEEEASE!›
‹TELL ME AND YOU DON'T HAVE TO HURT.›

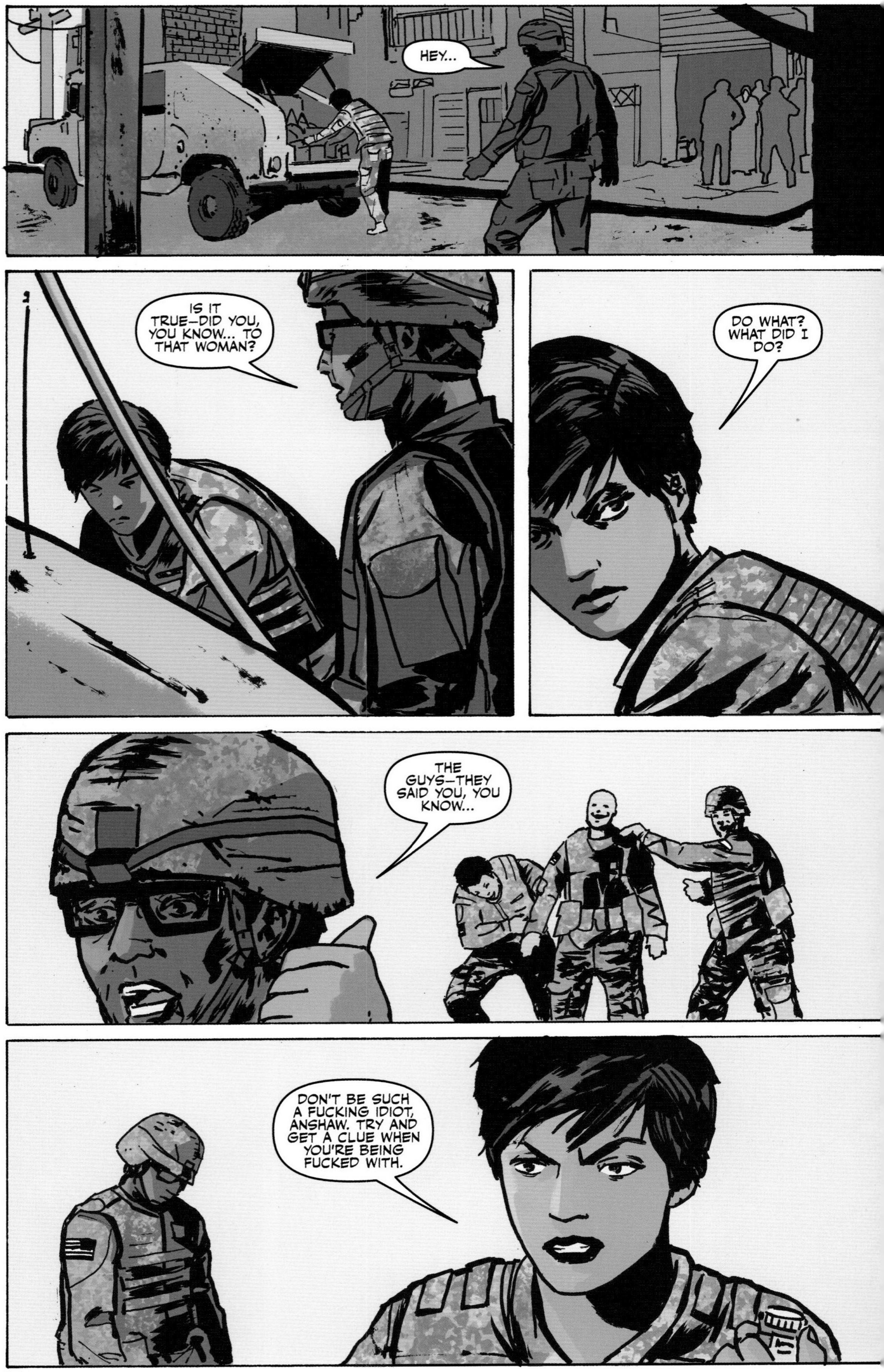
HEY...
IS IT TRUE—DID YOU, YOU KNOW... TO THAT WOMAN?
DO WHAT? WHAT DID I DO?
THE GUYS—THEY SAID YOU, YOU KNOW...
DON'T BE SUCH A FUCKING IDIOT, ANSHAW. TRY AND GET A CLUE WHEN YOU'RE BEING FUCKED WITH.

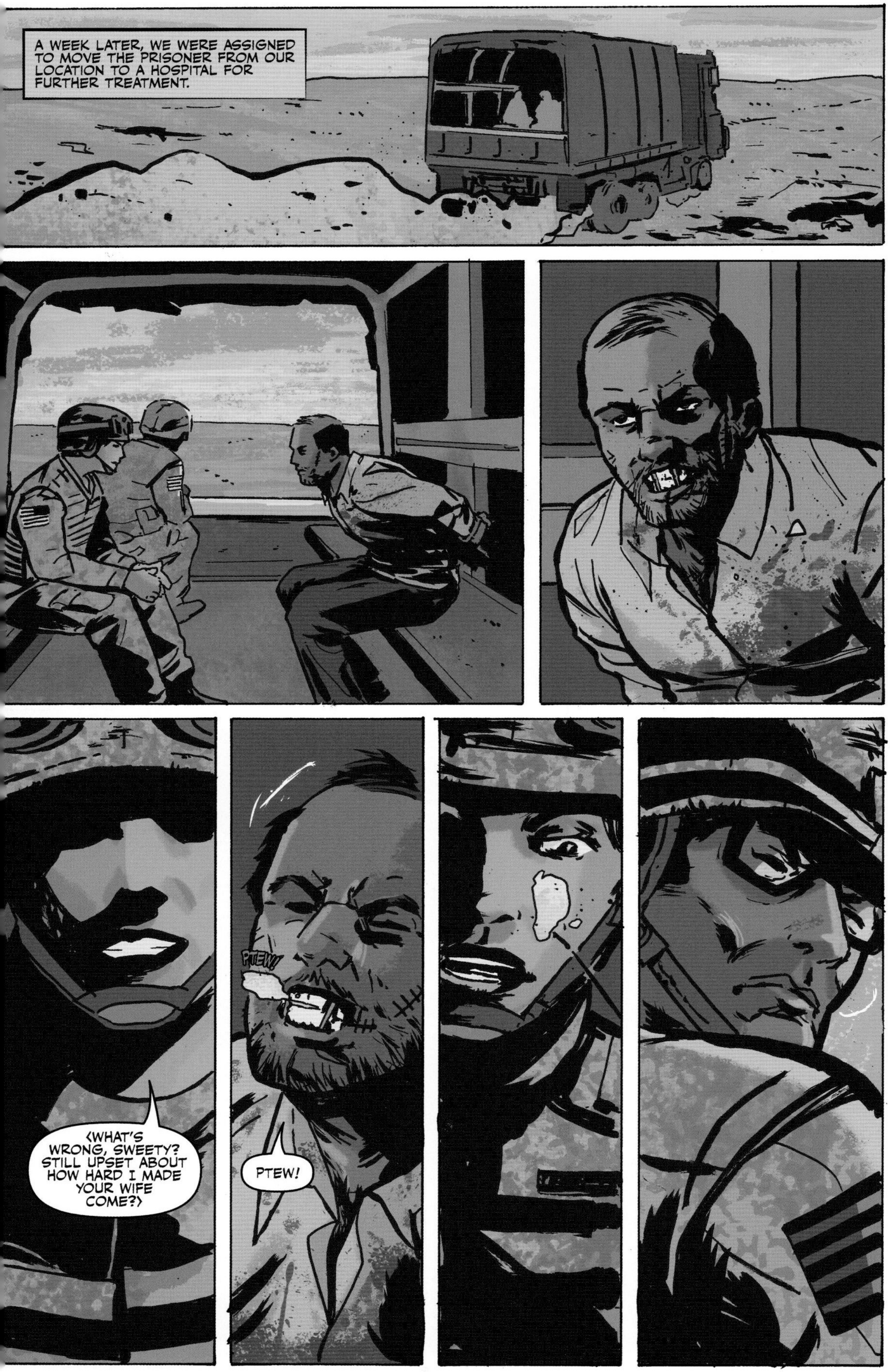
A WEEK LATER, WE WERE ASSIGNED TO MOVE THE PRISONER FROM OUR LOCATION TO A HOSPITAL FOR FURTHER TREATMENT.
<WHAT'S WRONG, SWEETY? STILL UPSET ABOUT HOW HARD I MADE YOUR WIFE COME?>
PTEW!
PTEW!

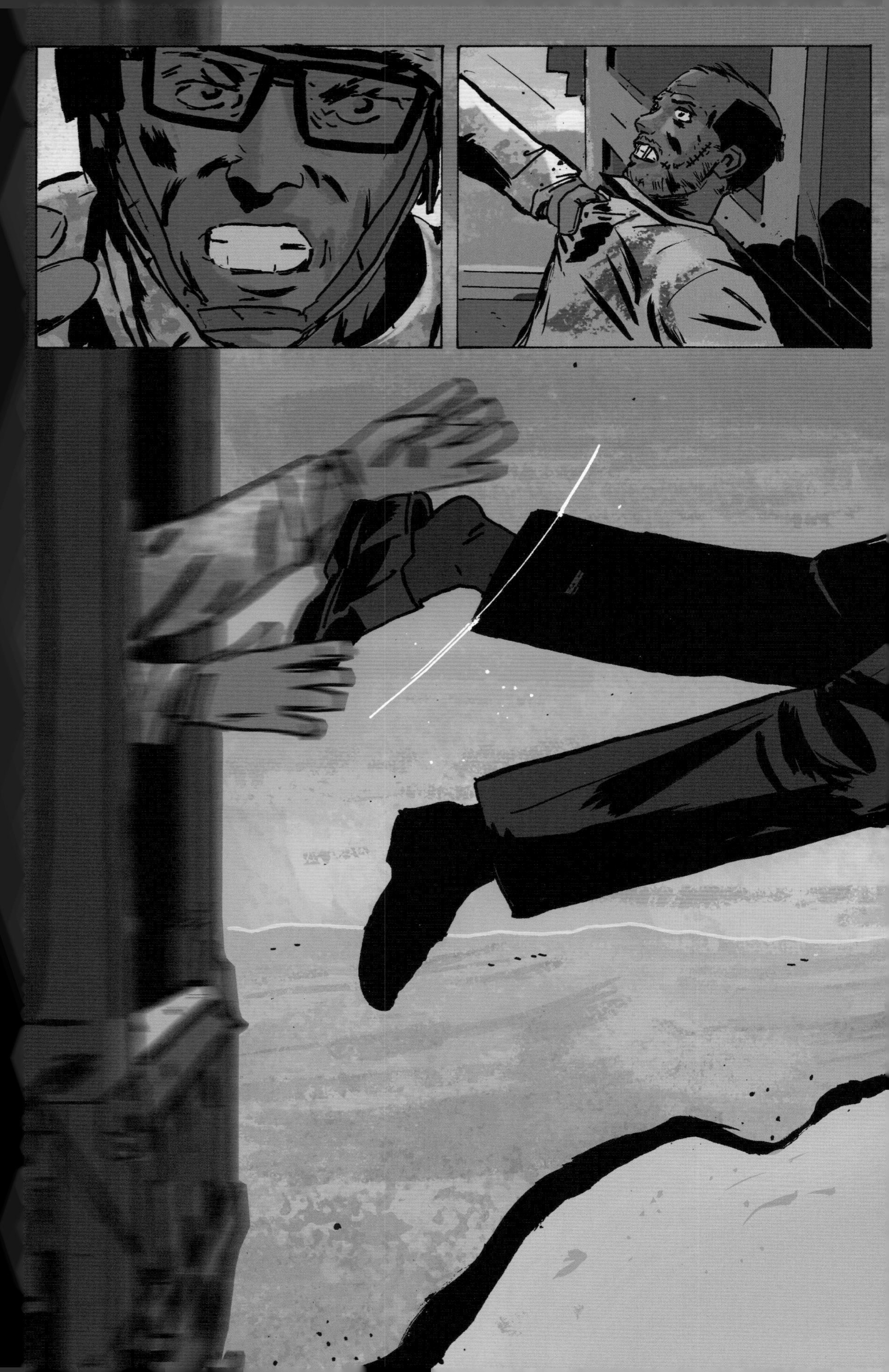

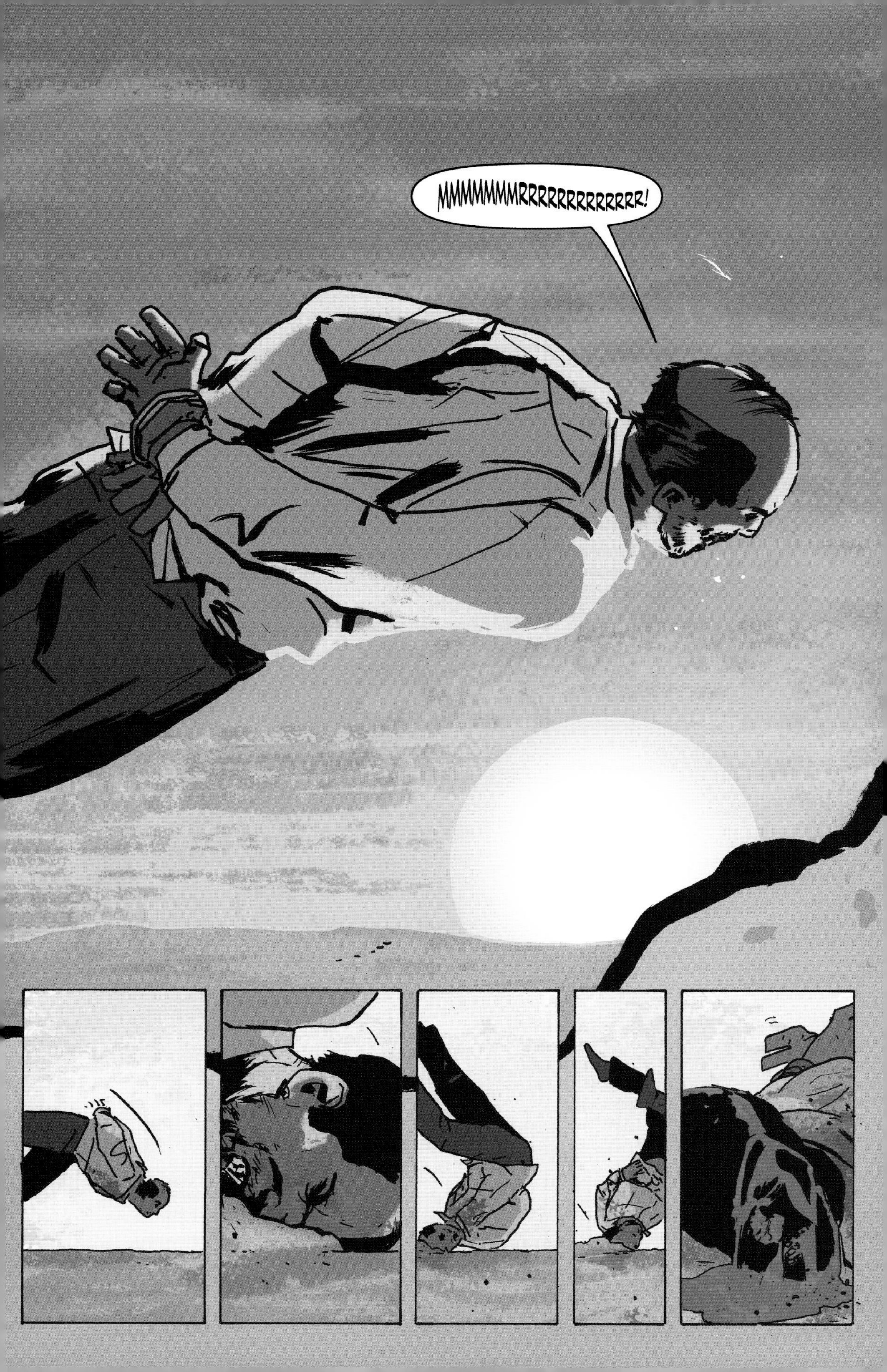
MMMMMMMMRRRRRRRRRRRRR!

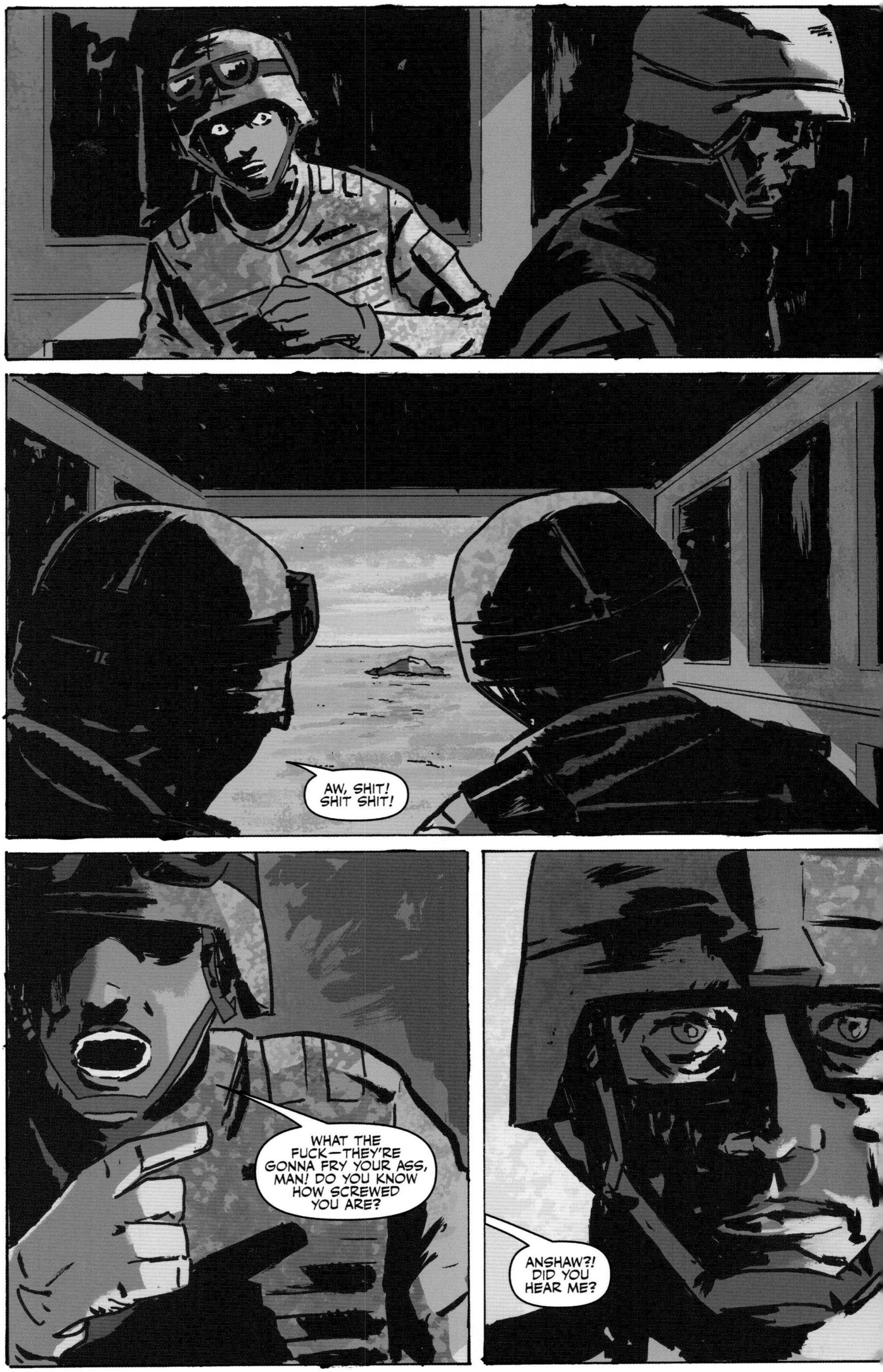
AW, SHIT! SHIT SHIT!
WHAT THE FUCK—THEY'RE GONNA FRY YOUR ASS, MAN! DO YOU KNOW HOW SCREWED YOU ARE?
ANSHAW?! DID YOU HEAR ME?

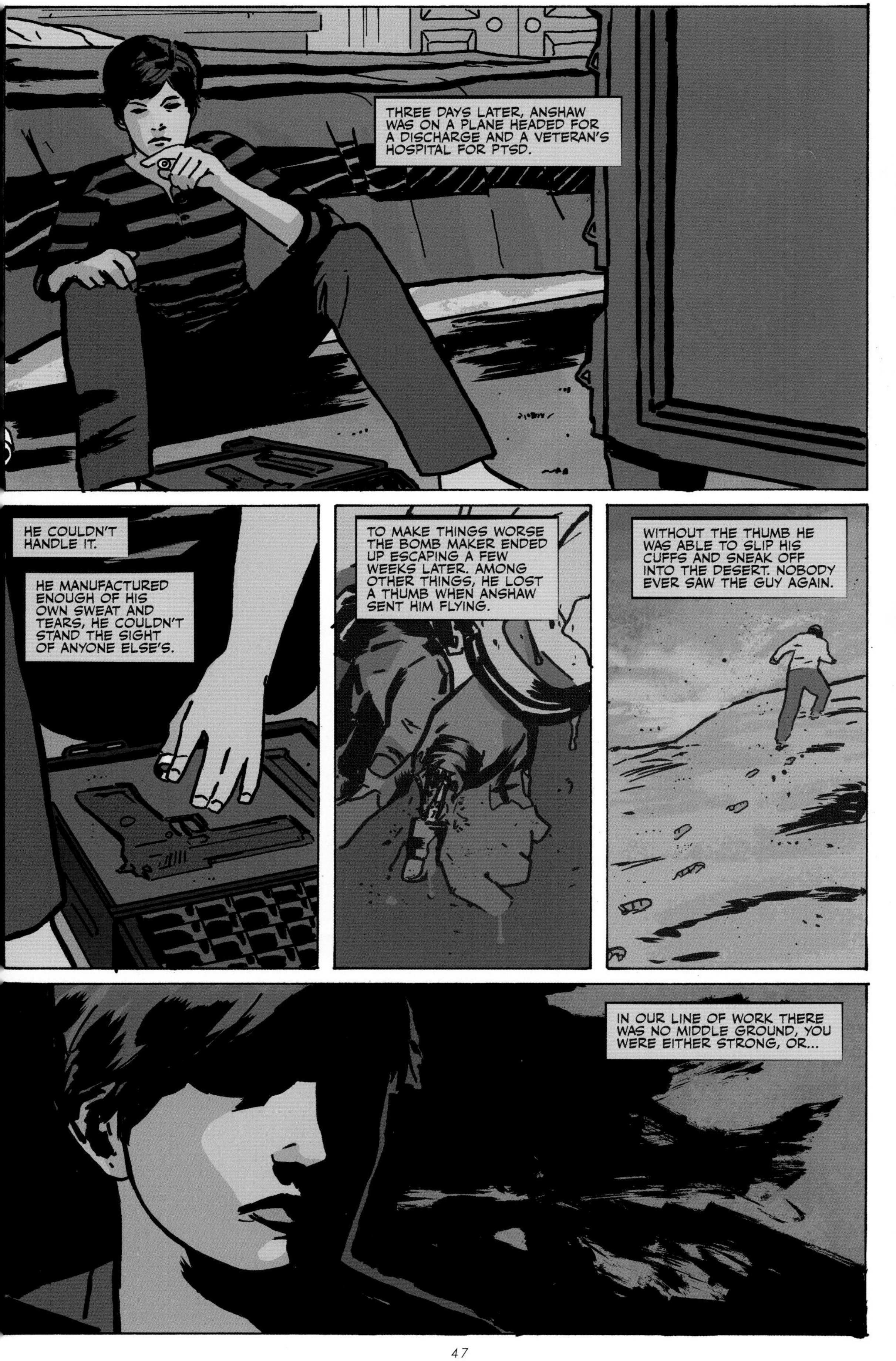
THREE DAYS LATER, ANSHAW WAS ON A PLANE HEADED FOR A DISCHARGE AND A VETERAN'S HOSPITAL FOR PTSD.
HE COULDN'T HANDLE IT.
HE MANUFACTURED ENOUGH OF HIS OWN SWEAT AND TEARS, HE COULDN'T STAND THE SIGHT OF ANYONE ELSE'S.
TO MAKE THINGS WORSE THE BOMB MAKER ENDED UP ESCAPING A FEW WEEKS LATER. AMONG OTHER THINGS, HE LOST A THUMB WHEN ANSHAW SENT HIM FLYING.
WITHOUT THE THUMB HE WAS ABLE TO SLIP HIS CUFFS AND SNEAK OFF INTO THE DESERT. NOBODY EVER SAW THE GUY AGAIN.
IN OUR LINE OF WORK THERE WAS NO MIDDLE GROUND, YOU WERE EITHER STRONG, OR...

...WEAK...

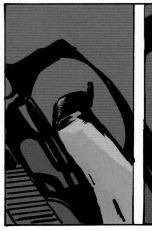

BLAM

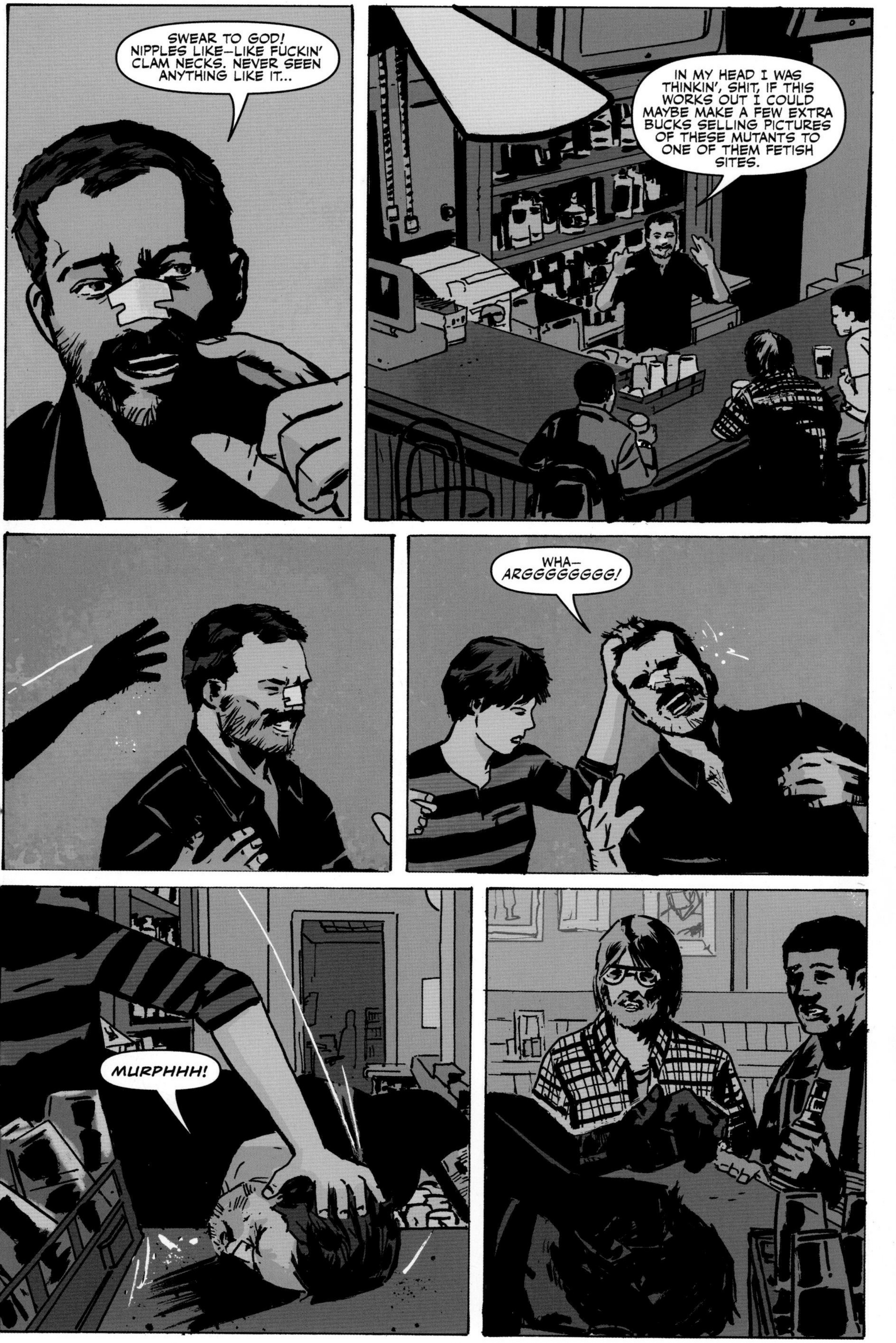
SWEAR TO GOD! NIPPLES LIKE--LIKE FUCKIN' CLAM NECKS. NEVER SEEN ANYTHING LIKE IT...
IN MY HEAD I WAS THINKIN', SHIT, IF THIS WORKS OUT I COULD MAYBE MAKE A FEW EXTRA BUCKS SELLING PICTURES OF THESE MUTANTS TO ONE OF THEM FETISH SITES.
WHA--ARGGGGGGGG!
MURPHHH!

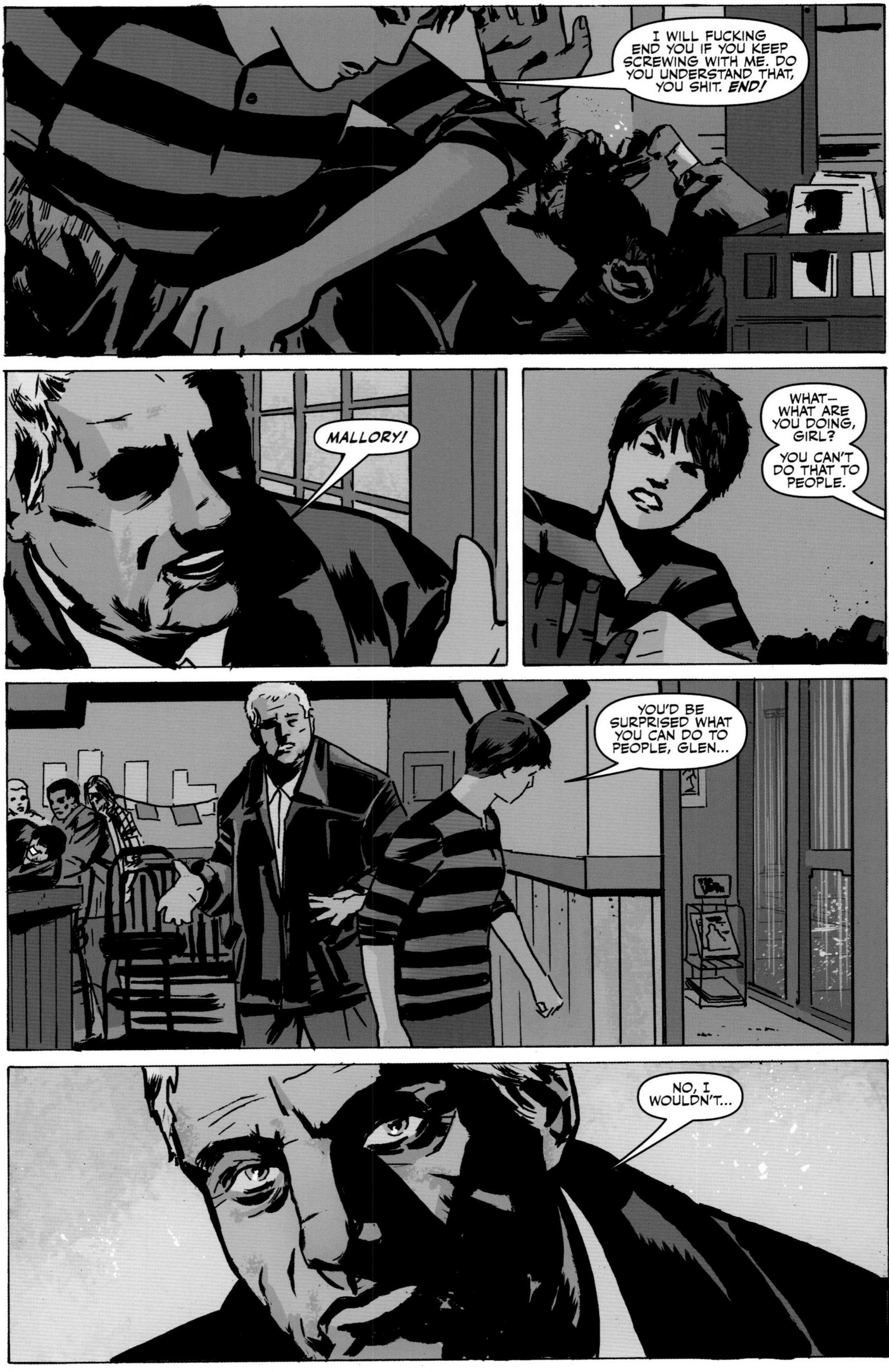
I WILL FUCKING END YOU IF YOU KEEP SCREWING WITH ME. DO YOU UNDERSTAND THAT, YOU SHIT. END!
MALLORY!
WHAT— WHAT ARE YOU DOING, GIRL?
YOU CAN'T DO THAT TO PEOPLE.
YOU'D BE SURPRISED WHAT YOU CAN DO TO PEOPLE, GLEN...
NO, I WOULDN'T...

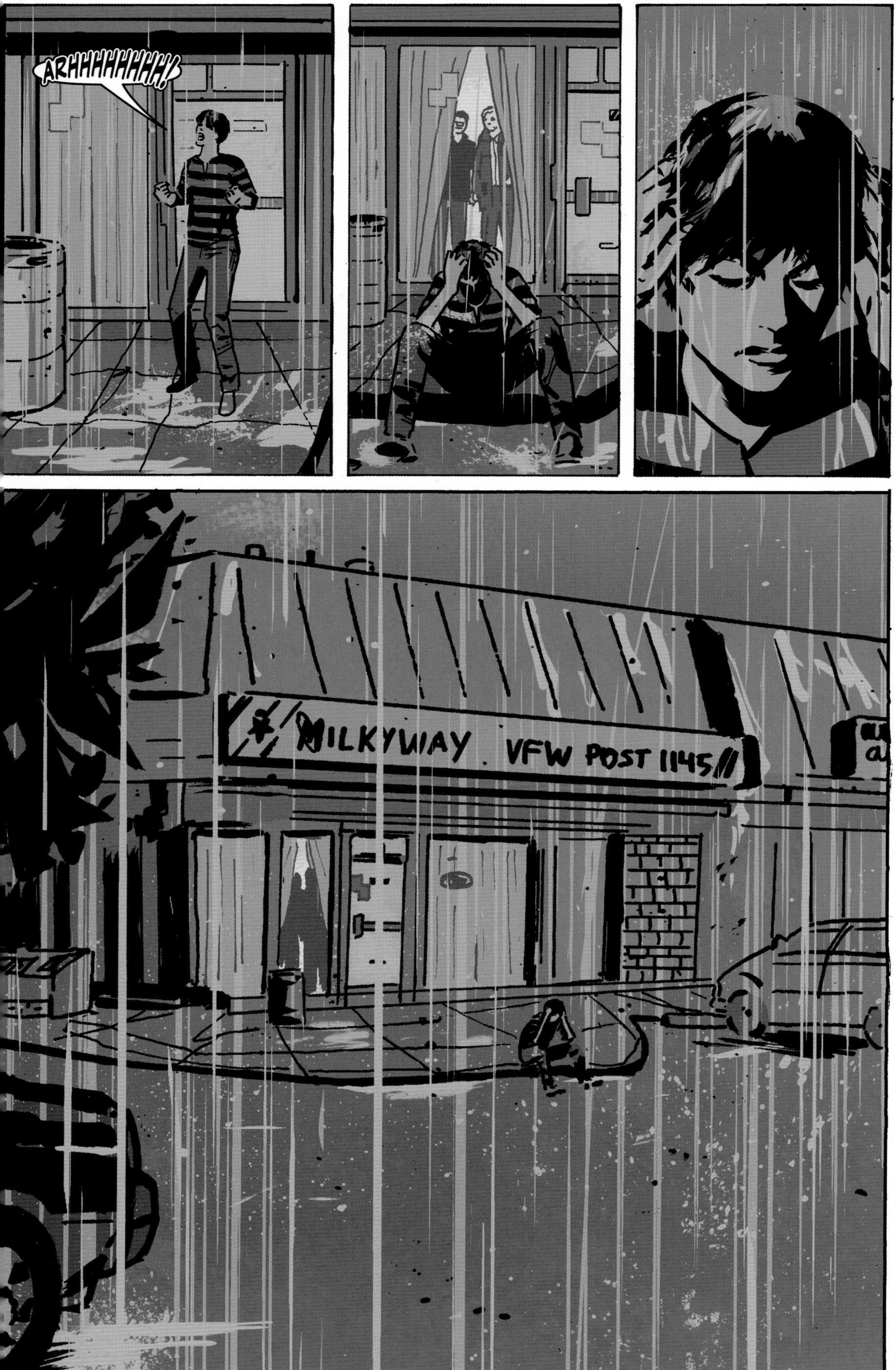
ARHHHHHHHH!
MILKYWAY
VFW POST 1145

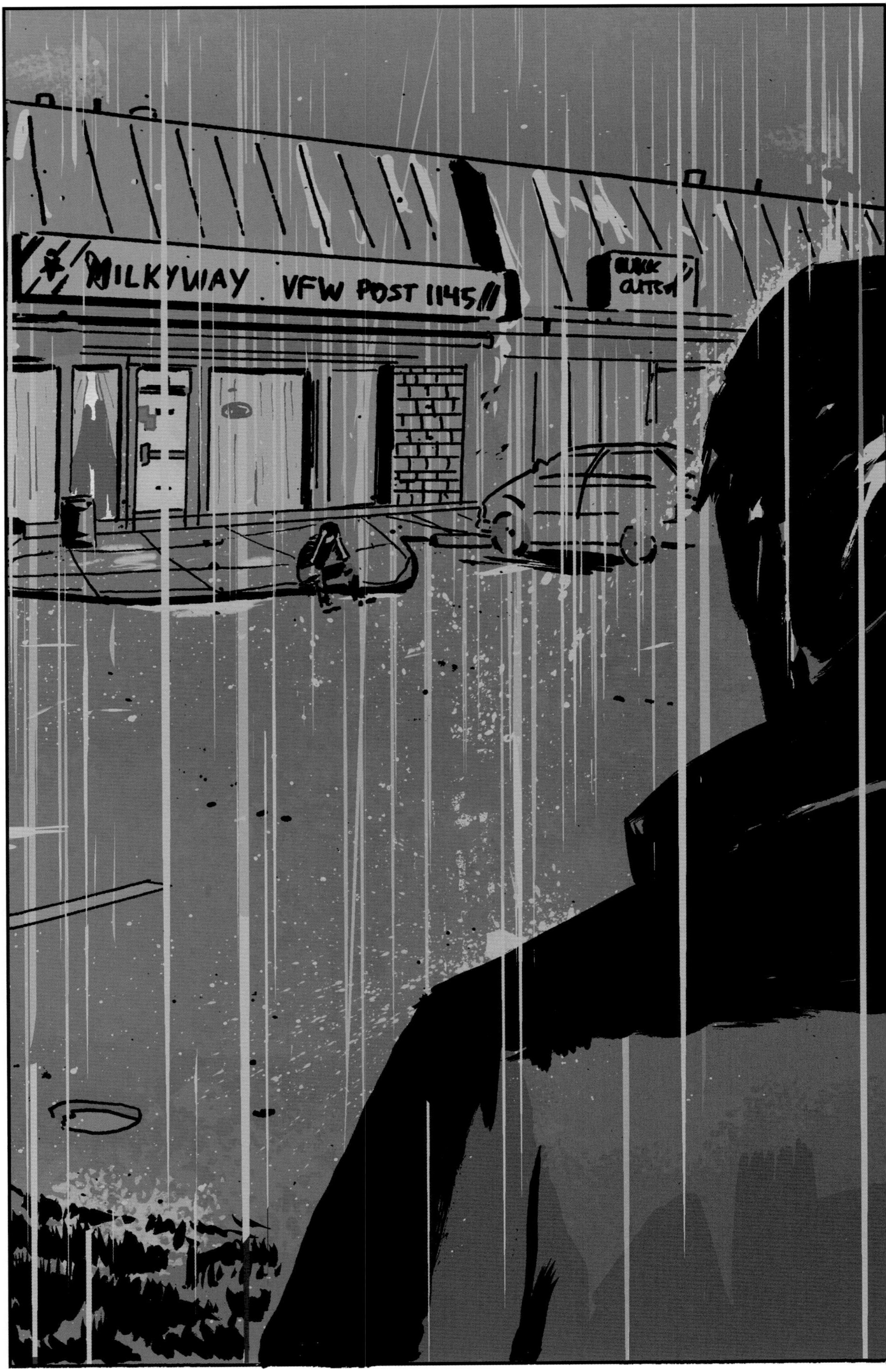
MILKYWAY
VFW POST 1145

Chapter 3

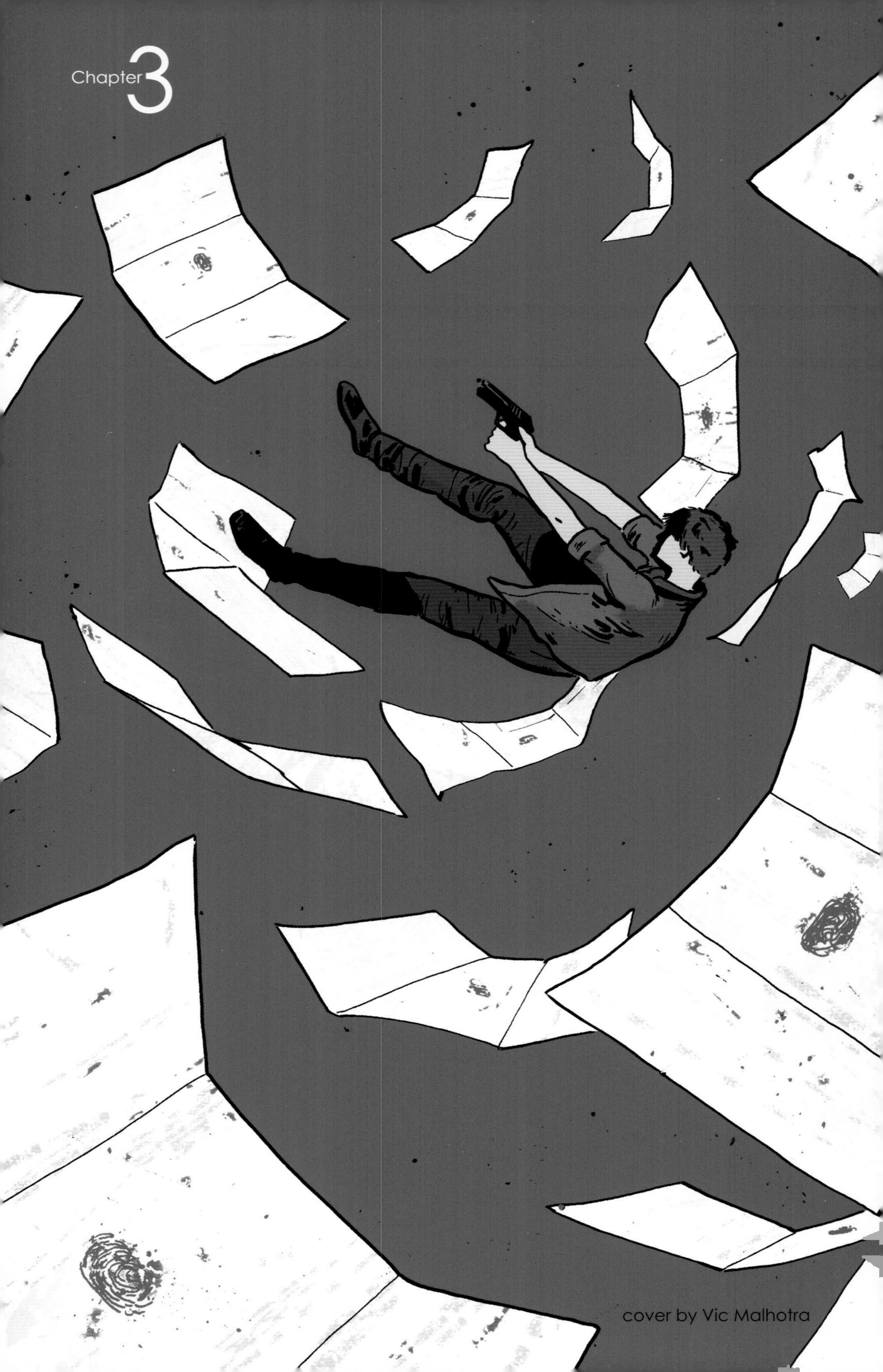

cover by Vic Malhotra

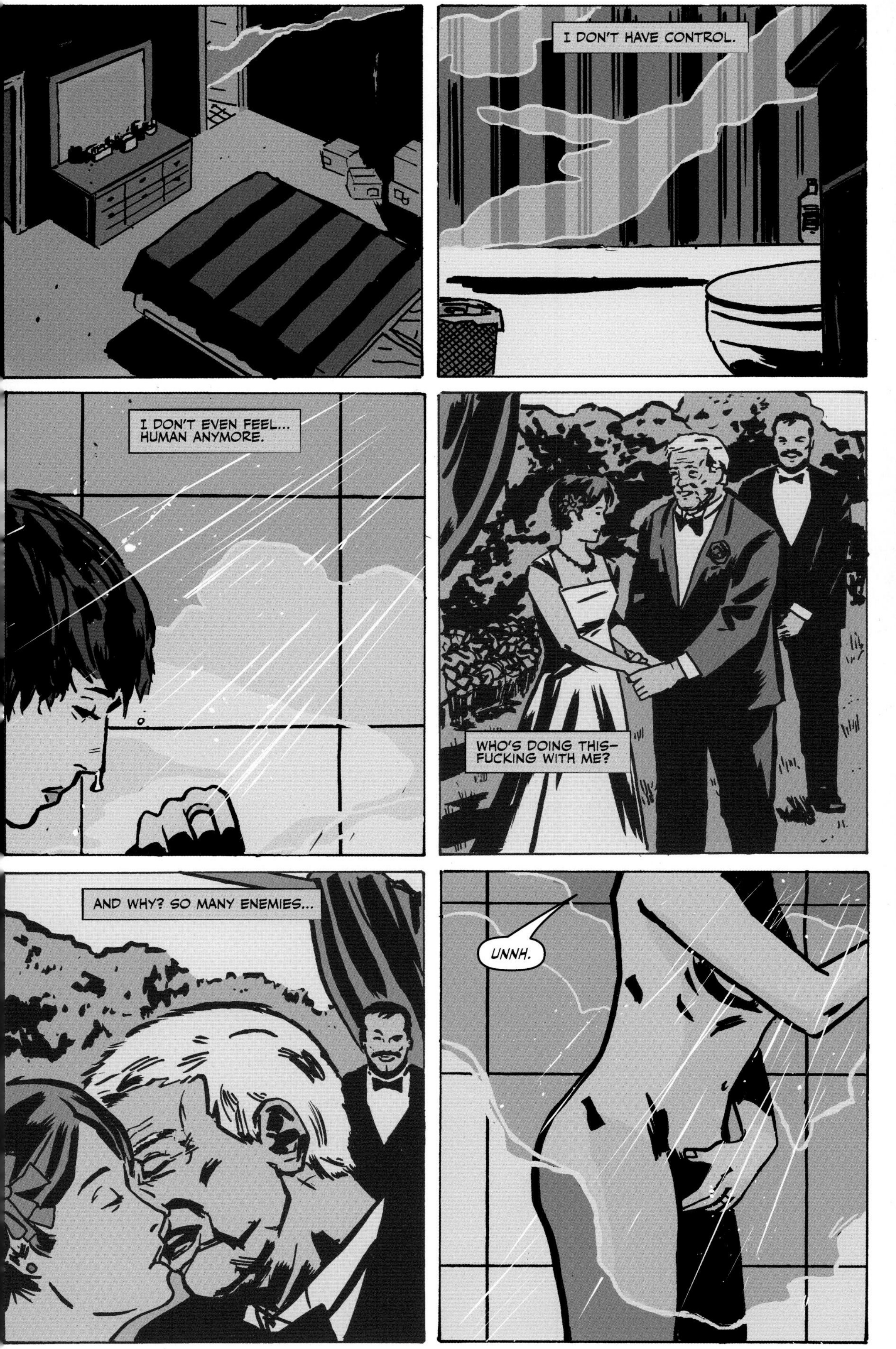
I DON'T HAVE CONTROL.
I DON'T EVEN FEEL... HUMAN ANYMORE.
WHO'S DOING THIS— FUCKING WITH ME?
AND WHY? SO MANY ENEMIES...
UNNH.

I SHOULD BE DISGUSTED WITH MYSELF, BUT I DON'T FEEL A DAMN THING.

UGH!

SMAK

UGH!

SMAK

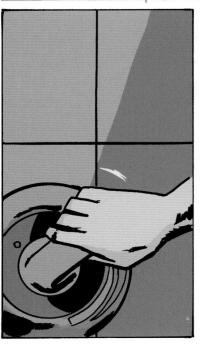

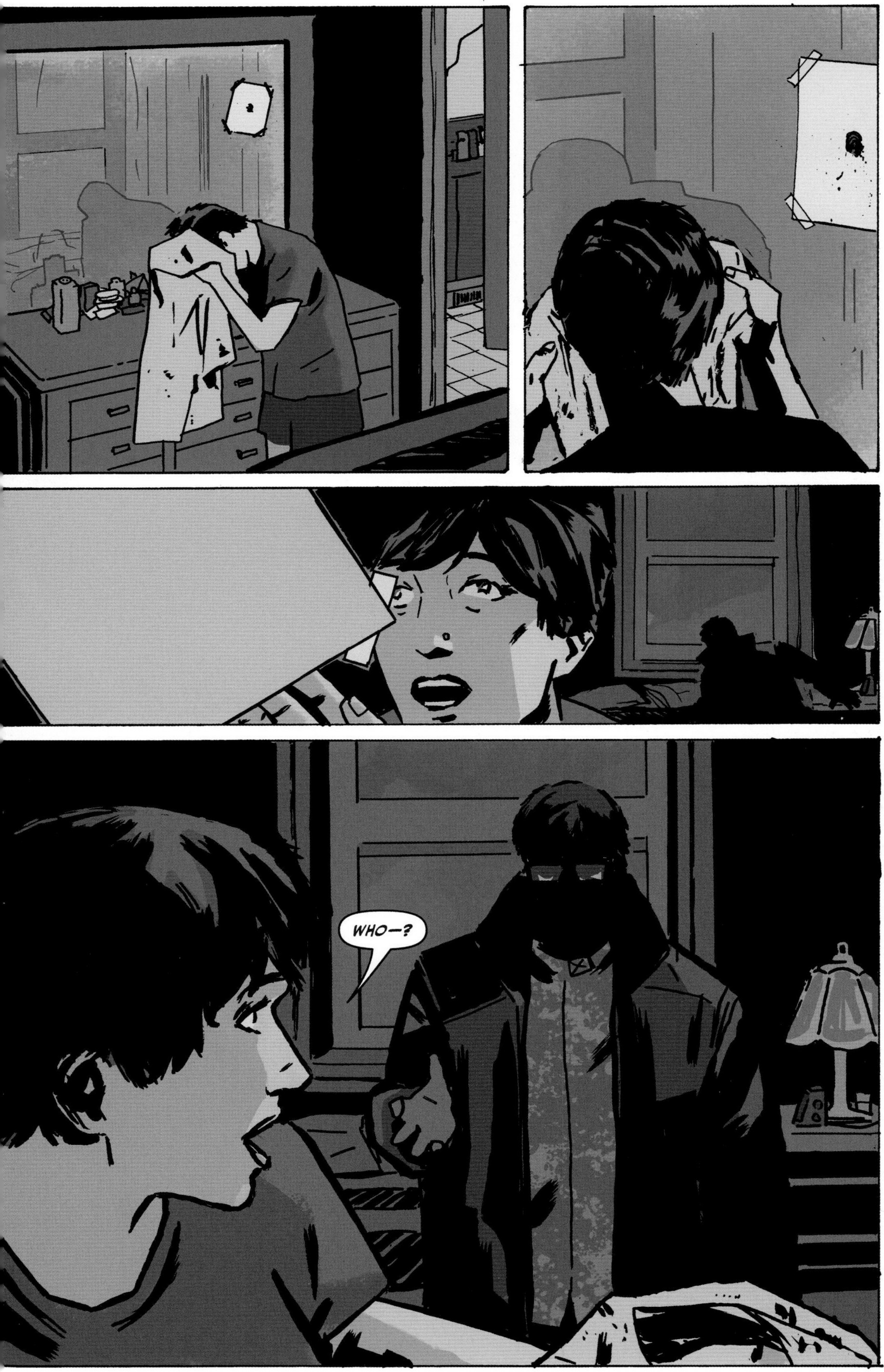
WHO—?

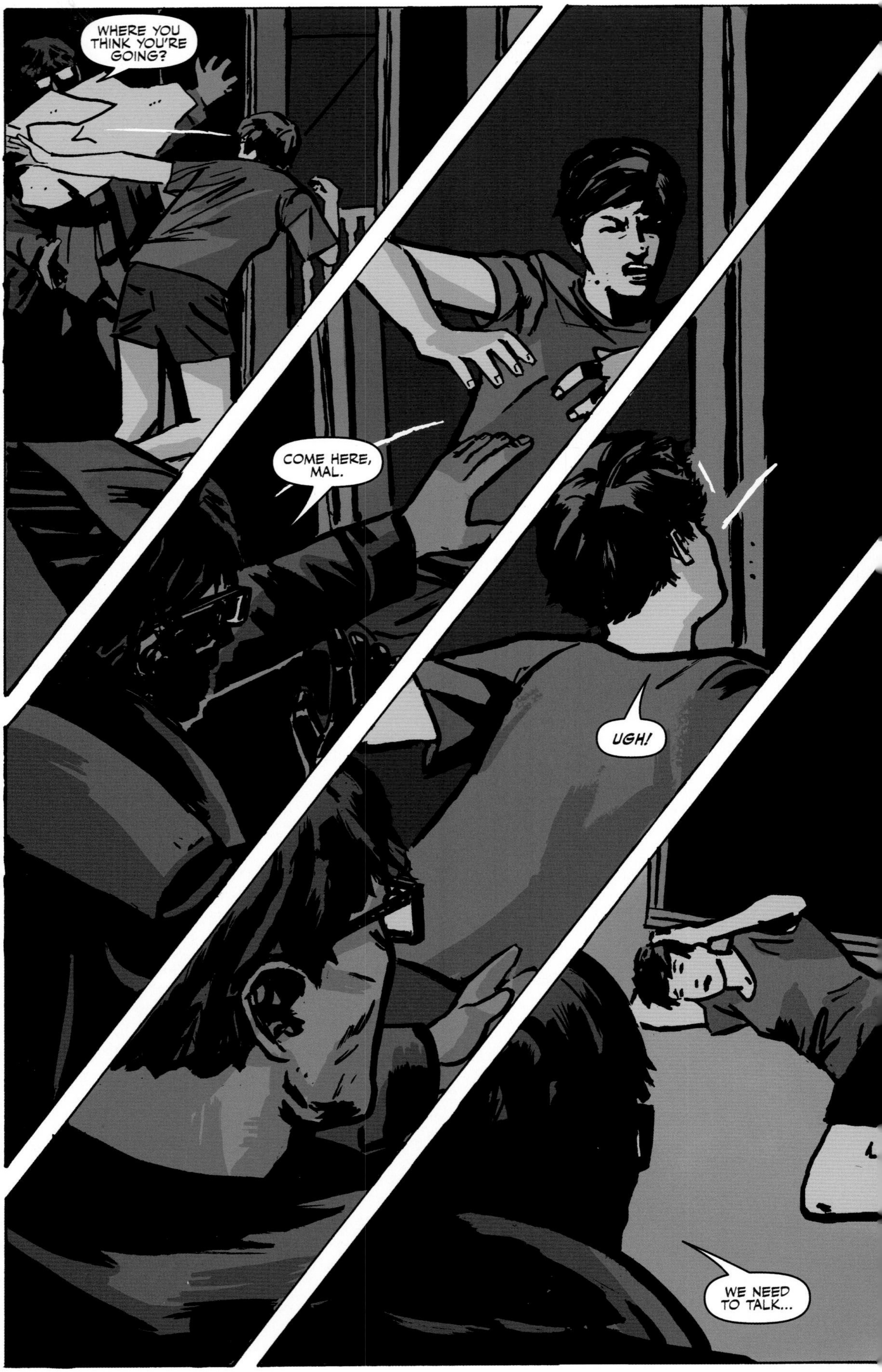
WHERE YOU THINK YOU'RE GOING?
COME HERE, MAL.
UGH!
WE NEED TO TALK...

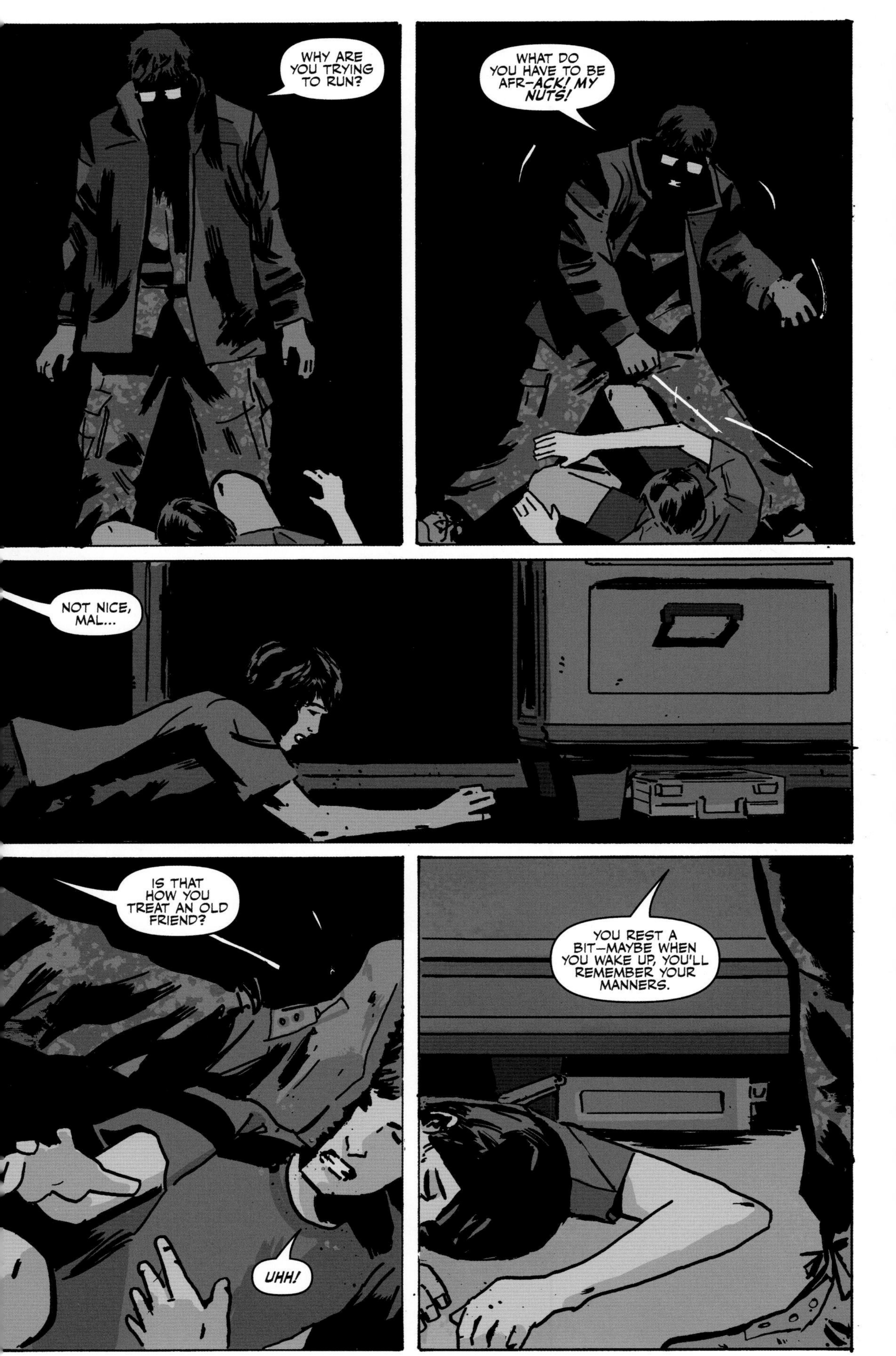
WHY ARE YOU TRYING TO RUN?
WHAT DO YOU HAVE TO BE AFR-ACK! MY NUTS!
NOT NICE, MAL...
IS THAT HOW YOU TREAT AN OLD FRIEND?
UHH!
YOU REST A BIT—MAYBE WHEN YOU WAKE UP, YOU'LL REMEMBER YOUR MANNERS.

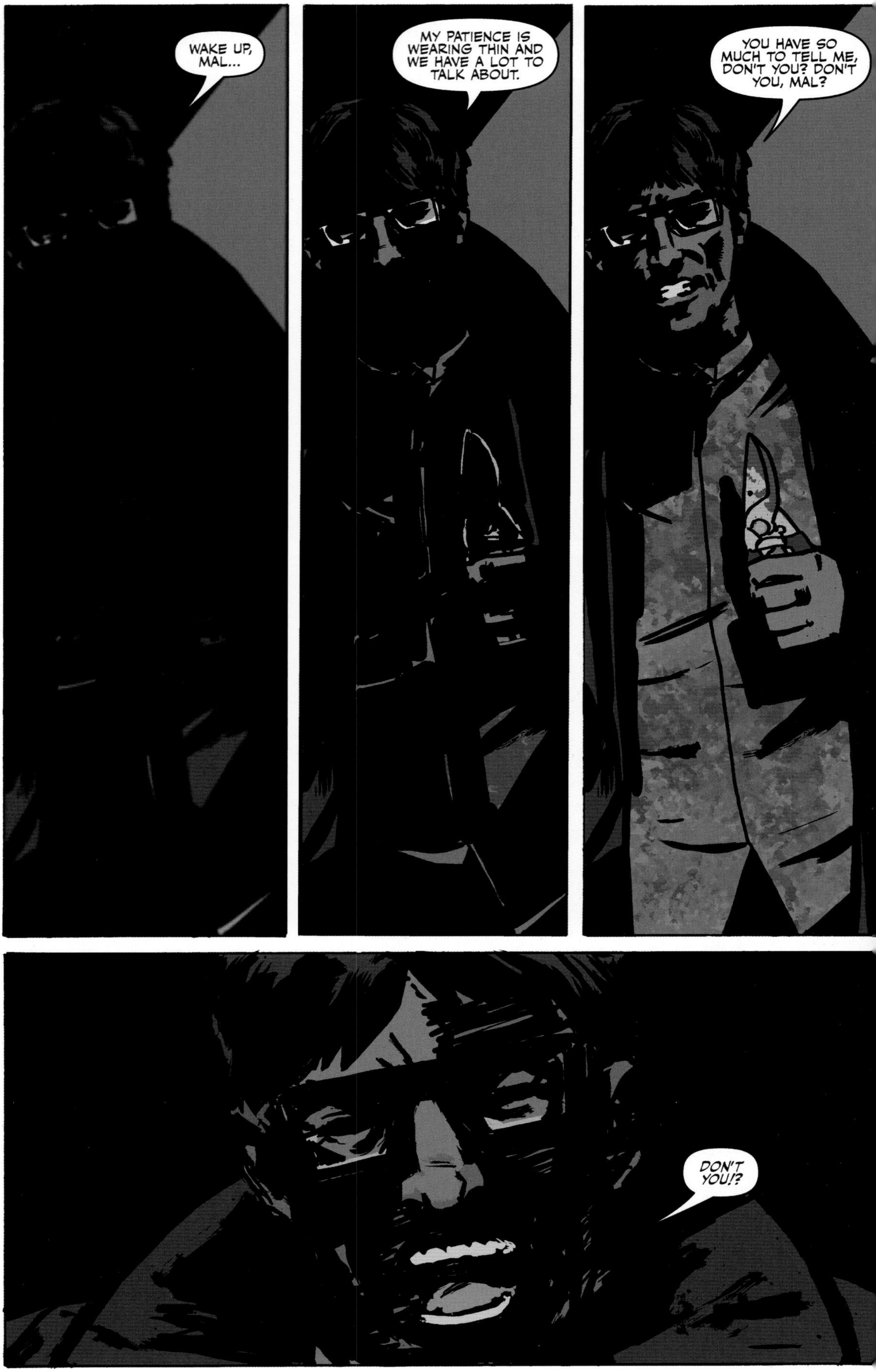
WAKE UP, MAL...
MY PATIENCE IS WEARING THIN AND WE HAVE A LOT TO TALK ABOUT.
YOU HAVE SO MUCH TO TELL ME, DON'T YOU? DON'T YOU, MAL?
DON'T YOU!?

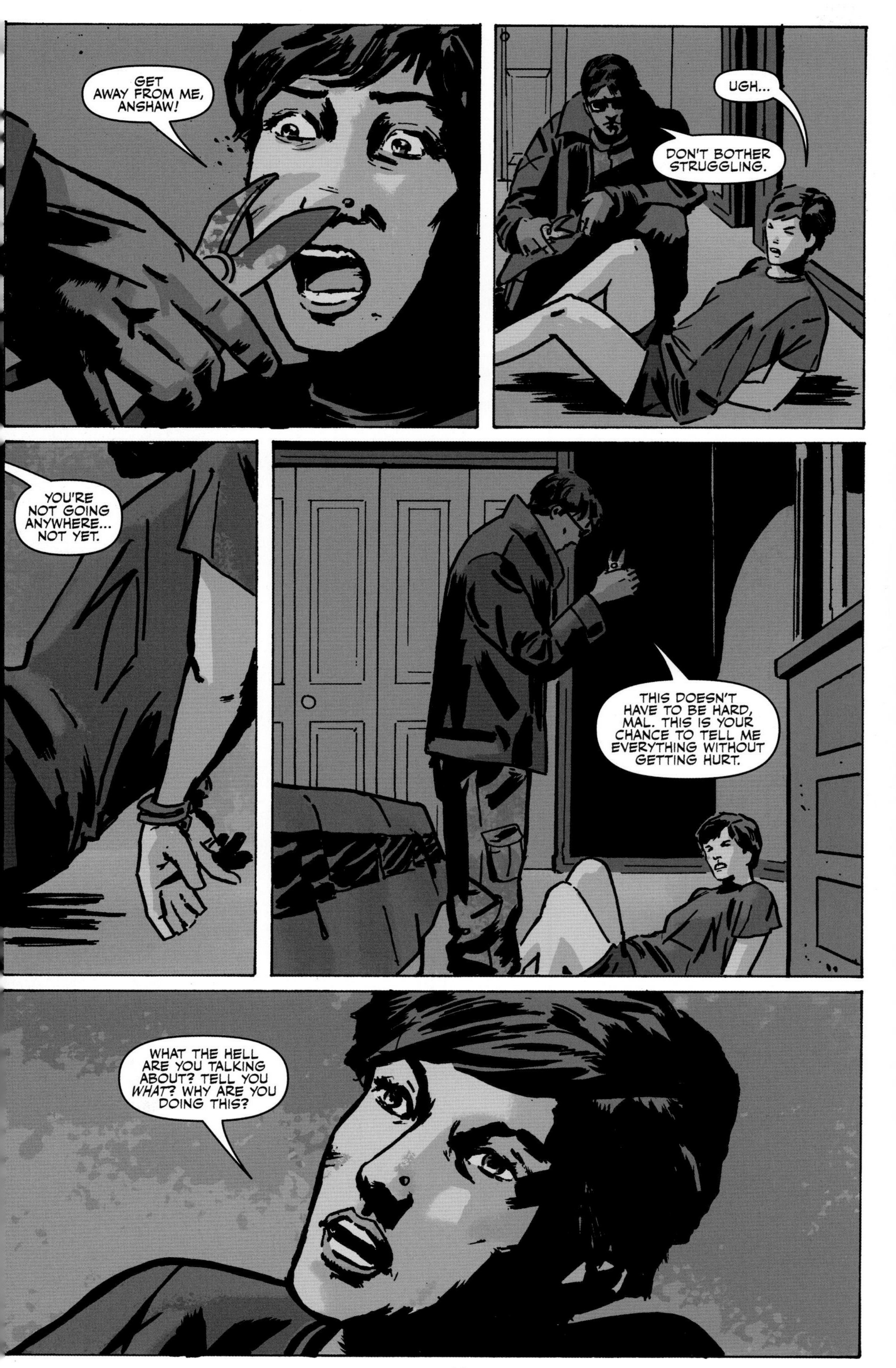
GET AWAY FROM ME, ANSHAW!
UGH...
DON'T BOTHER STRUGGLING.
YOU'RE NOT GOING ANYWHERE... NOT YET.
THIS DOESN'T HAVE TO BE HARD, MAL. THIS IS YOUR CHANCE TO TELL ME EVERYTHING WITHOUT GETTING HURT.
WHAT THE HELL ARE YOU TALKING ABOUT? TELL YOU *WHAT*? WHY ARE YOU DOING THIS?

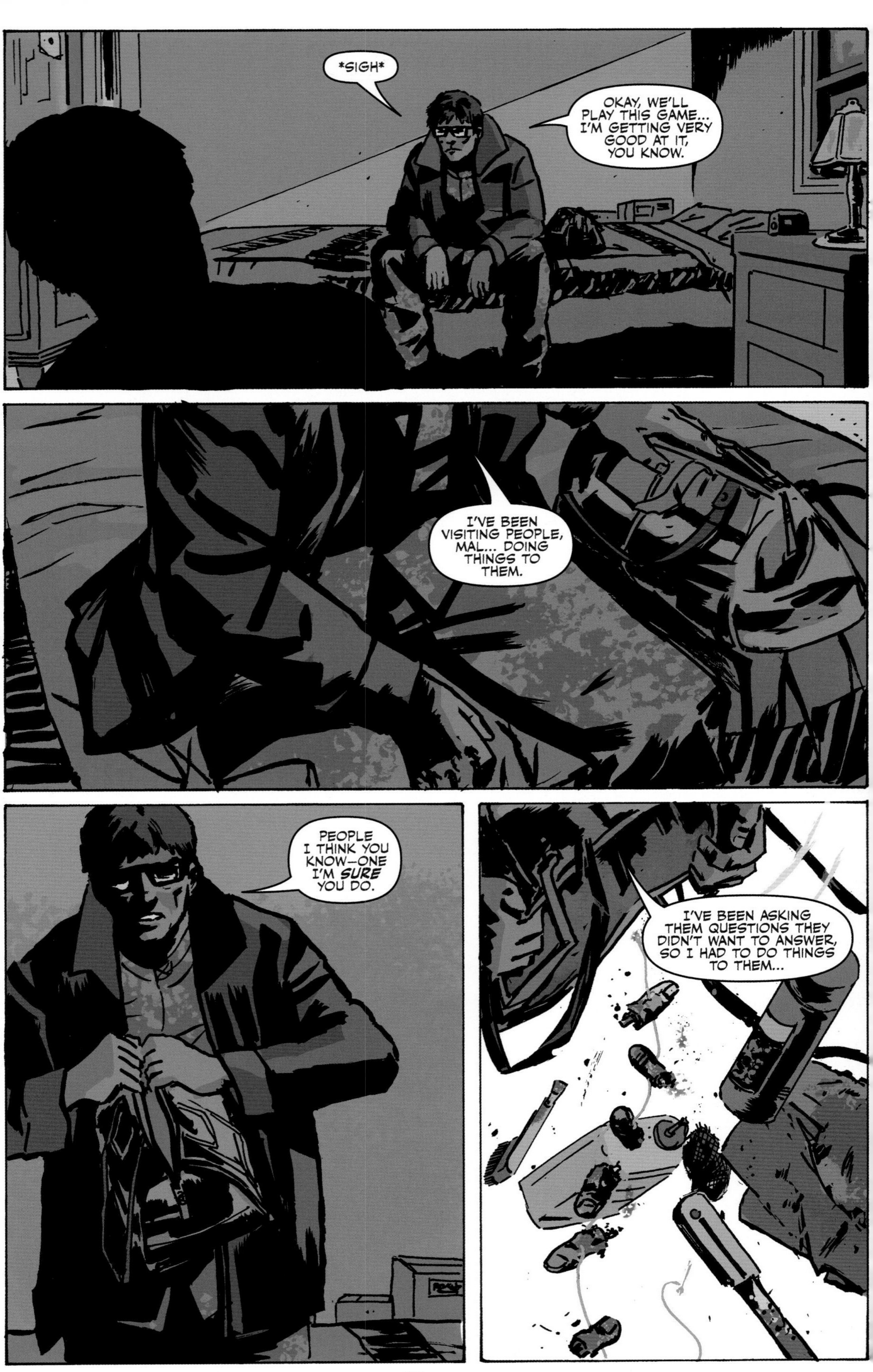
SIGH
OKAY, WE'LL PLAY THIS GAME... I'M GETTING VERY GOOD AT IT, YOU KNOW.
I'VE BEEN VISITING PEOPLE, MAL... DOING THINGS TO THEM.
PEOPLE I THINK YOU KNOW—ONE I'M ***SURE*** YOU DO.
I'VE BEEN ASKING THEM QUESTIONS THEY DIDN'T WANT TO ANSWER, SO I HAD TO DO THINGS TO THEM...

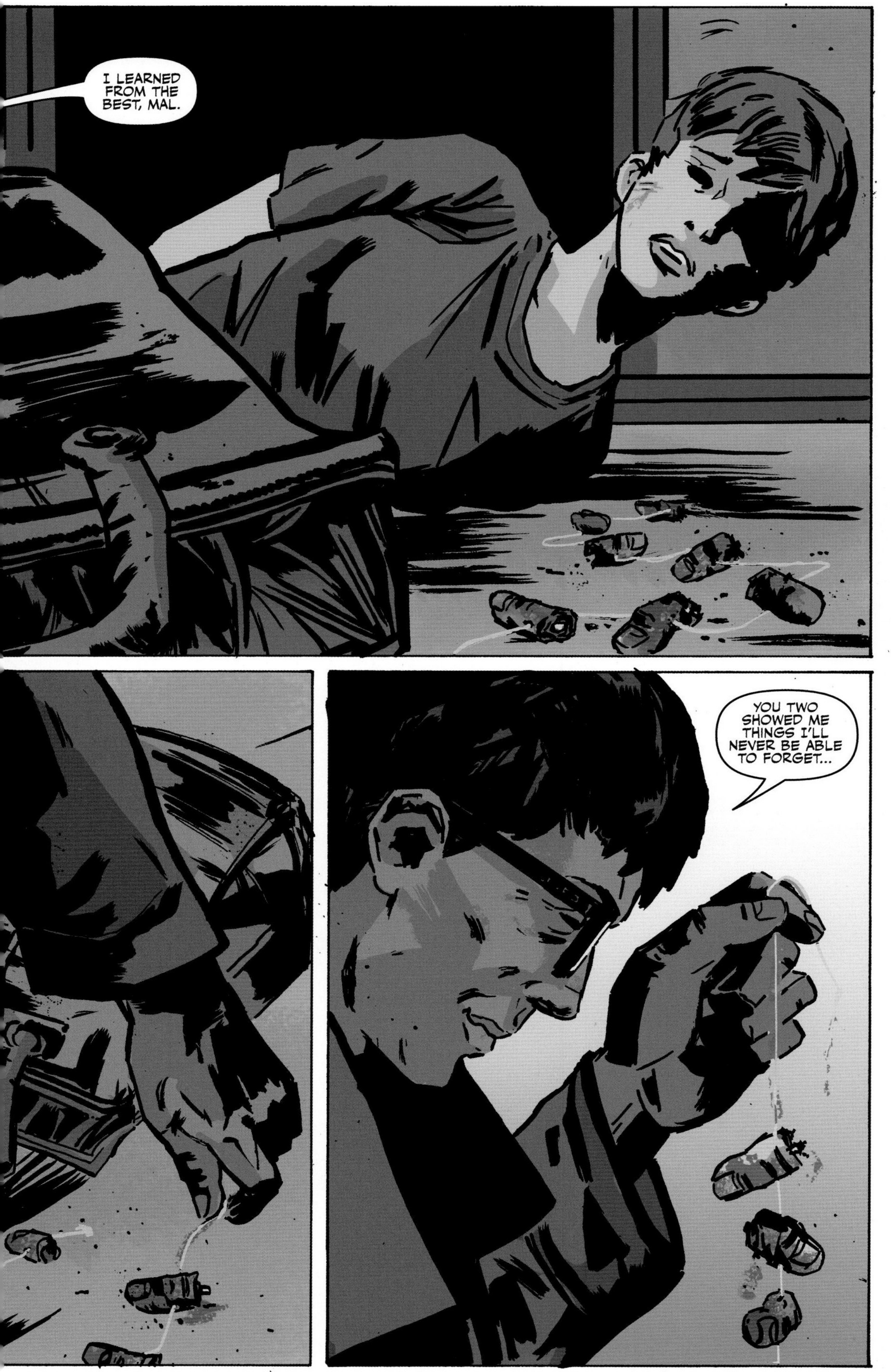
I LEARNED FROM THE BEST, MAL.
YOU TWO SHOWED ME THINGS I'LL NEVER BE ABLE TO FORGET...

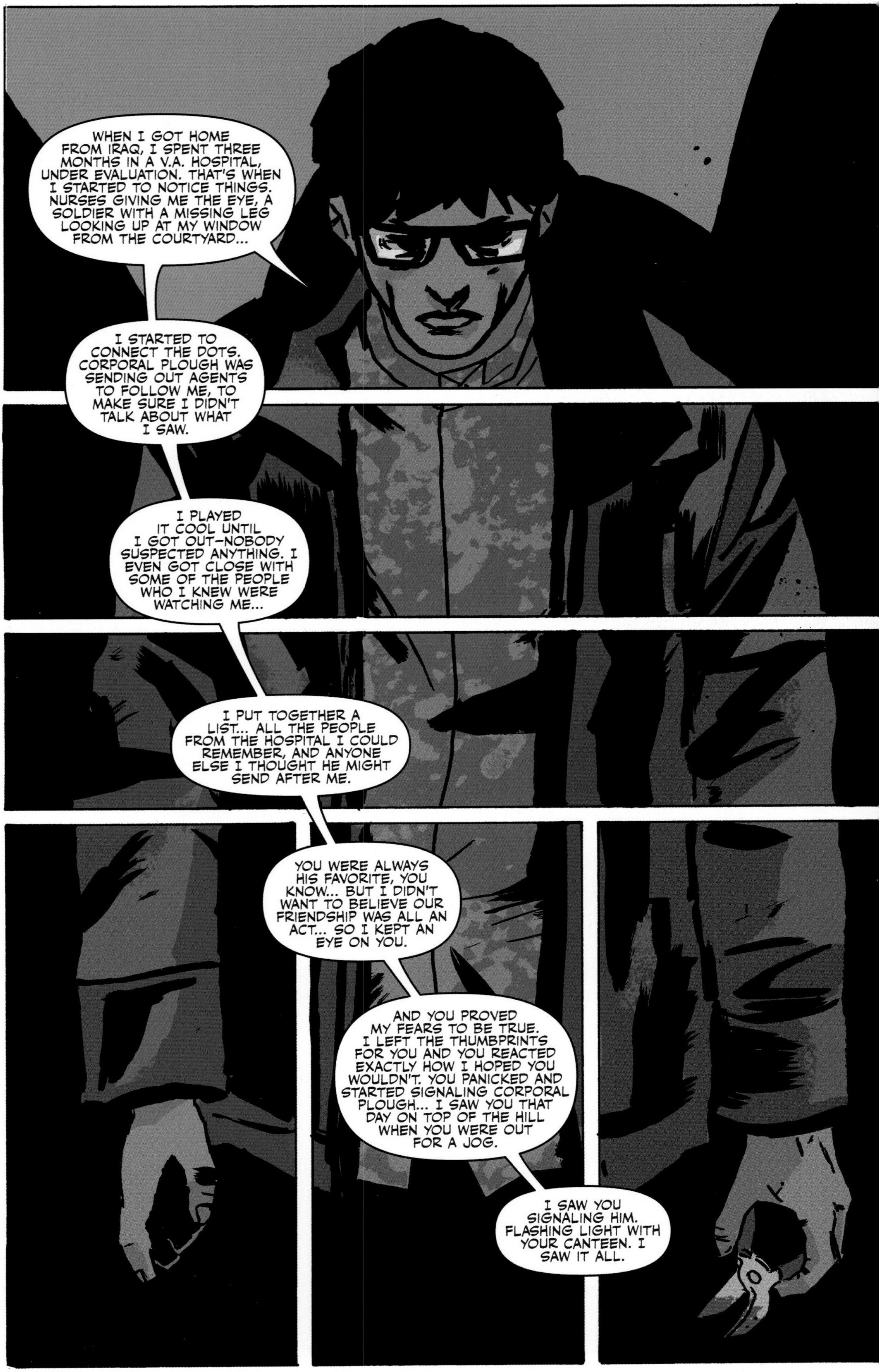
WHEN I GOT HOME FROM IRAQ, I SPENT THREE MONTHS IN A V.A. HOSPITAL, UNDER EVALUATION. THAT'S WHEN I STARTED TO NOTICE THINGS. NURSES GIVING ME THE EYE, A SOLDIER WITH A MISSING LEG LOOKING UP AT MY WINDOW FROM THE COURTYARD...
I STARTED TO CONNECT THE DOTS. CORPORAL PLOUGH WAS SENDING OUT AGENTS TO FOLLOW ME, TO MAKE SURE I DIDN'T TALK ABOUT WHAT I SAW.
I PLAYED IT COOL UNTIL I GOT OUT--NOBODY SUSPECTED ANYTHING. I EVEN GOT CLOSE WITH SOME OF THE PEOPLE WHO I KNEW WERE WATCHING ME...
I PUT TOGETHER A LIST... ALL THE PEOPLE FROM THE HOSPITAL I COULD REMEMBER, AND ANYONE ELSE I THOUGHT HE MIGHT SEND AFTER ME.
YOU WERE ALWAYS HIS FAVORITE, YOU KNOW... BUT I DIDN'T WANT TO BELIEVE OUR FRIENDSHIP WAS ALL AN ACT... SO I KEPT AN EYE ON YOU.
AND YOU PROVED MY FEARS TO BE TRUE. I LEFT THE THUMBPRINTS FOR YOU AND YOU REACTED EXACTLY HOW I HOPED YOU WOULDN'T. YOU PANICKED AND STARTED SIGNALING CORPORAL PLOUGH... I SAW YOU THAT DAY ON TOP OF THE HILL WHEN YOU WERE OUT FOR A JOG.
I SAW YOU SIGNALING HIM. FLASHING LIGHT WITH YOUR CANTEEN. I SAW IT ALL.

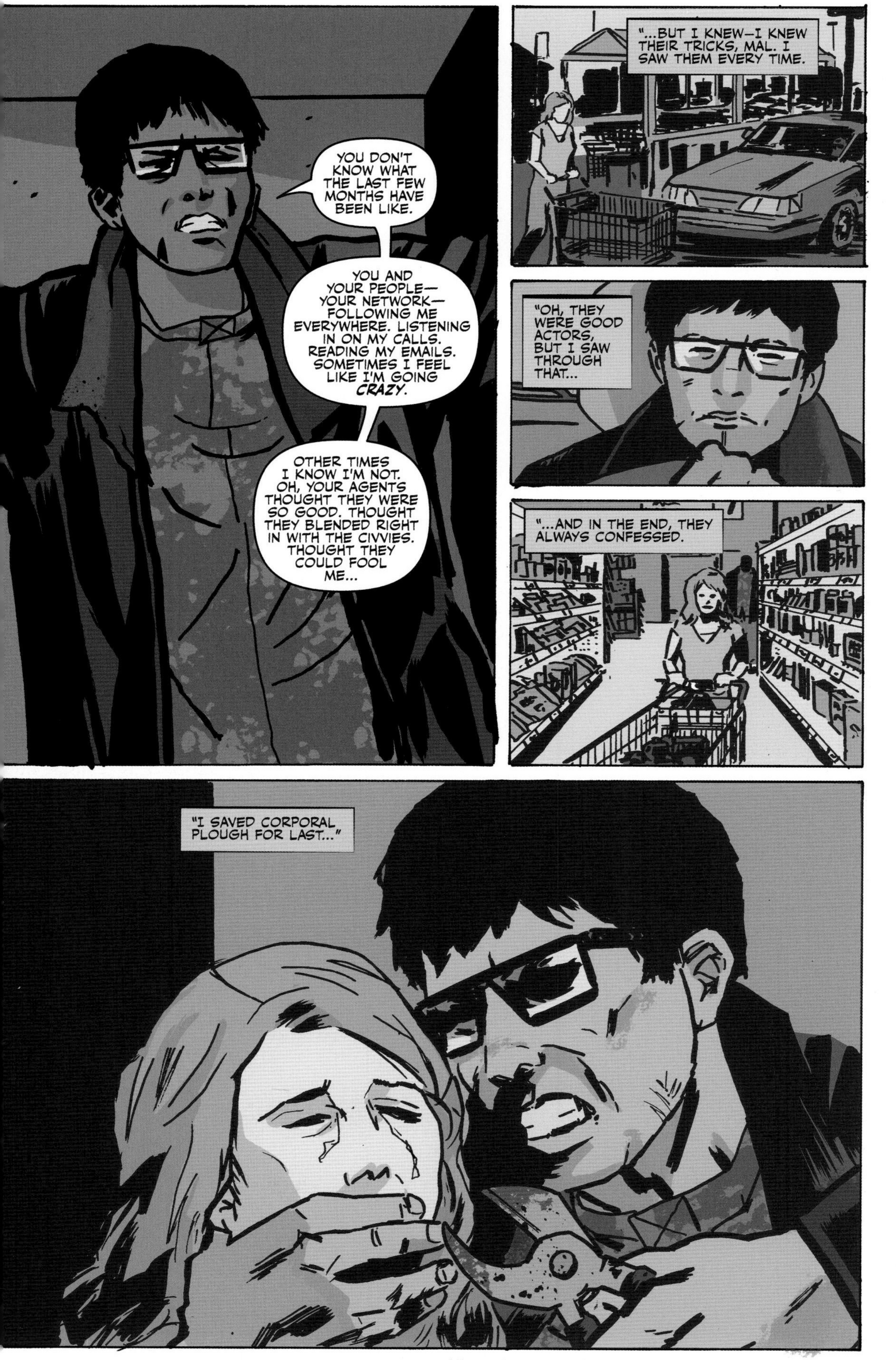
YOU DON'T KNOW WHAT THE LAST FEW MONTHS HAVE BEEN LIKE.
YOU AND YOUR PEOPLE— YOUR NETWORK— FOLLOWING ME EVERYWHERE. LISTENING IN ON MY CALLS. READING MY EMAILS. SOMETIMES I FEEL LIKE I'M GOING *CRAZY*.
OTHER TIMES I KNOW I'M NOT. OH, YOUR AGENTS THOUGHT THEY WERE SO GOOD. THOUGHT THEY BLENDED RIGHT IN WITH THE CIVVIES. THOUGHT THEY COULD FOOL ME...
"...BUT I KNEW—I KNEW THEIR TRICKS, MAL. I SAW THEM EVERY TIME.
"OH, THEY WERE GOOD ACTORS, BUT I SAW THROUGH THAT...
"...AND IN THE END, THEY ALWAYS CONFESSED.
"I SAVED CORPORAL PLOUGH FOR LAST..."

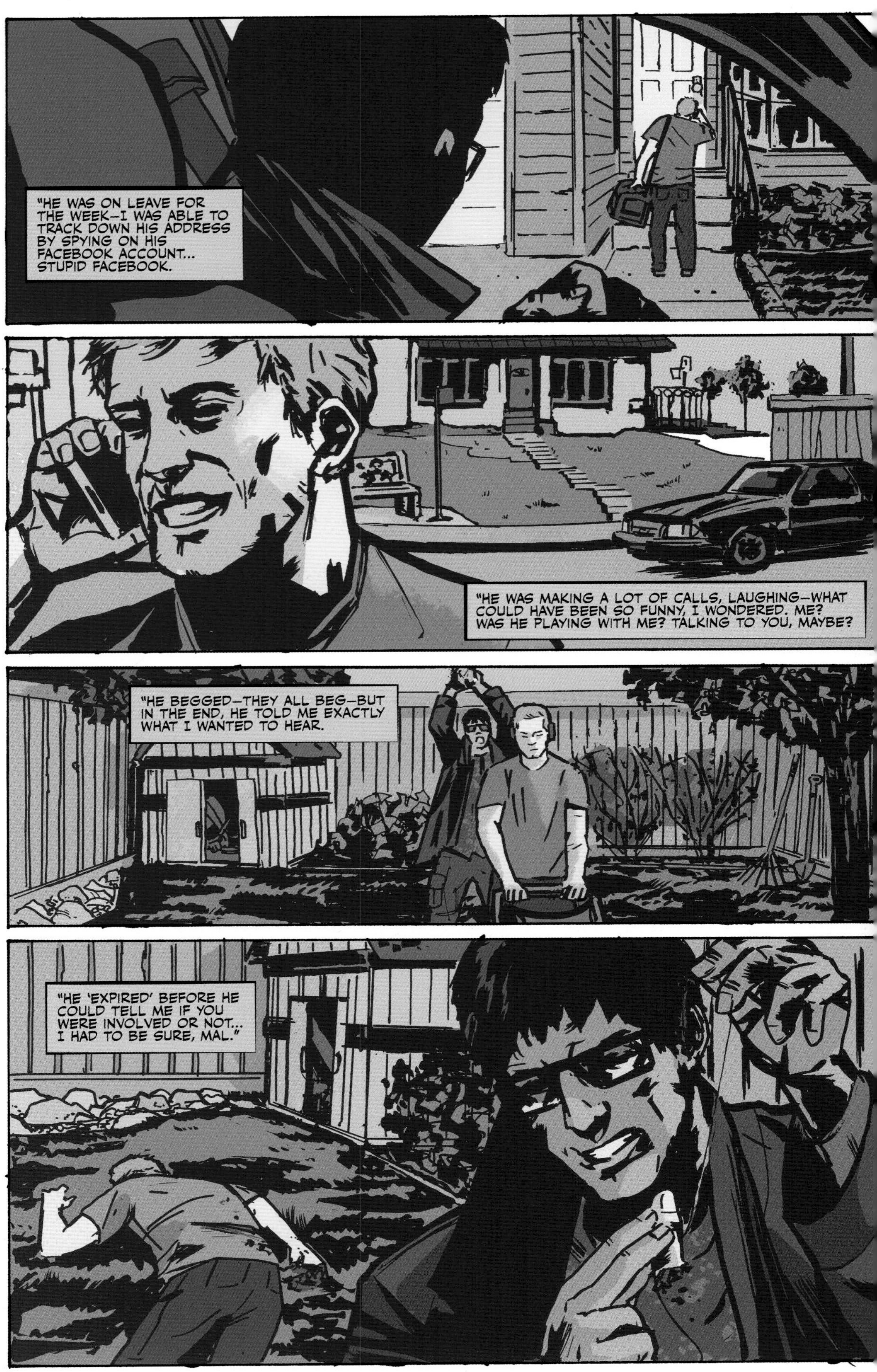
"HE WAS ON LEAVE FOR THE WEEK—I WAS ABLE TO TRACK DOWN HIS ADDRESS BY SPYING ON HIS FACEBOOK ACCOUNT... STUPID FACEBOOK.
"HE WAS MAKING A LOT OF CALLS, LAUGHING—WHAT COULD HAVE BEEN SO FUNNY, I WONDERED. ME? WAS HE PLAYING WITH ME? TALKING TO YOU, MAYBE?
"HE BEGGED—THEY ALL BEG—BUT IN THE END, HE TOLD ME EXACTLY WHAT I WANTED TO HEAR.
"HE 'EXPIRED' BEFORE HE COULD TELL ME IF YOU WERE INVOLVED OR NOT... I HAD TO BE SURE, MAL."

YOU'RE FUCKING INSANE... YOU KNOW THAT?

NOBODY'S WATCHING YOU. YOU KNOW WHY? BECAUSE YOU'RE NOBODY, ANSHAW.

I WAS AFRAID YOU WERE GOING TO SAY THAT... I REALLY WISH YOU HADN'T—I DON'T LIKE DOING THIS.

STOP IT! STOP!

THEY TRAINED YOU WELL... I KNOW YOU'LL NEVER COME CLEAN UNLESS I PERSUADE YOU.

LAST CHANCE, MAL. THIS IS THE LAST TIME I'M GOING TO ASK NICELY. IF YOU LIE TO ME AGAIN, I WILL CUT YOU.

I DON'T KNOW WHAT THE FUCK YOU'RE TALKING ABOUT!

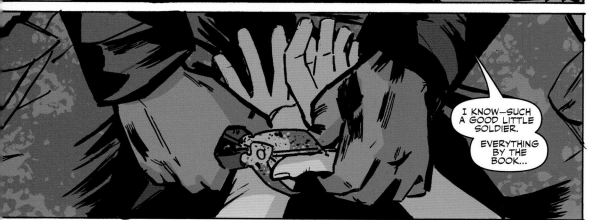

I KNOW—SUCH A GOOD LITTLE SOLDIER.

EVERYTHING BY THE BOOK...

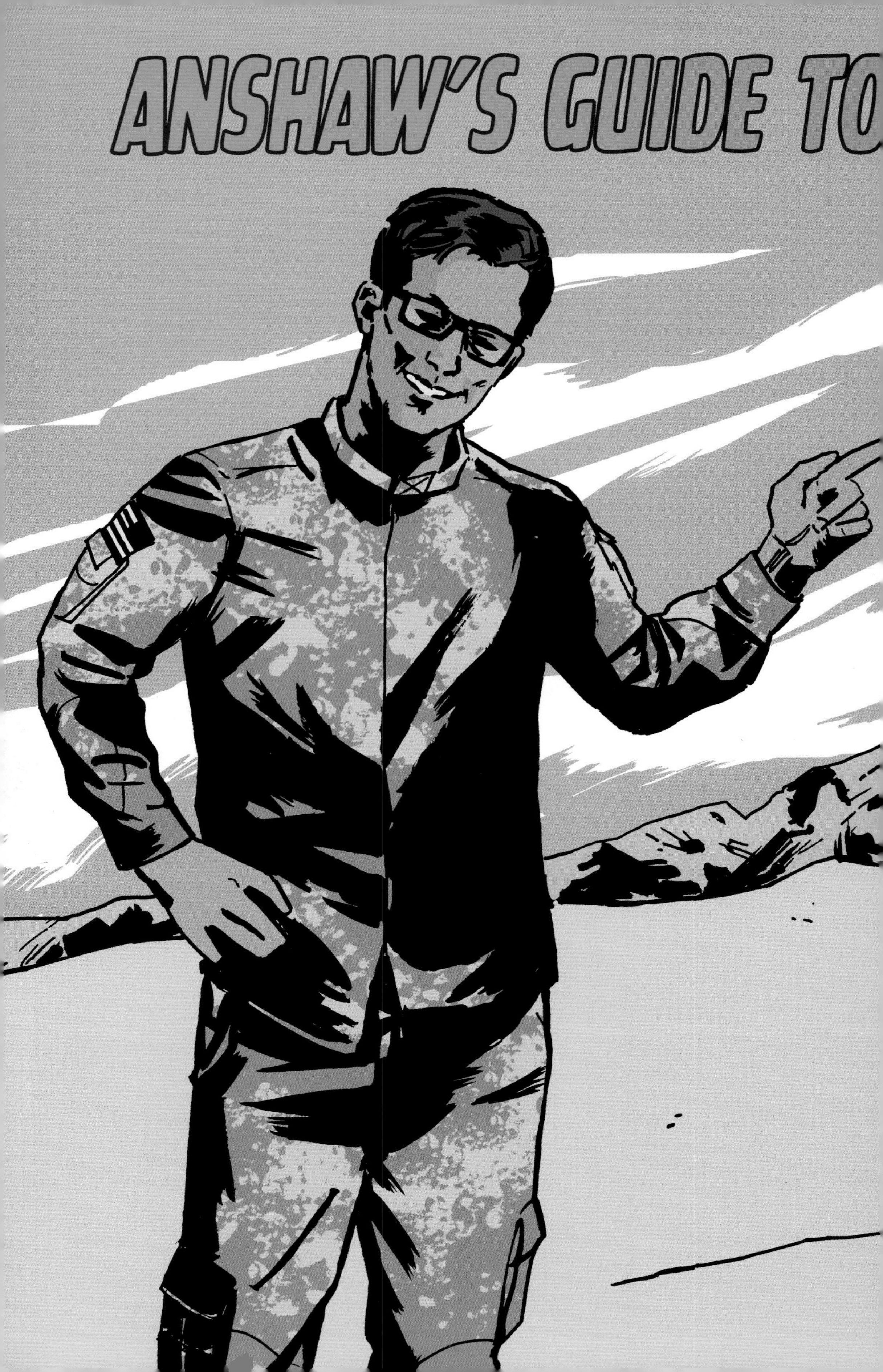
ANSHAW'S GUIDE TO

EASY THUMB REMOVAL

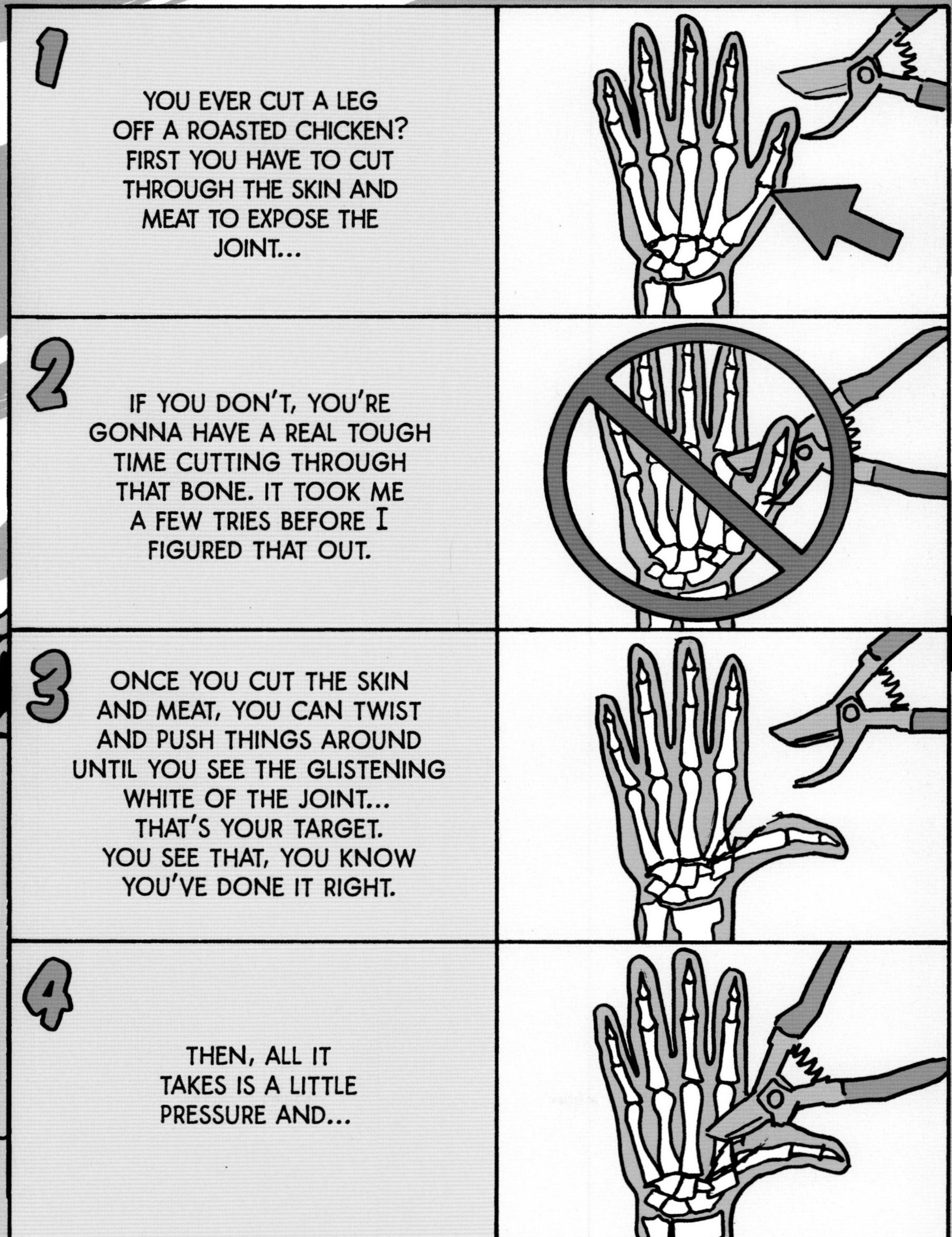

1 YOU EVER CUT A LEG OFF A ROASTED CHICKEN? FIRST YOU HAVE TO CUT THROUGH THE SKIN AND MEAT TO EXPOSE THE JOINT...

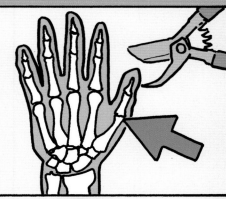

2 IF YOU DON'T, YOU'RE GONNA HAVE A REAL TOUGH TIME CUTTING THROUGH THAT BONE. IT TOOK ME A FEW TRIES BEFORE I FIGURED THAT OUT.

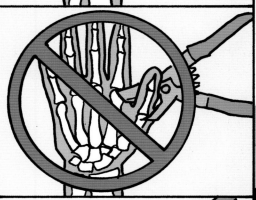

3 ONCE YOU CUT THE SKIN AND MEAT, YOU CAN TWIST AND PUSH THINGS AROUND UNTIL YOU SEE THE GLISTENING WHITE OF THE JOINT... THAT'S YOUR TARGET. YOU SEE THAT, YOU KNOW YOU'VE DONE IT RIGHT.

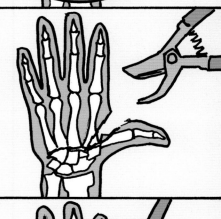

4 THEN, ALL IT TAKES IS A LITTLE PRESSURE AND...

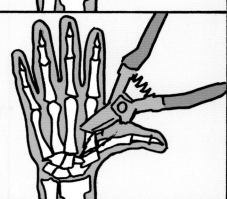

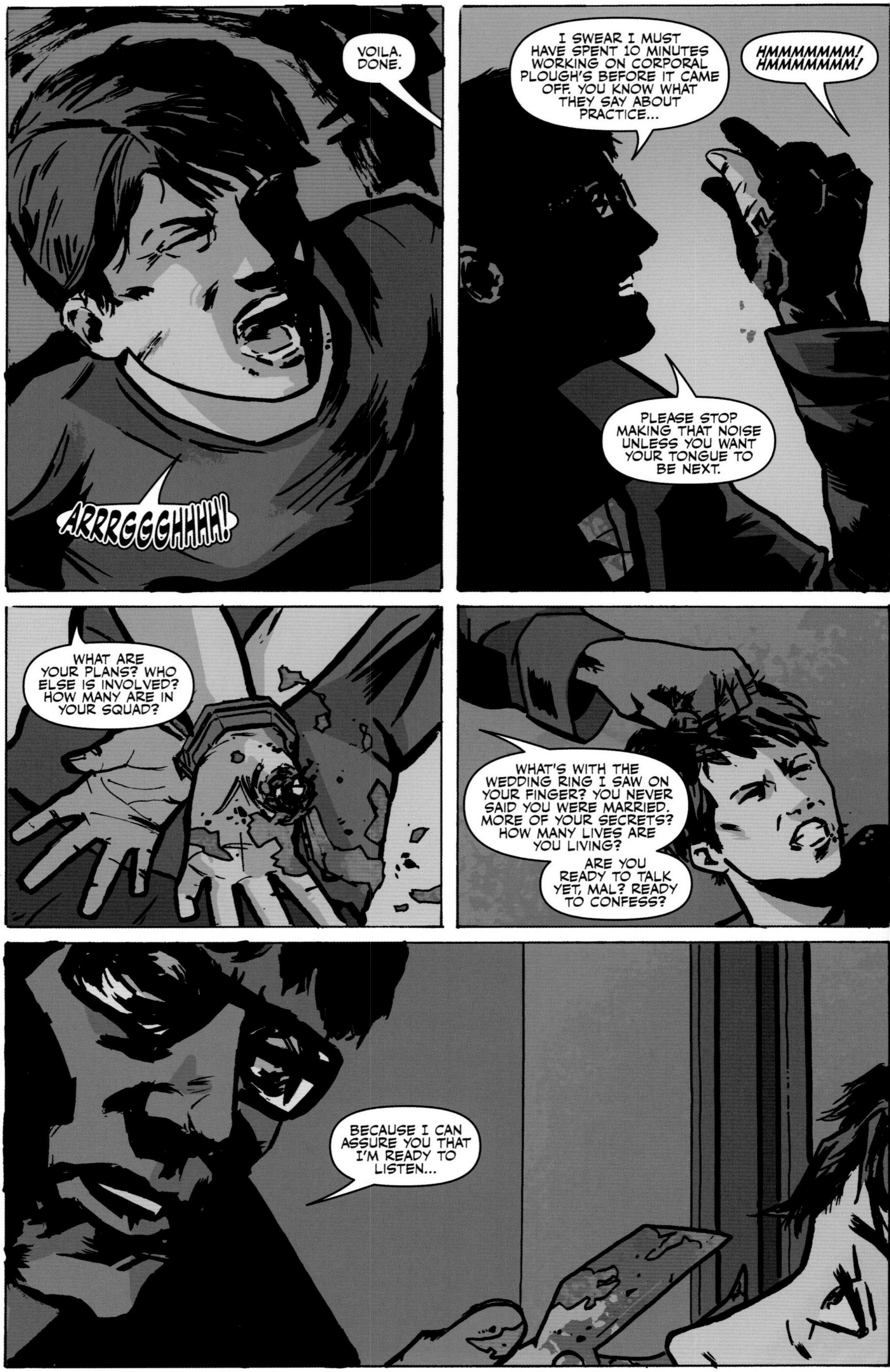
VOILA. DONE.
ARRRGGGHHHH!
I SWEAR I MUST HAVE SPENT 10 MINUTES WORKING ON CORPORAL PLOUGH'S BEFORE IT CAME OFF. YOU KNOW WHAT THEY SAY ABOUT PRACTICE...
HMMMMMMM! HMMMMMMM!
PLEASE STOP MAKING THAT NOISE UNLESS YOU WANT YOUR TONGUE TO BE NEXT.
WHAT ARE YOUR PLANS? WHO ELSE IS INVOLVED? HOW MANY ARE IN YOUR SQUAD?
WHAT'S WITH THE WEDDING RING I SAW ON YOUR FINGER? YOU NEVER SAID YOU WERE MARRIED. MORE OF YOUR SECRETS? HOW MANY LIVES ARE YOU LIVING?
ARE YOU READY TO TALK YET, MAL? READY TO CONFESS?
BECAUSE I CAN ASSURE YOU THAT I'M READY TO LISTEN...

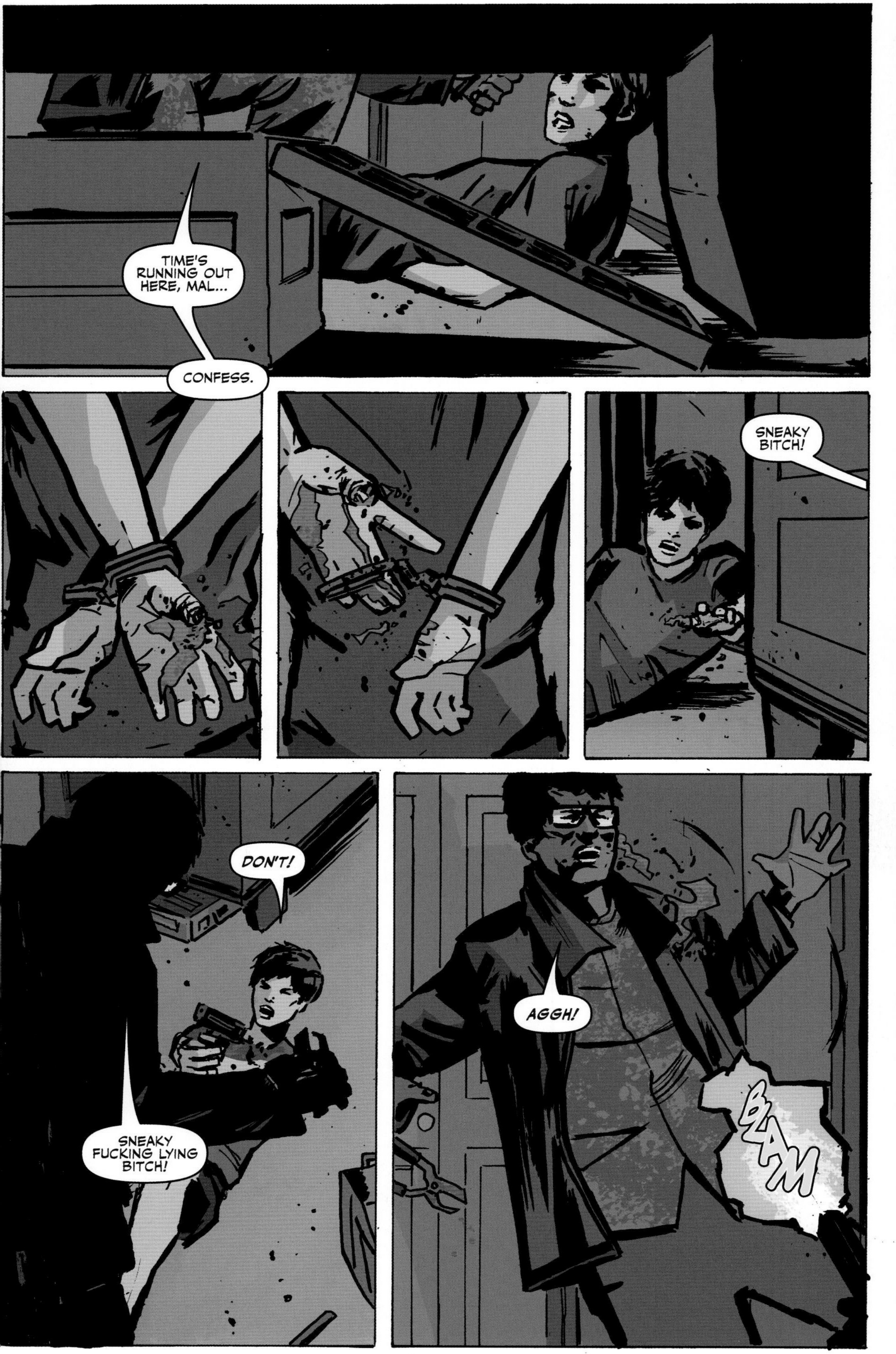
TIME'S RUNNING OUT HERE, MAL...
CONFESS.
SNEAKY BITCH!
DON'T!
SNEAKY FUCKING LYING BITCH!
AGGH!
BLAM

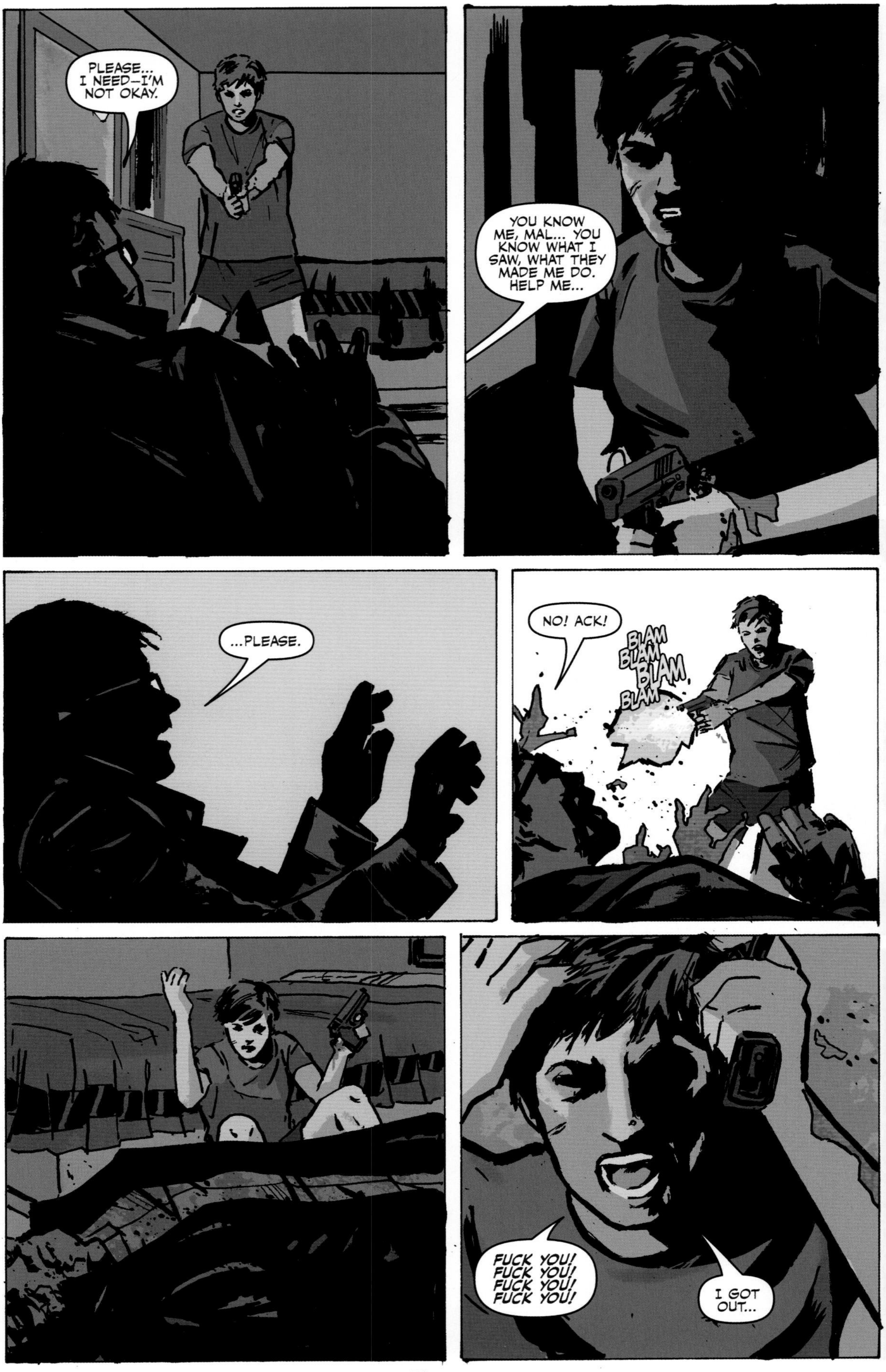
PLEASE... I NEED—I'M NOT OKAY.
YOU KNOW ME, MAL... YOU KNOW WHAT I SAW, WHAT THEY MADE ME DO. HELP ME...
...PLEASE.
NO! ACK!
BLAM BLAM BLAM BLAM BLAM
FUCK YOU! FUCK YOU! FUCK YOU! FUCK YOU!
I GOT OUT...

...I GOT AWAY...

ANY REASON YOU CAN THINK OF WHY HE WOULD COME AFTER YOU? ANYTHING AT ALL THAT MIGHT HELP US?

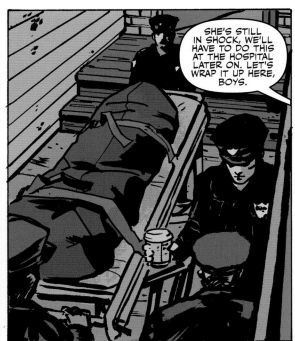

SHE'S STILL IN SHOCK, WE'LL HAVE TO DO THIS AT THE HOSPITAL LATER ON. LET'S WRAP IT UP HERE, BOYS.

THIS WILL HELP WITH THE PAIN...

NO...

...IT WONT.

73

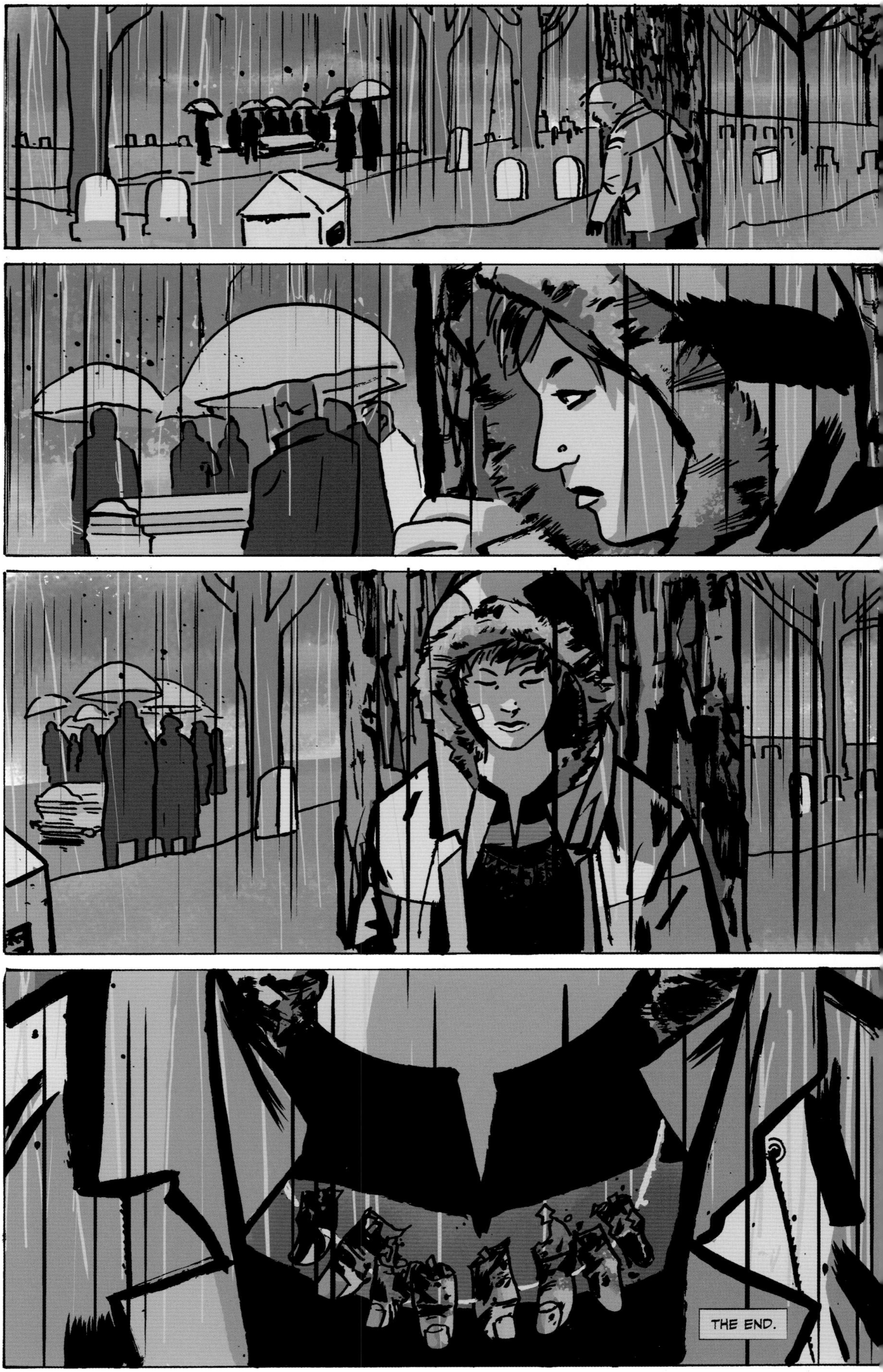
THE END.

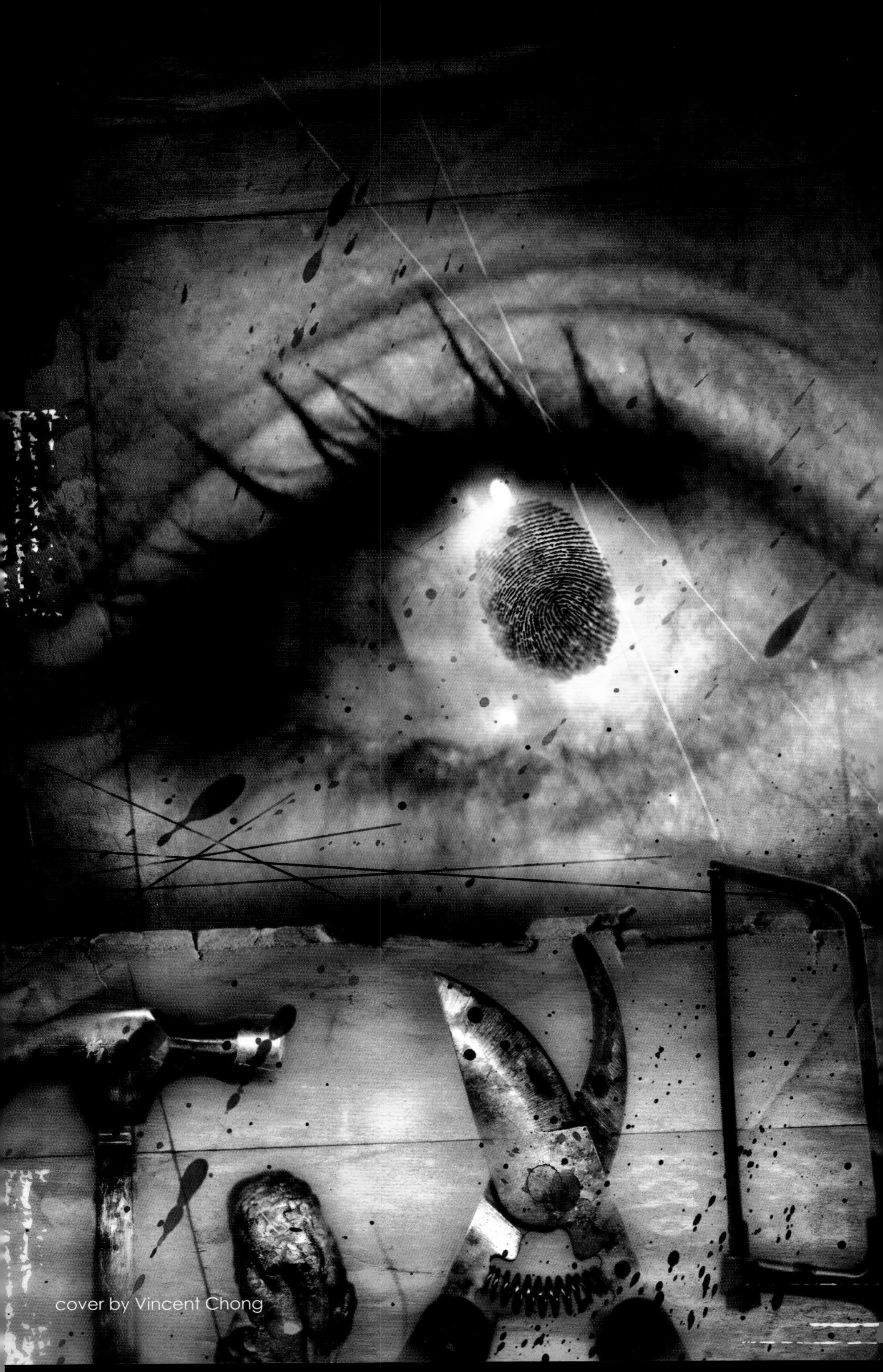

cover by Vincent Chong

Thumbprint

by JOE HILL

The first thumbprint came in the mail.

Mal was eight months back from Abu Ghraib, where she had done things she regretted. She had returned to Hammett, New York, just in time to bury her father. He died ten hours before her plane touched down in the States, which was maybe all for the best. After the things she had done, she wasn't sure she could've looked him in the eye. Although a part of her had wanted to talk to him about it and to see in his face how he judged her. Without him there was no one to hear her story, no one whose judgment mattered.

The old man had served, too, in Vietnam, as a medic. Her father had saved lives, jumped from a helicopter and dragged kids out of the paddy grass, under heavy fire. He called them kids, although he had been only twenty-five himself at the time. He'd been awarded a Purple Heart and a Silver Star.

They hadn't been offering Mal any medals when they sent her on her way. At least she hadn't been identifiable in any of the photographs of Abu Ghraib—just her boots in that one shot Graner took, with the men piled naked on top of each other, a pyramid of stacked ass and hanging sac. If Graner had just tilted the camera up a little, Mal would have been headed home a lot sooner, only it would have been in handcuffs.

She got back her old job at the Milky Way, keeping bar, and moved into her father's house. It was all he had to leave her, that and the car. The old man's ranch was set three hundred yards from Hatchet Hill Road, backed against the town woods. In the fall Mal ran in the forest, wearing a full ruck, three miles through the evergreens.

She kept the M4A1 in the downstairs bedroom, broke it down and put it together every morning, a job she could complete by the count of twelve. When she was done, she put the components back in their case with the bayonet, cradling them neatly in their foam cutouts—you didn't attach the bayonet unless you were about to be overrun. Her M4 had come back to the U.S. with a civilian contractor, who brought it with him on his company's private jet. He had been an interrogator for hire—there'd been a lot of them at Abu Ghraib in the final months before the arrests—and he said it was the least he could do, that she had earned it for services rendered, a statement that left her cold.

Come one night in November, Mal walked out of the Milky Way with John Petty, the other bartender, and they found Glen Kardon passed out in the front seat of his Saturn. The driver's-side door was open, and Glen's butt was in the air, his legs hanging from the car, feet twisted in the gravel, as if he had just been clubbed to death from behind.

Not even thinking, she told Petty to keep an eye out, and then Mal straddled Glen's hips and dug out his wallet. She helped herself to a hundred and twenty dollars cash, dropped the wallet back on the passenger-side seat. Petty hissed at her to hurry the fuck up, while Mal wiggled the wedding ring off Glen's finger.

"His wedding ring?" Petty asked when they were in her car together. Mal gave him half the money for being her lookout but kept the ring for herself. "Jesus, you're a demented bitch."

Petty put his hand between her legs and ground his thumb hard into the crotch of her black jeans while she drove. She let him do that for a while, his other hand groping her breast. Then she elbowed him off her.

"That's enough," she said.

"No it isn't."

She reached into his jeans, ran her hand down his hard-on, then took his balls and began to apply pressure until he let out a little moan, not entirely of pleasure.

"It's plenty," she said. She pulled her hand from his pants. "You want more than that, you'll have to wake up your wife. Give her a thrill."

Mal let him out of the car in front of his home and peeled away, tires throwing gravel at him.

Back at her father's house, she sat on the kitchen counter, looking at the wedding ring in the cup of her palm. A simple gold band, scuffed and scratched, all the shine dulled out of it. She wondered why she had taken it.

Mal knew Glen Kardon, Glen and his wife, Helen, both. The three of them were the same age, had all gone to school together. Glen had a magician at his tenth birthday party, who had escaped from handcuffs and a straitjacket as his final trick. Years later Mal would become well acquainted with another escape artist who managed to slip out of a pair of handcuffs, a Ba'athist. Both of his thumbs had been broken, making it possible for him to squeeze out of the cuffs. It was easy if you could bend your thumb in any direction—all you had to do was ignore the pain.

And Helen had been Mal's lab partner in sixth-grade biology. Helen took notes in her delicate cursive, using different colored inks to brighten up their reports, while Mal sliced things open. Mal liked the scalpel, the way the skin popped apart at the slightest touch of the blade to show what was hidden behind it. She had an instinct for it, always somehow knew just where to put the cut.

Mal shook the wedding ring in one hand for a while and finally dropped it down the sink. She didn't know what to do with it, wasn't sure where to fence it. Had no use for it, really.

When she went down to the mailbox the next morning, she found an oil bill, a real estate flyer, and a plain white envelope. Inside the envelope was a crisp sheet of typing paper, neatly folded, blank except for a single thumbprint in black ink. The print was a clean impression, and among the whorls and lines was a scar, like a fishhook. There was nothing on the envelope—no stamp, no addresses, no mark of any kind. The postman had not left it.

In her first glance, she knew it was a threat and that whoever had put the envelope in her mailbox might still be watching. Mal felt her vulnerability in the sick clench of her insides and had to struggle against the conditioned impulse to get low and find cover. She looked to either side but saw only the trees, their branches waving in the cold swirl of a light breeze. There was no traffic along the road and no sign of life anywhere.

The whole long walk back to the house, she was aware of a weakness in her legs. She didn't look at the thumbprint again but carried it inside and left it with the other mail on the kitchen counter. She let her shaky legs carry her on into her father's bedroom, her bedroom now. The M4 was in its case in the closet, but her father's .45 automatic was even closer—she slept with it under the pillow—and it didn't need to be assembled. Mal slid the action back to pump a bullet into the chamber. She got her field glasses from her ruck.

Mal climbed the carpeted stairs to the second floor and opened the door into her old bedroom under the eaves. She hadn't been in there since coming home, and the air had a musty, stale quality. A tatty poster of Alan Jackson was stuck up on the inverted slant of the roof. Her dolls—the blue corduroy bear, the pig with the queer silver-button eyes that gave him a look of blindness—were set neatly in the shelves of a bookcase without books.

Her bed was made, but when she went close, she was surprised to find the shape of a body pressed into it, the pillow dented in the outline of someone's head. The idea occurred that whoever had left the thumbprint had been inside the house while she was out, and had taken a nap up here. Mal didn't slow down but stepped straight up onto the mattress, unlocked the window over it, shoved it open, and climbed through.

In another minute she was sitting on the roof, holding the binoculars to her eyes with one hand, the gun in the other. The asbestos shingles had been warming all day in the sun and provided a pleasant ambient heat beneath her. From where she sat on the roof, she could see in every direction.

She remained there for most of an hour, scanning the trees, following the passage of cars along Hatchet Hill Road. Finally she knew she was looking for someone who wasn't there anymore. She hung the binoculars from her neck and leaned back on the hot shingles and closed her eyes. It had been cold down in the driveway, but up on the roof, on the lee side of the house, out of the wind, she was comfortable, a lizard on a rock.

When Mal swung her body back into the bedroom, she sat for a while on the sill, holding the gun in both hands and considering the impression of a human body on her blankets and pillow. She picked up the pillow and pressed her face into it. Very faintly she could smell a trace of her father, his cheap corner-store cigars, the waxy tang of that shit he put in his hair, same stuff Reagan had used. The thought that he had sometimes been up here, dozing in her bed, gave her a little chill. She wished she were still the kind of person who could hug a pillow and weep over what she had lost. But in truth maybe she had never been that kind of person.

When she was back in the kitchen, Mal looked once more at the thumbprint on the plain white sheet of paper. Against all logic or sense, it seemed somehow familiar to her. She didn't like that.

He had been brought in with a broken tibia, the Iraqi everyone called the Professor, but a few hours after they put him in a cast, he was judged well enough to sit for an interrogation. In the early morning, before sunrise, Corporal Plough came to get him.

Mal was working in Block 1A then and went with Anshaw to collect the Professor. He was in a cell with eight other men: sinewy, unshaved Arabs, most of them dressed in Fruit of the Loom jockey shorts and nothing else. Some others, who had been uncooperative with CI, had been given pink--flowered panties to wear. The panties fit more snugly than the jockeys, which were all extra large and baggy. The prisoners skulked in the gloom of their stone chamber, giving Mal looks so feverish and sunken-eyed they appeared deranged. Glancing in at them, Mal didn't know whether to laugh or flinch.

"Walk away from the bars, women," she said in her clumsy Arabic. "Walk away." She crooked her finger at the Professor. "You. Come to here."

He hopped forward, one hand on the wall to steady himself. He wore a hospital johnny, and his left leg was in a cast from ankle to knee. Anshaw had brought a pair of aluminum crutches for him. Mal and Anshaw were coming to the end of a twelve-hour shift, in a week of twelve-hour shifts. Escorting the prisoner to CI with Corporal Plough would be their last job of the night. Mal was twitchy from all the Vivarin in her system, so much she could hardly stand still. When she looked at lamps, she saw rays of hard-edged, rainbow-shot light emanating from them, as if she were peering through crystal.

The night before, a patrol had surprised some men planting an IED in the red, hollowed-out carcass of a German shepherd, on the side of the road back to Baghdad. The bombers scattered, yelling, from the spotlights on the Hummers, and a contingent of men went after them.

An engineer named Leeds stayed behind to have a look at the bomb inside the dog. He was three steps from the animal when a cell phone went off inside the dog's bowels, three bars of "Oops! . . . I Did It Again." The dog ruptured in a belch of flame and with a heavy thud that people standing thirty feet away could feel in the marrow of their bones. Leeds dropped to his knees, holding his face, smoke coming out from under his gloves. The first soldier to get to him said his face peeled off like a cheap black rubber mask that had been stuck to the sinew beneath with rubber cement.

Not long after, the patrol grabbed the Professor—so named because of his horn-rimmed glasses and because he insisted he was a teacher—two blocks from the site of the explosion. He broke his leg jumping off a high berm, running away after the soldiers fired over his head and ordered him to halt.

Now the Professor lurched along on the crutches, Mal and Anshaw flanking him and Plough walking behind. They made their way out of 1A and into the predawn morning. The Professor paused, beyond the doors, to take a breath. That was when Plough kicked the left crutch out from under his arm.

The Professor went straight down and forward with a cry, his johnny flapping open to show the soft paleness of his ass. Anshaw reached to help him back up. Plough said to leave him.

"Sir?" Anshaw asked. Anshaw was just nineteen. He had been over as long as Mal, but his skin was oily and white, as if he had never been out of his chemical suit.

"Did you see him swing that crutch at me?" Plough asked Mal.

Mal did not reply but watched to see what would happen next. She had spent the last two hours bouncing on her heels, chewing her fingernails down to the skin, too wired to stop moving. Now, though, she felt stillness spreading through her, like a drop of ink in water, calming her restless hands, her nervous legs.

Plough bent over and pulled the string at the back of the johnny, unknotting it so it fell off the Professor's shoulders and down to his wrists. His ass was spotted with dark moles and relatively hairless. His sac was drawn tight to his perineum. The Professor glanced up over his shoulder, his eyes too large in his face, and spoke rapidly in Arabic.

"What's he saying?" Plough asked. "I don't speak Sand Nigger."

"He said don't," Mal answered, translating automatically. "He says he hasn't done anything. He was picked up by accident."

Plough kicked away the other crutch. "Get those."

Anshaw picked up the crutches.

Plough put his boot in the Professor's fleshy ass and shoved.

"Get going. Tell him get going."

A pair of MPs walked past, turned their heads to look at the Professor as they went by. He was trying to cover his crotch with one hand, but Plough kicked him in the ass again, and he had to start crawling. His crawl was awkward stuff, what with his left leg sticking out straight in its cast and the bare foot dragging in the dirt. One of the MPs laughed, and then they moved away into the night.

The Professor struggled to pull his johnny up onto his shoulders as he crawled, but Plough stepped on it and it tore away.

"Leave it. Tell him leave it and hurry up."

Mal told him. The prisoner couldn't look at her. He looked at Anshaw instead and began pleading with him, asking for something to wear and saying his leg hurt while Anshaw stared down at him, eyes bulging, as if he were choking on something. Mal wasn't surprised that the Professor was addressing Anshaw instead of her. Part of it was a cultural thing. The Arabs couldn't cope with being humiliated in front of a woman. But also Anshaw had something about him that signified to others, even the enemy, that he was approachable. In spite of the nine-millimeter strapped to his outer thigh, he gave an impression of stumbling, unthreatening cluelessness. In the barracks he blushed when other guys were ogling centerfolds; he often could be seen praying during heavy mortar attacks.

The prisoner had stopped crawling once more. Mal poked the barrel of her M4 in the Professor's ass to get him going again, and the Iraqi jerked, gave a shrill sort of sob. Mal didn't mean to laugh, but there was something funny about the convulsive clench of his butt cheeks, something that sent a rush of blood to her head. Her blood was racy and strange with Vivarin, and watching the prisoner's ass bunch up like that was the most hilarious thing she had seen in weeks.

The Professor crawled past the wire fence, along the edge of the road. Plough told Mal to ask him where his friends were now, his friends who blew up the American GI. He said if the Professor would tell about his friends, he could have his crutches and his johnny back.

The prisoner said he didn't know anything about the IED. He said he ran because other men were running and soldiers were shooting. He said he was a teacher of literature, that he had a little girl. He said he had taken his twelve-year-old to Disneyland Paris once.

"He's fucking with us," Plough said. "What's a professor of literature doing out at two A.M. in the worst part of town? Your queer-fuck bin Laden friends blew the face right off an American GI, a good man, a man with a pregnant wife back home. Where do your friends—Mal, make him understand he's going to tell us where his friends are hiding. Let him know it would be better to tell us now, before we get where we're going. Let him know this is the easy part of his day. CI wants this motherfucker good and soft before we get him there."

Mal nodded, her ears buzzing. She told the Professor he didn't have a daughter, because he was a known homosexual. She asked him if he liked the barrel of her gun in his ass, if it excited him. She said, "Where is the house of your partners who make the dogs into bombs? Where do your homosexual friends go after murdering Americans with their trick dogs? Tell me if you don't want the gun in the hole of your ass."

"I swear by the life of my little girl I don't know who those other men were. Please. My child is named Alaya. She is ten years old. There was a picture of her in my pants. Where are my pants? I will show you."

She stepped on his hand and felt the bones compress unnaturally under her heel. He shrieked.

"Tell," she said. "Tell."

"I can't."

A steely clashing sound caught Mal's attention. Anshaw had dropped the crutches. He looked green, and his hands were hooked into claws, raised almost but not quite to cover his ears.

"You okay?" she asked.

"He's lying," Anshaw said. Anshaw's Arabic was not as good as hers, but not bad. "He said his daughter was twelve the first time."

She stared at Anshaw, and he stared back, and while they were looking at each other, there came a high, keening whistle, like air being let out of some giant balloon . . . a sound that made Mal's racy blood feel as if it were fizzing with oxygen, made her feel carbonated inside. She flipped her M4 around to hold it by the barrel in both hands, and when the mortar struck—out beyond the perimeter but still hitting hard enough to cause the earth to shake underfoot—she drove the butt of the gun straight down into the Professor's broken leg, clubbing at it as if she were trying to drive a stake into the ground. Over the shattering thunder of the exploding mortar, not even Mal could hear him screaming.

Mal pushed herself hard on her Friday-morning run, out in the woods, driving herself up Hatchet Hill, reaching ground so steep she was really climbing, not running. She kept going until she was short of breath and the sky seemed to spin, as if it were the roof of a carousel.

When she finally paused, she felt faint. The wind breathed in her face, chilling her sweat, a curiously pleasant sensation. Even the feeling of lightheadedness, of being close to exhaustion and collapse, was somehow satisfying to her.

The army had her for four years before Mal left to become a part of the reserves. On her second day of basic training, she had done push-ups until she was sick, then was so weak she collapsed in it. She wept in front of others, something she could now hardly bear to remember.

Eventually she learned to like the feeling that came right before collapse: the way the sky got big, and sounds grew far away and tinny, and all the colors seemed to sharpen to a hallucinatory brightness. There was an intensity of sensation when you were on the edge of what you could handle, when you were physically tested and made to fight for each breath, that was somehow exhilarating.

At the top of the hill, Mal slipped the stainless-steel canteen out of her ruck, her father's old camping canteen, and filled her mouth with ice water. The canteen flashed, a silver mirror in the late-morning sun. She poured water onto her face, wiped her eyes with the hem of her T-shirt, put the canteen away, and ran on, ran for home.

She let herself in through the front door, didn't notice the envelope until she stepped on it and heard the crunch of paper underfoot. She stared down at it, her mind blank for one dangerous moment, trying to think who would've come up to the house to slide a bill under the door when it would've been easier to just leave it in the mailbox. But it wasn't a bill, and she knew it.

Mal was framed in the door, the outline of a soldier painted into a neat rectangle, like the human-silhouette targets they shot at on the range. She made no sudden moves, however. If someone meant to shoot her, he would have done it—there had been plenty of time—and if she was being watched, she wanted to show she wasn't afraid.

She crouched, picked up the envelope. The flap was not sealed. She tapped out the sheet of paper inside and unfolded it. Another thumbprint, this one a fat black oval, like a flattened spoon. There was no fishhook-shaped scar on this thumb. This was a different thumb entirely. In some ways that was more unsettling to her than anything.

No—the most unsettling thing was that this time he had slipped his message under her door, while last time he had left it a hundred yards down the road, in the mailbox. It was maybe his way of saying he could get as close to her as he wanted.

Mal thought police but discarded the idea. She had been a cop herself, in the army, knew how cops thought. Leaving a couple thumbprints on unsigned sheets of paper wasn't a crime. It was probably a prank, they would say, and you couldn't waste manpower investigating a prank. She felt now, as she had when she saw the first thumbprint, that these messages were not the perverse joke of some local snotnose but a malicious promise, a warning to be on guard. Yet it was an irrational feeling, unsupported by any evidence. It was soldier knowledge, not cop knowledge.

Besides, when you called the cops, you never knew what you were going to get. There were cops like her out there. People you didn't want getting too interested in you.

She balled up the thumbprint, took it onto the porch. Mal cast her gaze around, scanning the bare trees, the straw-colored weeds at the edge of the woods. She stood there for close to a minute. Even the trees were perfectly still, no wind to tease their branches into motion, as if the whole world were in a state of suspension, waiting to see what would happen next—only nothing happened next.

She left the balled-up paper on the porch railing, went back inside, and got the M4 from the closet. Mal sat on the bedroom floor, assembling and disassembling it, three times, twelve seconds each time. Then she set the parts back in the case with the bayonet and slid it under her father's bed.

Two hours later Mal ducked down behind the bar at the Milky Way to rack clean glasses. They were fresh from the dishwasher and so hot they burned her fingertips.

When she stood up with the empty tray, Glen Kardon was on the other side of the counter, staring at her with red-rimmed, watering eyes. He looked in a kind of stupor, his face puffy, his combover disheveled, as if he had just stumbled out of bed.

"I need to talk to you about something," he said. "I was trying to think if there was some way I could get my wedding ring back. Any way at all."

All the blood seemed to rush from Mal's brain, as if she had stood up too quickly. She lost some of the feeling in her hands, too, and for a moment her palms were overcome with a cool, almost painful tingling.

She wondered why he hadn't arrived with cops, whether he meant to give her some kind of chance to settle the matter without the involvement of the police. She wanted to say something to him, but there were no words for this. She could not remember the last time she had felt so helpless, had been caught so exposed, in such indefensible terrain.

Glen went on. "My wife spent the morning crying about it. I heard her in the bedroom, but when I tried to go in and talk to her, the door was locked. She wouldn't let me in. She tried to play it off like she was all right, talking to me through the door. She told me to go to work, don't worry. It was her father's wedding ring, you know. He died three months before we got married. I guess that sounds a little—what do you call it? Oedipal. Like in marrying me she was marrying Daddy. Oedipal isn't right, but you know what I'm saying. She loved that old man."

Mal nodded.

"If they only took the money, I'm not sure I even would've told Helen. Not after I got so drunk. I drink too much. Helen wrote me a note a few months ago, about how much I've been drinking. She wanted to know if it was because I was unhappy with her. It would be easier if she was the kind of woman who'd just scream at me. But I got drunk like that, and the wedding ring she gave me that used to belong to her daddy is gone, and all she did was hug me and say thank God they didn't hurt me."

Mal said, "I'm sorry." She was about to say she would give it all back, ring and money both, and go with him to the police if he wanted—then caught herself. He had said "they": "If they only took the money" and "they didn't hurt me." Not "you."

Glen reached inside his coat and took out a white business envelope, stuffed fat. "I been sick to my stomach all day at work, thinking about it. Then I thought I could put up a note here in the bar. You know, like one of these flyers you see for a lost dog. Only for my lost ring. The guys who robbed me must be customers here. What else would they have been doing down in that lot, that hour of the night? So next time they're in, they'll see my note."

She stared. It took a few moments for what he'd said to register. When it did—when she understood he had no idea she was guilty of anything—she was surprised to feel an odd twinge of something like disappointment.

"Electra," she said.

"Huh?"

"A love thing between father and daughter," Mal said. "Is an Electra complex. What's in the envelope?"

He blinked. Now he was the one who needed some processing time. Hardly anyone knew or remembered that Mal had been to college, on Uncle Sam's dime. She had learned Arabic there and psychology too, although in the end she had wound up back here behind the bar of the Milky Way without a degree. The plan had been to collect her last few credits after she got back from Iraq, but sometime during her tour she had ceased to give a fuck about the plan.

At last Glen came mentally unstuck and replied, "Money. Five hundred dollars. I want you to hold on to it for me."

"Explain."

"I was thinking what to say in my note. I figure I should offer a cash reward for the ring. But whoever stole the ring isn't ever going to come up to me and admit it. Even if I promise not to prosecute, they wouldn't believe me. So I figured out what I need is a middleman. This is where you come in. So the note would say to bring Mallory Grennan the ring and she'll give you the reward money, no questions asked. It'll say they can trust you not to tell me or the police who they are. People know you. I think most folks around here will believe that." He pushed the envelope at her.

"Forget it, Glen. No one is bringing that ring back."

"Let's see. Maybe they were drunk, too, when they took it. Maybe they feel remorse."

She laughed.

He grinned, awkwardly. His ears were pink. "It's possible."

She looked at him a moment longer, then put the envelope under the counter. "Okay. Let's write your note. I can copy it on the fax machine. We'll stick it up around the bar, and after a week, when no one brings you your ring, I'll give you your money back and a beer on the house."

"Maybe just a ginger ale," Glen said.

Glen had to go, but Mal promised she'd hang a few flyers in the parking lot. She had just finished taping them up to the streetlamps when she spotted a sheet of paper, folded into thirds and stuck under the windshield wiper of her father's car.

The thumbprint on this one was delicate and slender, an almost perfect oval, feminine in some way, while the first two had been squarish and blunt. Three thumbs, each of them different from the others.

She pitched it at a wire garbage can attached to a telephone pole, hit the three-pointer, got out of there.

The Eighty-second had finally arrived at Abu Ghraib, to provide force protection and try to nail the fuckers who were mortaring the prison every night. Early in the fall, they began conducting raids in the town around the prison. The first week of operations, they had so many patrols out and so many raids going that they needed backup, so General Karpinski assigned squads of MPs to accompany them. Corporal Plough put in for the job and, when he was accepted, told Mal and Anshaw they were coming with him.

Mal was glad. She wanted away from the prison, the dark corridors of 1A and 1B, with their smell of old wet rock, urine, flop sweat. She wanted away from the tent cities that held the general prison population, the crowds pressed against the chain-links who pleaded with her as she walked along the perimeter, black flies crawling on their faces. She wanted to be in a Hummer with open sides, night air rushing in over her. Destination: any-fucking-where else on the planet.

In the hour before dawn, the platoon they had been tacked onto hit a private home, set within a grove of palms, a white stucco wall around the yard and a wrought-iron gate across the drive. The house was stucco, too, and had a swimming pool out back, a patio and grill, wouldn't have looked out of place in SoCal. Delta Team drove their Hummer right through the gate, which went down with a hard metallic bang, hinges shearing out of the wall with a spray of plaster.

That was all Mal saw of the raid. She was behind the wheel of a two-and-a-half-ton troop transport for carrying prisoners. No Hummer for her, and no action either. Anshaw had another truck. She listened for gunfire, but there was none, the residents giving up without a struggle.

When the house was secure, Corporal Plough left them, said he wanted to size up the situation. What he wanted to do was get his picture taken chewing on a stogie and holding his gun, with his boot on the neck of a hog-tied insurgent. She heard over the walkie-talkie that they had grabbed one of the Fedayeen Saddam, a Ba'athist lieutenant, and had found weapons, files, personnel information. There was a lot of cornpone whoop-ass on the radio. Everyone in the Eighty-second looked like Eminem—blue eyes, pale blond hair in a crew cut—and talked like one of the Duke boys.

Just after sunup, when the shadows were leaning long away from the buildings on the east side of the street, they brought the Fedayeen out and left him on the narrow sidewalk with Plough. The insurgent's wife was still inside the building, soldiers watching her while she packed a bag.

The Fedayeen was a big Arab with hooded eyes and a three-day shadow on his chin, and he wasn't saying anything except "Fuck you" in American. In the basement, Delta Team had found racked AK-47s and a table covered in maps, marked all over with symbols, numbers, Arabic letters. They discovered a folder of photographs, featuring U.S. soldiers in the act of establishing checkpoints, rolling barbed wire across different roads. There was also a picture in the folder of George Bush Sr., smiling a little foggily, posing with Steven Seagal.

Plough was worried that the pictures showed places and people the insurgents planned to strike. He had already been on the radio a couple times, back to base, talking with CI about it in a strained, excited voice. He was especially upset about Steven Seagal. Everyone in Plough's unit had been made to watch *Above the Law* at least once, and Plough claimed to have seen it more than a hundred times. After they brought the prisoner out, Plough stood over the Fedayeen, yelling at him and sometimes swatting him upside the head with Seagal's rolled-up picture. The Fedayeen said, "More fuck you."

Mal leaned against the driver's-side door of her truck for a while, wondering when Plough would quit hollering and swatting the prisoner. She had a Vivarin hangover, and her head hurt. Eventually she decided he wouldn't be done yelling until it was time to load up and go, and that might not be for another hour.

She left Plough yelling, walked over the flattened gate and up to the house. She let herself into the cool of the kitchen. Red tile floor, high ceilings, lots of windows so the place was filled with sunlight. Fresh bananas in a glass bowl. Where did they get fresh bananas? She helped herself to one and ate it on the toilet, the cleanest toilet she had sat on in a year.

She came back out of the house and started down to the road again. On the way there, she put her fingers in her mouth and sucked on them. She hadn't brushed her teeth in a week, and her breath had a human stink on it.

When she returned to the street, Plough had stopped swatting the prisoner long enough to catch his breath. The Ba'athist looked up at him from under his heavy-lidded eyes. He snorted and said, "Is talk. Is boring. You are no one. I say fuck you still no one."

Mal sank to one knee in front of him, put her fingers under his nose, and said in Arabic, "Smell that? That is the cunt of your wife. I fucked her myself like a lesbian, and she said it was better than your cock."

The Ba'athist tried to lunge at her from his knees, making a sound down in his chest, a strangled growl of rage, but Plough caught him across the chin with the stock of his M4. The sound of the Ba'athist's jaw snapping was as loud as a gunshot.

He lay on his side, twisted into a fetal ball. Mal remained crouched beside him.

"Your jaw is broken," Mal said. "Tell me about the photographs of the U.S. soldiers and I will bring a no-more-hurt pill."

It was half an hour before she went to get him the painkillers, and by then he'd told her when the pictures had been taken, coughed up the name of the photographer.

Mal was leaning into the back of her truck, digging in the first-aid kit, when Anshaw's shadow joined hers at the rear bumper.

"Did you really do it?" Anshaw asked her. The sweat on him glowed with an ill sheen in the noonday light. "The wife?"

"What? Fuck no. Obviously."

"Oh," Anshaw said, and swallowed convulsively. "Someone said . . ." he began, and then his voice trailed off.

"What did someone say?"

He glanced across the road, at two soldiers from the Eighty-second, standing by their Hummer. "One of the guys who was in the building said you marched right in and bent her over. Facedown on the bed."

She looked over at Vaughan and Henrichon, holding their M16s and struggling to contain their laughter. She flipped them the bird.

"Jesus, Anshaw. Don't you know when you're being fucked with?"

His head was down. He stared at his own scarecrow shadow, tilting into the back of the truck.

"No," he said.

Two weeks later Anshaw and Mal were in the back of a different truck, with that same Arab, the Ba'athist, who was being transferred from Abu Ghraib to a smaller prison facility in Baghdad. The prisoner had his head in a steel contraption, to clamp his jaw in place, but he was still able to open his mouth wide enough to hawk a mouthful of spit into Mal's face.

Mal was wiping it away when Anshaw got up and grabbed the Fedayeen by the front of his shirt and heaved him out the back of the truck, into the dirt road. The truck was doing thirty miles an hour at the time and was part of a convoy that included two reporters from MSNBC.

The prisoner survived, although most of his face was flayed off on the gravel, his jaw rebroken, his hands smashed. Anshaw said he leaped out on his own, trying to escape, but no one believed him, and three weeks later Anshaw was sent home.

The funny thing was that the insurgent really did escape, a week after that, during another transfer. He was in handcuffs, but with his thumbs broken he was able to slip his hands right out of them. When the MPs stepped from their Hummer at a checkpoint, to talk porno with some friends, the prisoner dropped out of the back of the transport. It was night. He simply walked into the desert and, as the stories go, was never seen again.

The band took the stage Friday evening and didn't come offstage until Saturday morning. Twenty minutes after one, Mal bolted the door behind the last customer. She started helping Candice wipe down tables, but she had been on since before lunch and Bill Rodier said to go home already.

Mal had her jacket on and was headed out when John Petty poked her in the shoulder with something.

"Mal," he said. "This is yours, right? Your name on it."

She turned. Petty was at the cash register, holding a fat envelope toward her. She took it.

"That the money Glen gave you, to swap for his wedding ring?" Petty turned away from her, shifting his attention back to the register. He pulled out stacks of bills, rubber-banded them, and lined them up on the bar. "That's something. Taking his money and fucking him all over again. You think I plop down five hundred bucks you'd fuck me just as nice?"

As he spoke, he put his hand back in the register. Mal reached under his elbow and slammed the drawer on his fingers. He squealed. The drawer began to slide open again on its own, but before he could get his mashed fingers out, Mal slammed it once more. He lifted one foot off the floor and did a comic little jig.

"Ohfuckgoddamnyouuglydyke," he said.

"Hey," said Bill Rodier, coming toward the bar carrying a trash barrel. "Hey."

She let Petty get his hand out of the drawer. He stumbled clumsily away from her, struck the bar with his hip, and wheeled to face her, clutching the mauled hand to his chest.

"You crazy bitch! I think you broke my fingers!"

"Jesus, Mal," Bill said, looking over the bar at Petty's hand. His fat fingers had a purple line of bruise across them. Bill turned his questioning gaze back in her direction. "I don't know what the hell John said, but you can't do that to people."

"You'd be surprised what you can do to people," she told him.

Outside, it was drizzling and cold. She was all the way to her car before she felt a weight in one hand and realized she was still clutching the envelope full of cash.

Mal kept on holding it, against the inside of her thigh, the whole drive back. She didn't put on the radio, just drove and listened to the rain tapping on the glass. She had been in the desert for two years, and she had seen it rain just twice during that time, although there was often a moist fog in the morning, a mist that smelled of eggs, of brimstone.

When she enlisted, she had hoped for war. She did not see the point of joining if you weren't going to get to fight. The risk to her life did not trouble her. It was an incentive. You received a two-hundred-dollar-a-month bonus for every month you spent in the combat zone, and a part of her had relished the fact that her own life was valued so cheap. Mal would not have expected more.

But it didn't occur to her, when she first learned she was going to Iraq, that they paid you that money for more than just the risk to your own life. It wasn't just a question of what could happen to you, but also a matter of what you might be asked to do to others. For her two-hundred-dollar bonus, she had left naked and bound men in stress positions for hours and told a nineteen-year-old girl that she would be gang-raped if she did not supply information about her boyfriend. Two hundred dollars a month was what it cost to make a torturer out of her. She felt now that she had been crazy there, that the Vivarin, the ephedra, the lack of sleep, the constant scream-and-thump of the mortars, had made her into someone who was mentally ill, a bad-dream version of herself. Then Mal felt the weight of the envelope against her thigh, Glen Kardon's payoff, and remembered taking his ring, and it came to her that she was having herself on, pretending she had been someone different in Iraq. Who she'd been then and who she was now were the same person. She had taken the prison home with her. She lived in it still.

Mal let herself into the house, soaked and cold, holding the envelope. She found herself standing in front of the kitchen counter with Glen's money. She could sell him back his own ring for five hundred dollars if she wanted, and it was more than she would get from any pawnshop. She had done worse, for less cash. She stuck her hand down the drain, felt along the wet smoothness of the trap, until her fingertips found the ring.

Mal hooked her ring finger through it, pulled her hand back out. She turned her wrist this way and that, considering how the ring looked on her crooked, blunt finger. With this I do thee wed. She didn't know what she'd do with Glen Kardon's five hundred dollars if she swapped it for his ring. It wasn't money she needed. She didn't need his ring either. She couldn't say what it was she needed, but the idea of it was close, a word on the tip of her tongue, maddeningly out of reach.

She made her way to the bathroom, turned on the shower, and let the steam gather while she undressed. Slipping off her black blouse, she noticed she still had the envelope in one hand, Glen's ring on the third finger of the other. She tossed the money next to the bathroom sink, left the ring on.

She glanced at the ring sometimes while she was in the shower. She tried to imagine being married to Glen Kardon, pictured him stretched out on her father's bed in boxers and a T-shirt, waiting for her to come out of the bathroom, his stomach aflutter with the anticipation of some late-night, connubial action. She snorted at the thought. It was as absurd as trying to imagine what her life would've been like if she had become an astronaut.

The washer and dryer were in the bathroom with her. She dug through the Maytag until she found her Curt Schilling T-shirt and a fresh pair of Hanes. She slipped back into the darkened bedroom, toweling her hair, and glanced at herself in the dresser mirror, only she couldn't see her face, because a white sheet of paper had been stuck into the top of the frame and it covered the place where her face belonged. A black thumbprint had been inked in the center. Around the edges of the sheet of paper, she could see reflected in the mirror a man stretched out on the bed, just as she had pictured Glen Kardon stretched out and waiting for her, only in her head Glen hadn't been wearing gray-and-black fatigues.

She lunged to her side, going for the kitchen door. But Anshaw was already moving, launching himself at her, driving his boot into her right knee. The leg twisted in a way it wasn't meant to go, and she felt her ACL pop behind her knee. Anshaw was right behind her by then, and he got a handful of her hair. As she went down, he drove her forward and smashed her head into the side of the dresser.

A black spoke of pain lanced down into her skull, a nail gun fired straight into the brain. She was down and flailing, and he kicked her in the head. That kick didn't hurt so much, but it took the life out of her, as if she were no more than an appliance and he had jerked the power cord out of the wall.

When he rolled her onto her stomach and twisted her arms behind her back, she had no strength in her to resist. He had the heavy-duty plastic ties, the flex cuffs they used on the prisoners in Iraq sometimes. He sat on her ass and squeezed her ankles together and put the flex cuffs on them, too, tightening until it hurt, and then some. Black flashes were still firing behind her eyes, but the fireworks were smaller and exploding less frequently now. She was coming back to herself, slowly. Breathe. Wait.

When her vision cleared, she found Anshaw sitting above her, on the edge of her father's bed. He had lost weight, and he hadn't any to lose. His eyes peeked out, too bright at the bottoms of deep hollows, moonlight reflected in the water at the bottom of a long well. In his lap was a bag, like an old-fashioned doctor's case, the leather pebbled and handsome.

"I observed you while you were running this morning," he began, without preamble. Using the word "observed," like he would in a report on enemy troop movements. "Who were you signaling when you were up on the hill?"

"Anshaw," Mal said. "What are you talking about, Anshaw? What is this?"

"You're staying in shape. You're still a soldier. I tried to follow you, but you outran me on the hill this morning. When you were on the crest, I saw you flashing a light. Two long flashes, one short, two long. You signaled someone. Tell me who."

At first she didn't know what he was talking about; then she did. Her canteen. Her canteen had flashed in the sunlight when she tipped it up to drink. She opened her mouth to reply, but before she could, he lowered himself to one knee beside her. Anshaw unbuckled his bag and dumped the contents onto the floor. He had a collection of tools: a pair of heavy-duty shears, a Taser, a hammer, a hacksaw, a portable vise. Mixed in with the tools were five or six human thumbs.

Some of the thumbs were thick and blunt and male, and some were white and slender and female, and some were too shriveled and darkened with rot to provide much of any clue about the person they had belonged to. Each thumb ended in a lump of bone and sinew. The inside of the bag had a smell, a sickly-sweet, almost floral stink of corruption.

Anshaw selected the heavy-duty shears.

"You went up the hill and signaled someone this morning. And tonight you came back with a lot of money. I looked in the envelope while you were in the shower. So you signaled for a meeting, and at the meeting you were paid for intel. Who did you meet? CIA?"

"I went to work. At the bar. You know where I work. You followed me there."

"Five hundred dollars. Is that supposed to be tips?"

She didn't have a reply. She couldn't think. She was looking at the thumbs mixed in with his mess of tools.

He followed her gaze, prodded a blackened and shriveled thumb with the blade of the shears. The only identifiable feature remaining on the thumb was a twisted, silvery fishhook scar.

"Plough," Anshaw said. "He had helicopters doing flyovers of my house. They'd fly over once or twice a day. They used different kinds of helicopters on different days to try and keep me from putting two and two together. But I knew what they were up to. I started watching them from the kitchen with my field glasses, and one day I saw Plough at the controls of a radio-station traffic copter. I didn't even know he knew how to pilot a bird until then. He was wearing a black helmet and sunglasses, but I still recognized him."

As Anshaw spoke, Mal remembered Corporal Plough trying to open a bottle of Red Stripe with the blade of his bayonet and the knife slipping, catching him across the thumb, Plough sucking on it and saying around his thumb, Motherfuck, someone open this for me.

"No, Anshaw. It wasn't him. It was just someone who looked like him. If he could fly a helicopter, they would've had him piloting Apaches over there."

"Plough admitted it. Not at first. At first he lied. But eventually he told me everything, that he was in the helicopter, that they'd been keeping me under surveillance ever since I came home." Anshaw moved the tip of the shears to point at another thumb, shriveled and brown, with the texture and appearance of a dried mushroom. "This was his wife. She admitted it, too. They were putting dope in my water to make me sluggish and stupid. Sometimes I'd be driving home and I'd forget what my own house looked like. I'd spend twenty minutes cruising around my development before I realized I'd gone by my place twice."

He paused, moved the tip of the shears to a fresher thumb, a woman's, the nail painted red. "She followed me into a supermarket in Poughkeepsie. This was while I was on my way north, to see you. To see if you had been compromised. This woman in the supermarket, she followed me aisle to aisle, always whispering on her cell phone. Pretending not to look at me. Then, later, I went into a Chinese place and noticed her parked across the street, still on the phone. She was the toughest to get solid information out of. I almost thought I was wrong about her. She told me she was a first-grade teacher. She told me she didn't even know my name and that she wasn't following me. I almost believed her. She had a photo in her purse, of her sitting on the grass with a bunch of little kids. But it was tricked up. They used Photoshop to stick her in that picture. I even got her to admit it in the end."

"Plough told you he could fly helicopters so you wouldn't keep hurting him. The first-grade teacher told you the photo was faked to make you stop. People will tell you anything if you hurt them badly enough. You're having some kind of break with reality, Anshaw. You don't know what's true anymore."

"You would say that. You're part of it. Part of the plan to make me crazy, make me kill myself. I thought the thumbprints would startle you into getting in contact with your handler, and they did. You went straight to the hills to send him a signal. To let him know I was close. But where's your backup now?"

"I don't have backup. I don't have a handler."

"We were friends, Mal. You got me through the worst parts of being over there, when I thought I was going crazy. I hate that I have to do this to you. But I need to know who you were signaling. And you're going to tell. Who did you signal, Mal?"

"No one," she said, trying to squirm away from him on her belly.

He grabbed her hair and wrapped it around his fist, to keep her from going anywhere. She felt a tearing along her scalp. He pinned her with a knee in her back. She went still, head turned, right cheek mashed against the nubbly rug on the floor.

"I didn't know you were married. I didn't notice the ring until just tonight. Is he coming home? Is he part of it? Tell me." Tapping the ring on her finger with the blade of the shears.

Mal's face was turned so she was staring under the bed at the case with her M4 and bayonet in it. She had left the clasps undone.

Anshaw clubbed her in the back of the head, at the base of the skull, with the handles of the shears. The world snapped out of focus, went to a soft blur, and then slowly her vision cleared and details regained their sharpness, until at last she was seeing the case under the bed again, not a foot away from her, the silver clasps hanging loose.

"Tell me, Mal. Tell me the truth now."

In Iraq the Fedayeen had escaped the handcuffs after his thumbs were broken. Cuffs wouldn't hold a person whose thumb could move in any direction . . . or someone who didn't have a thumb at all.

Mal felt herself growing calm. Her panic was like static on a radio, and she had just found the volume, was slowly dialing it down. He would not begin with the shears, of course, but would work his way up to them. He meant to beat her first. At least. She drew a long, surprisingly steady breath. Mal felt almost as if she were back on Hatchet Hill, climbing with all the will and strength she had in her, for the cold, open blue of the sky.

"I'm not married," she said. "I stole this wedding ring off a drunk. I was just wearing it because I like it."

He laughed: a bitter, ugly sound. "That isn't even a good lie."

And another breath, filling her chest with air, expanding her lungs to their limit. He was about to start hurting her. He would force her to talk, to give him information, to tell him what he wanted to hear. She was ready. She was not afraid of being pushed to the edge of what could be endured. She had a high tolerance for pain, and her bayonet was in arm's reach, if only she had an arm to reach.

"It's the truth," she said, and with that, PFC Mallory Grennan began her confession.

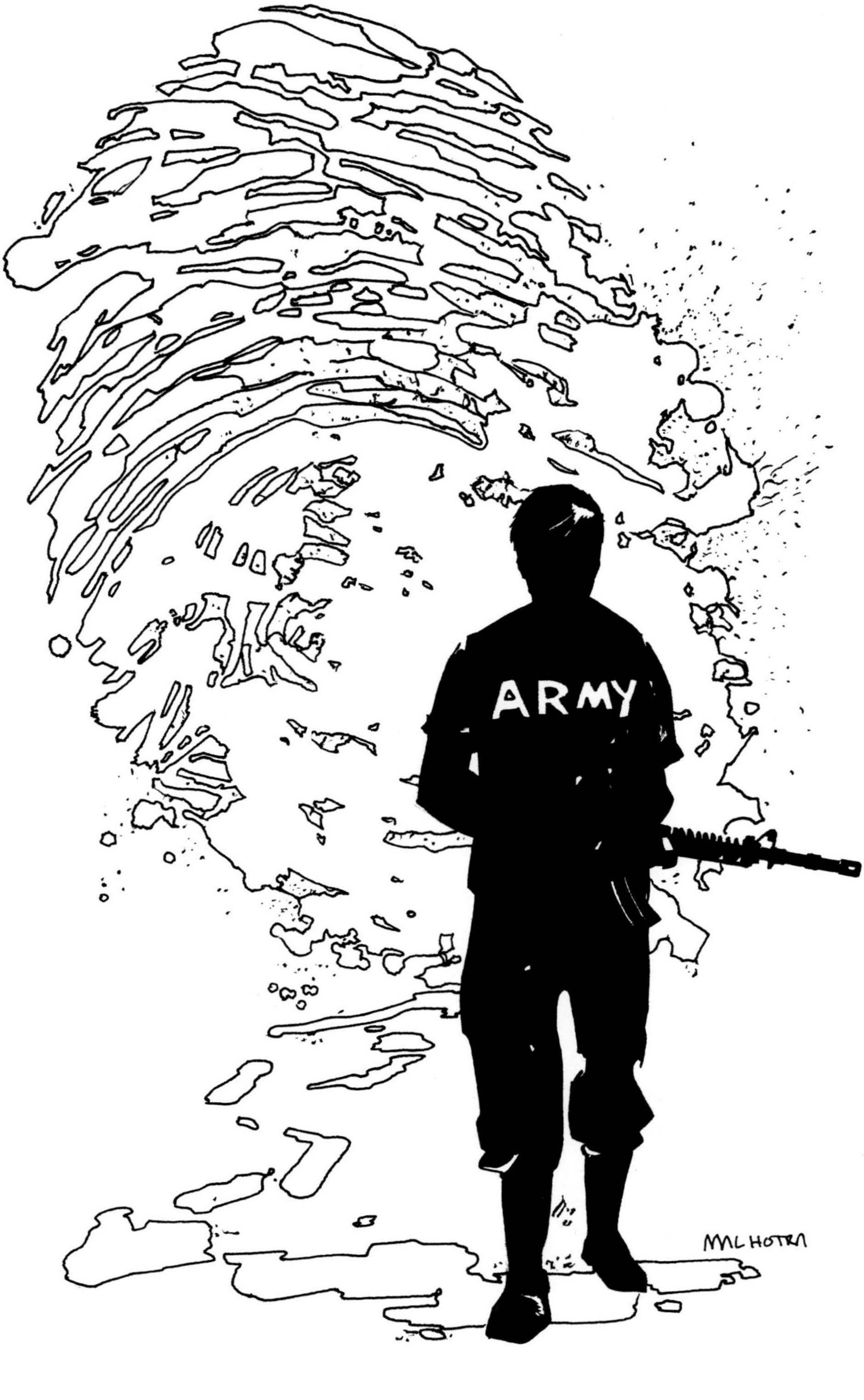
ARMY
MALHOTRA

Vic Malhotra
Art Gallery

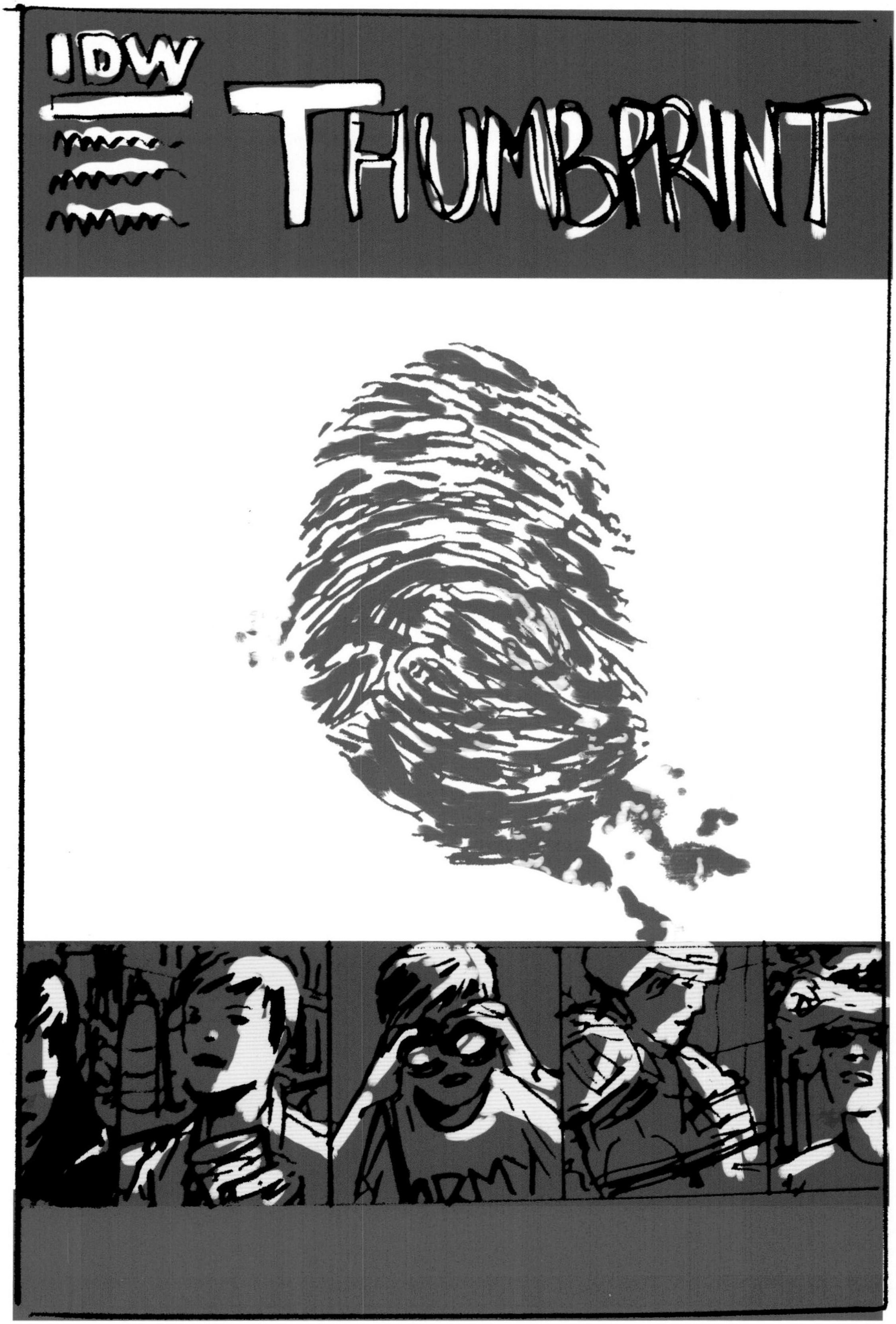
IDW
THUMBPRINT

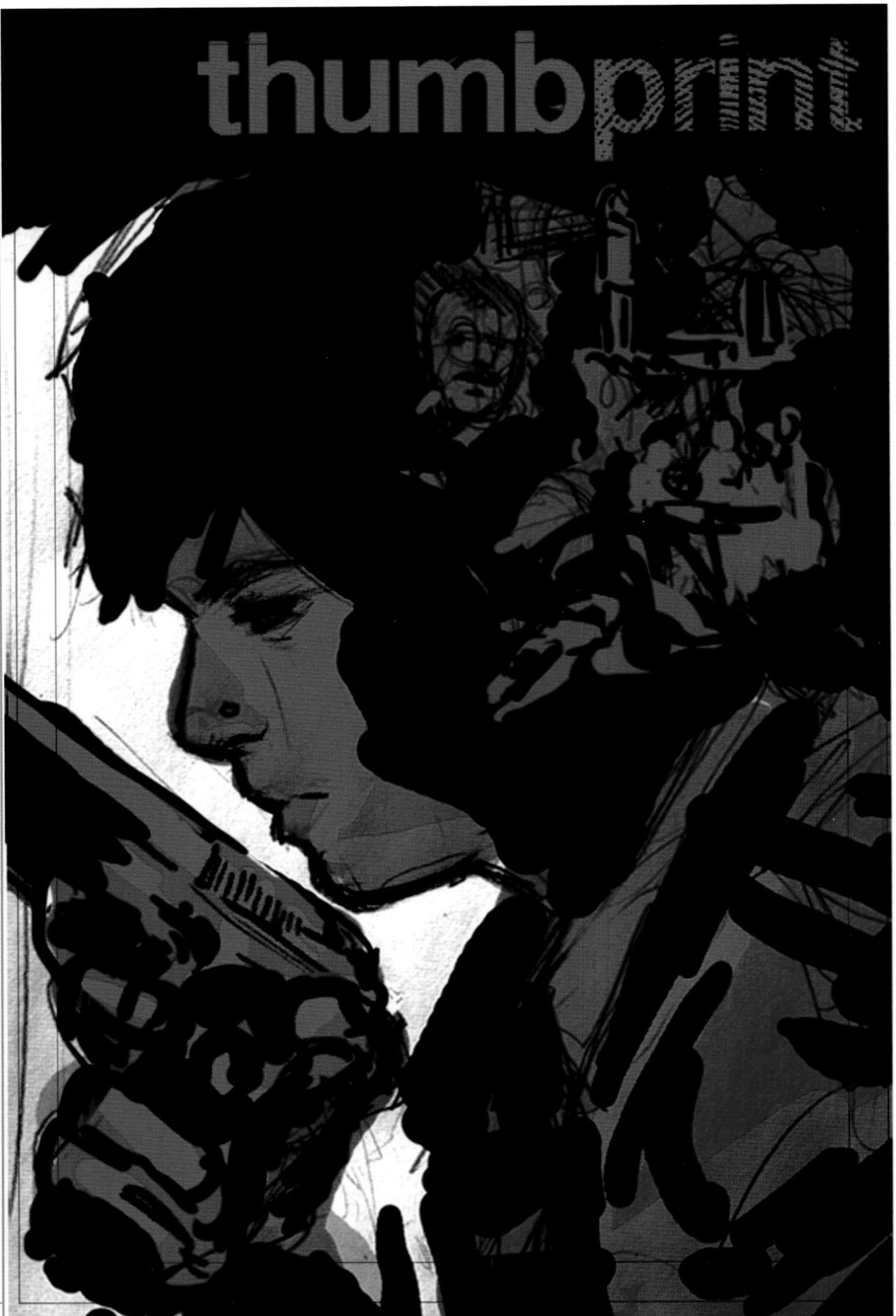
thumbprint

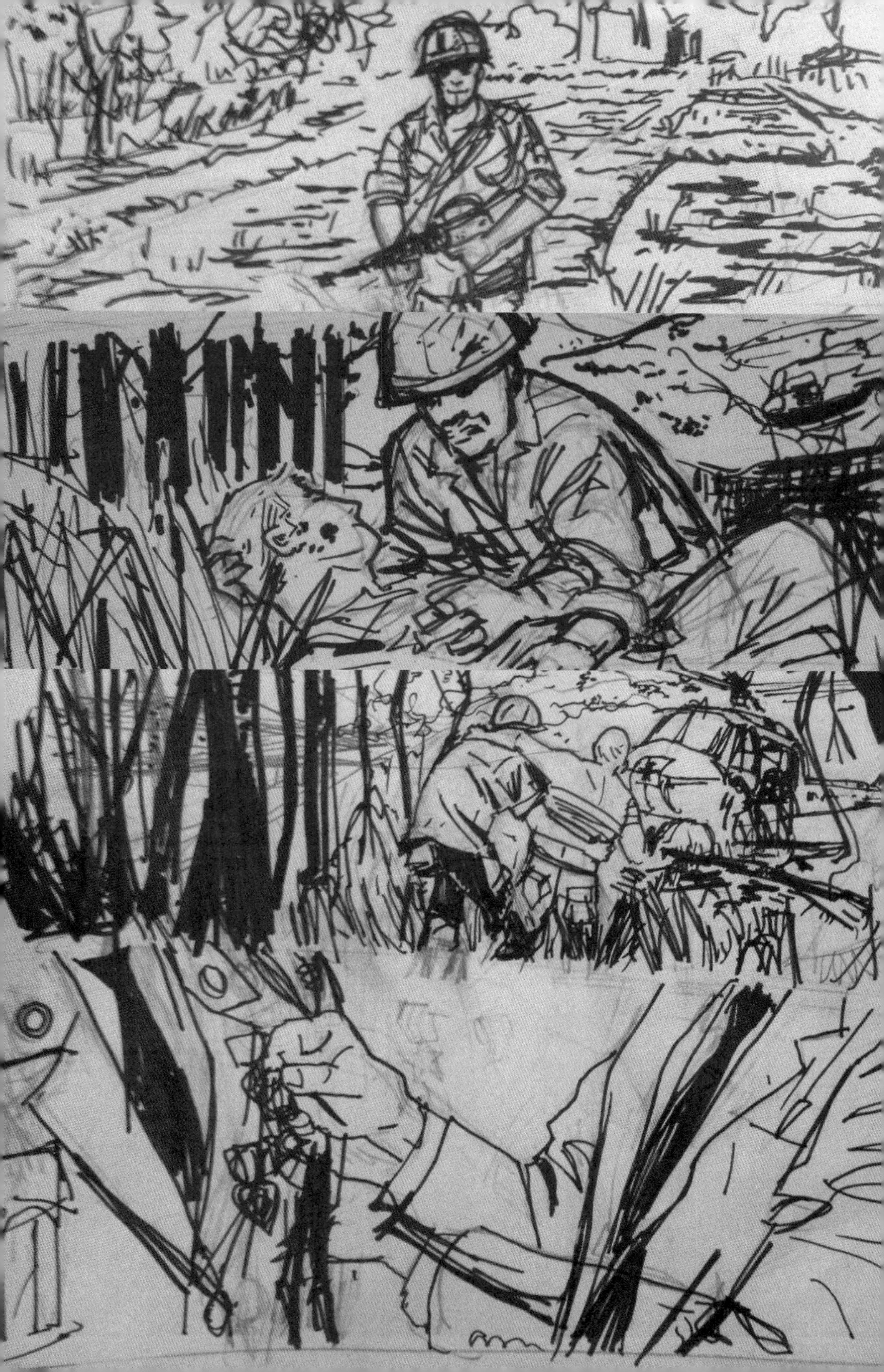

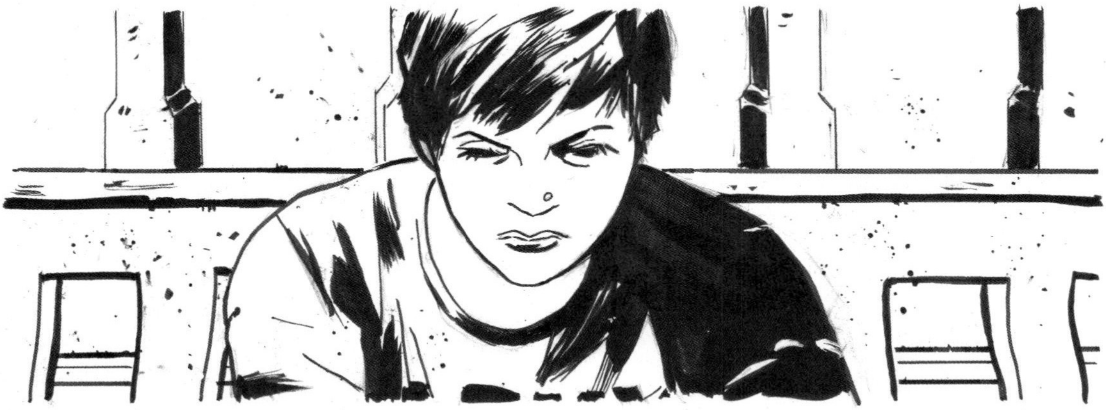

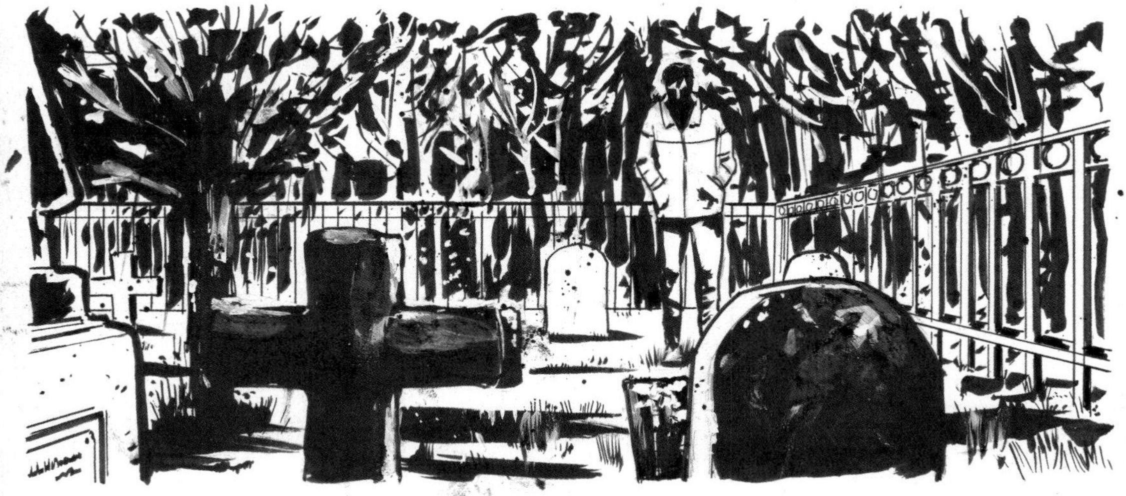

THUMBPRINT - MAL

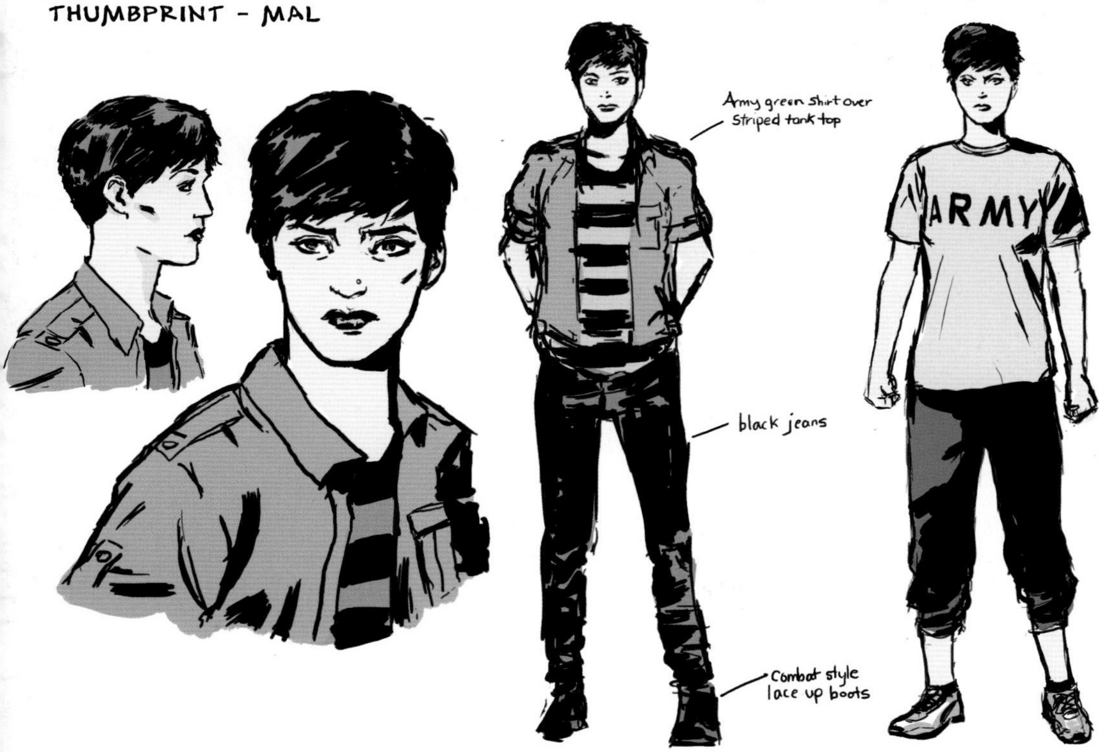

Army green shirt over
Striped tank top
black jeans
Combat style
lace up boots
ARMY

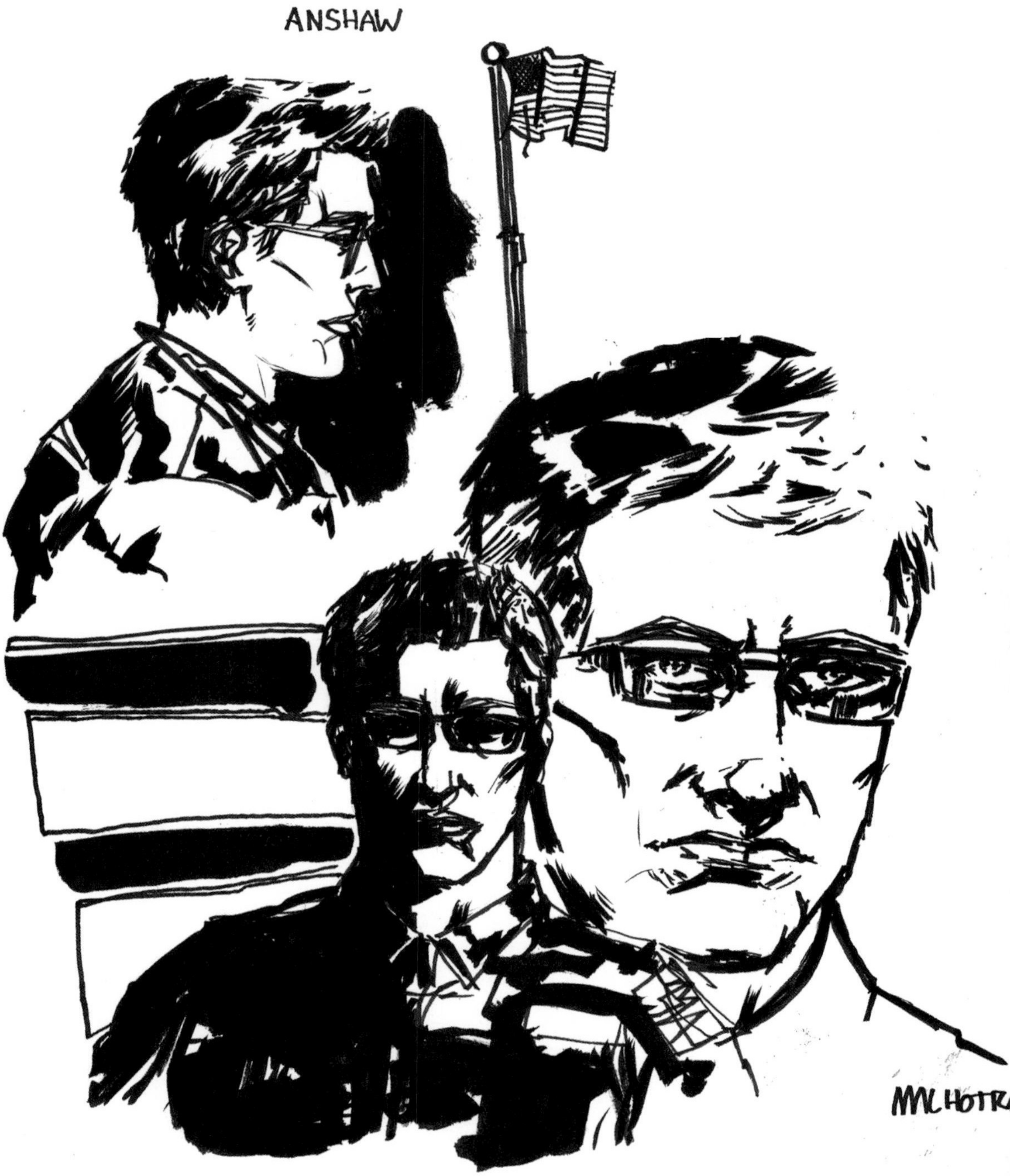
ANSHAW

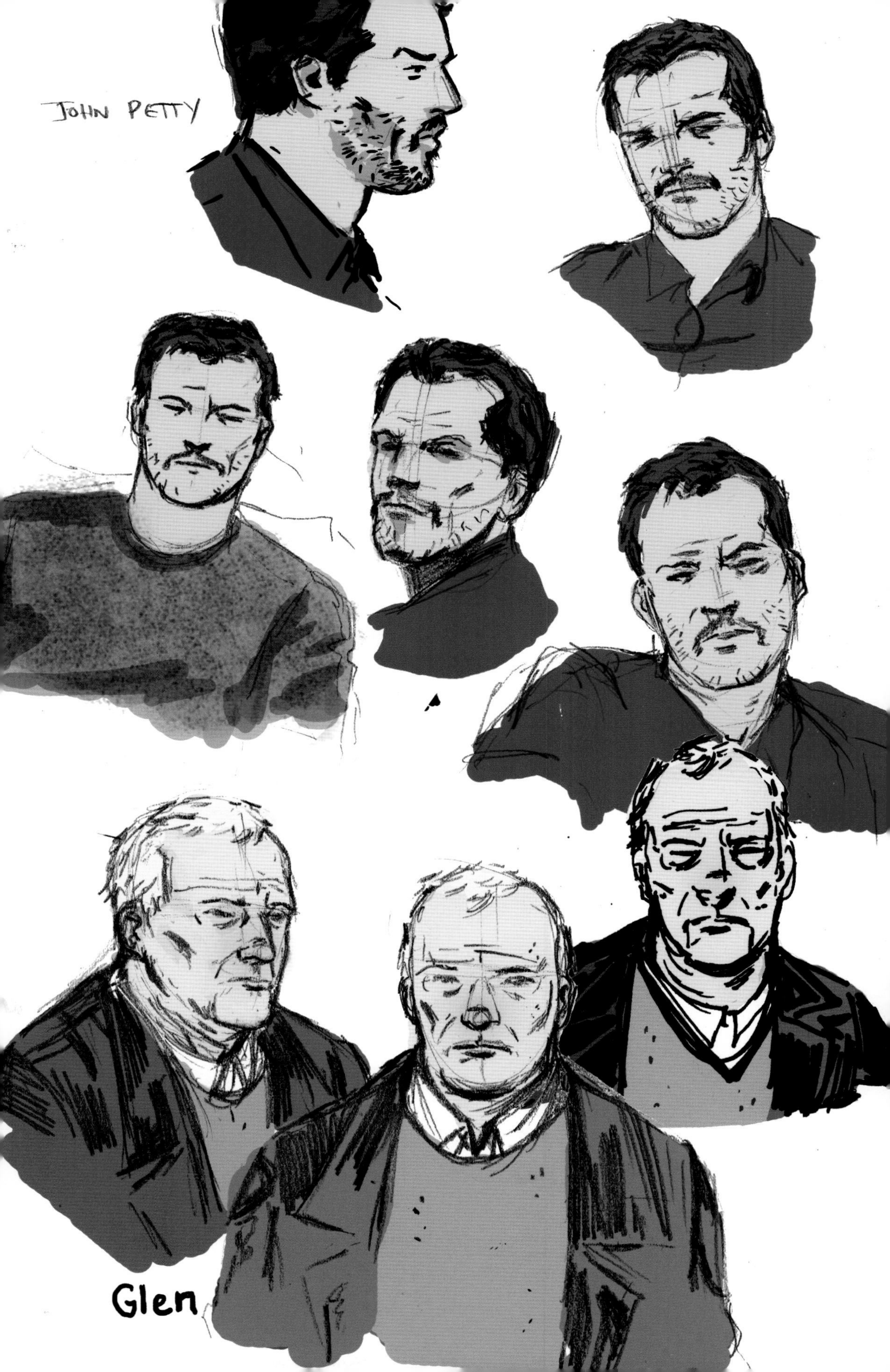
JOHN PETTY
Glen

PENCILLER ____ INKER ____ PAGE# ____ **INTERIORS**

TITLE ____ ISSUE # ____ MONTH ____

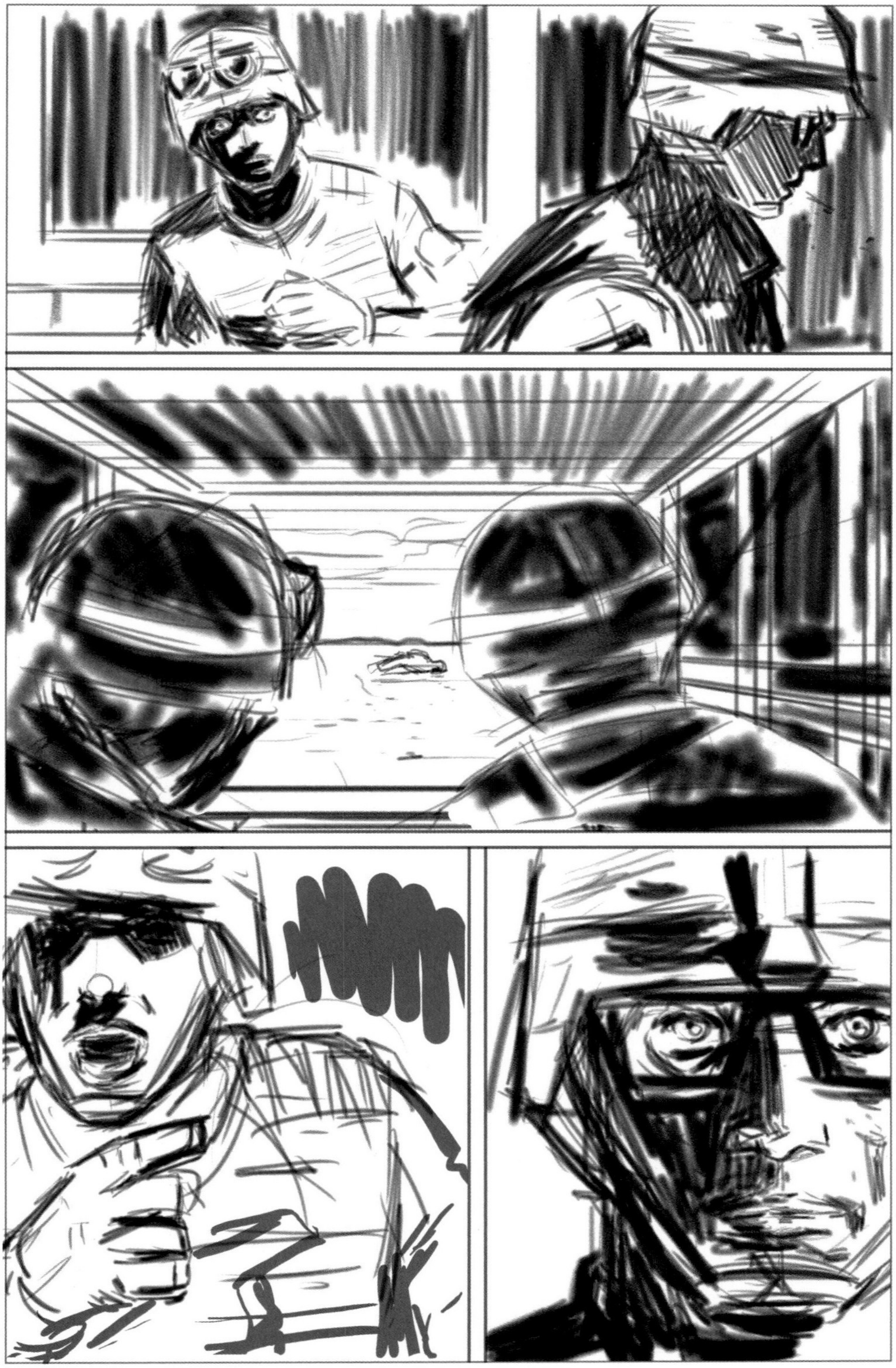

< CUT RIGHT HAND PAGE AT THIS LINE

DOUBLE PAGE SPREAD: CUT AS SHOWN, ABUT PAGE EDGE, TAPE ON BACK, DO NOT OVERLAP

CUT LEFT HAND PAGE AT THIS LINE >

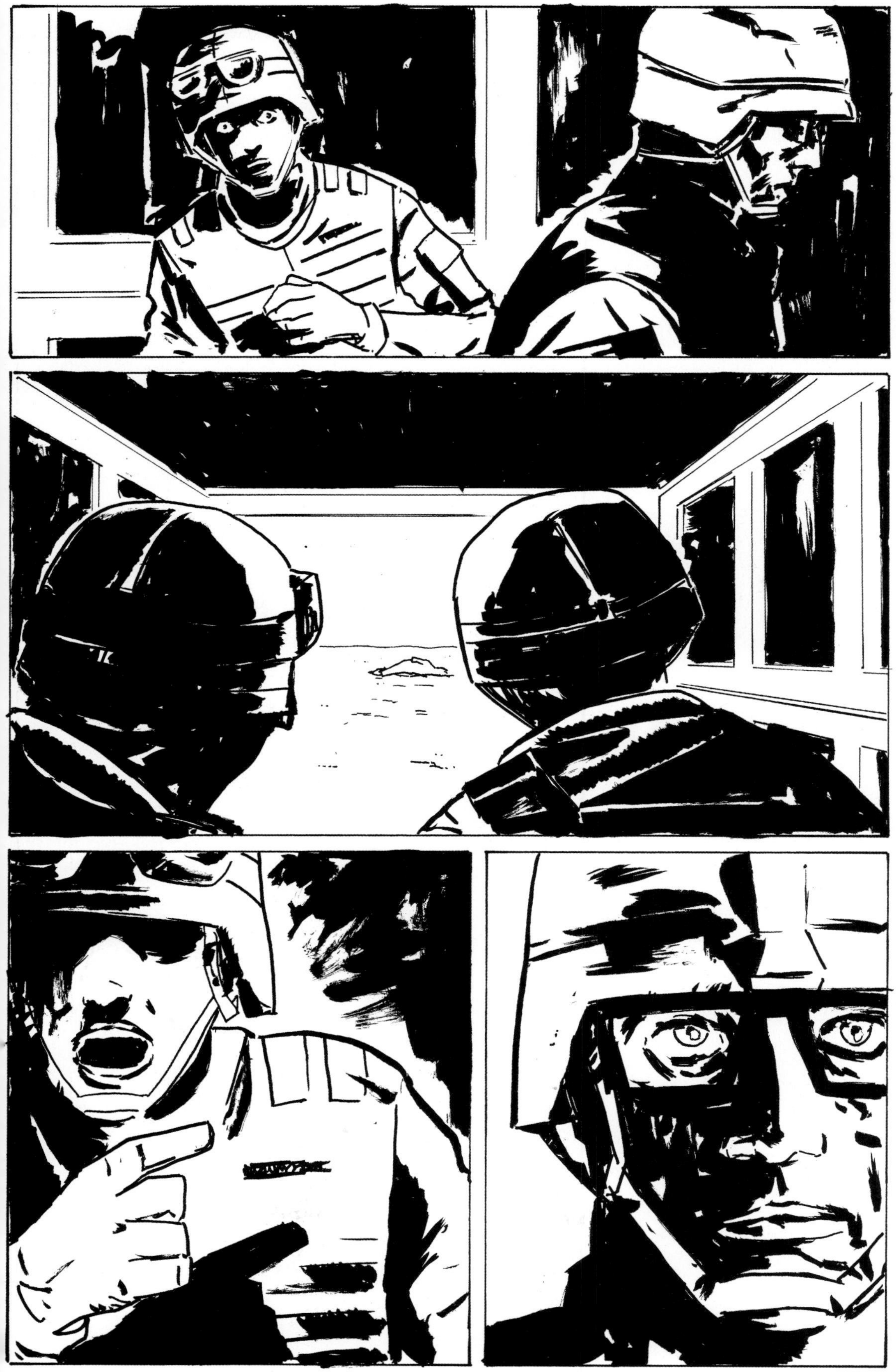

KODIAK

WRITTEN BY JOE HILL AND JASON CIARAMELLA
ART BY NAT JONES · COLORS BY JAY FOTOS
LETTERS BY ROBBIE ROBBINS · EDITS BY CHRIS RYALL

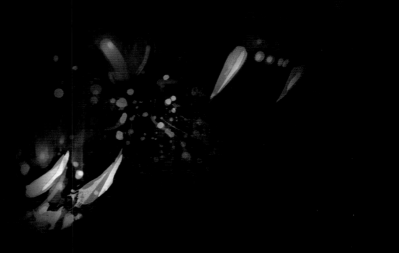

A note from Joe -

Adapting another writer's work is nerve-wracking business. Imagine you're grooming a bear for the circus, trying to comb the knots out of its fur while the thing sleeps and farts and snores. The act of adaptation is roughly as soothing as that. One wrong tug and the bad-smelling son-of-a-bitch might wake up and show you his teeth. And every sentence—that's another stroke of the comb. What are you going to do if he stirs, rolls over, and opens his eyes? You're in his cave. You're in reach of his paws.

Maybe it's no easier if the bear belongs to you—if the work of fiction is your own original piece—but at least you're more familiar with its ways and habits. You raised that one from a cub. This other bear... who knows what kind of temper it has? Who knows how mean it might be if you yank his fur the wrong way?

But you have to do the work—you have to somehow make that animal presentable for your big top—and the only way to do the work is to risk your own voice. Nothing makes for a sorry story like a writer so intent on honoring his source material, he never allows himself to have any fun, never allows himself to take that other person's story and make it his own. That's a recipe to get something that sits there dead on the page, not fooling anyone. Sure, you managed to comb out the bear's fur, but you had to kill it and fill it with sawdust first. The reader can always tell the difference between what's alive and what just came back from the taxidermist.

To his credit, Jason has had his own voice from the beginning. *KODIAK* was based on my plot, but it's his story and his sound: effortless, laid back, wry, charming, not trying too hard... and all forward motion. This was the first time Jason took one of my stories, groomed it for the comics, and taught it to juggle while balancing on a ball. Mostly Jason writes his own stuff now, but it was a pleasure to see what he did with this one, and *THE CAPE*, and eventually *THUMBPRINT*.

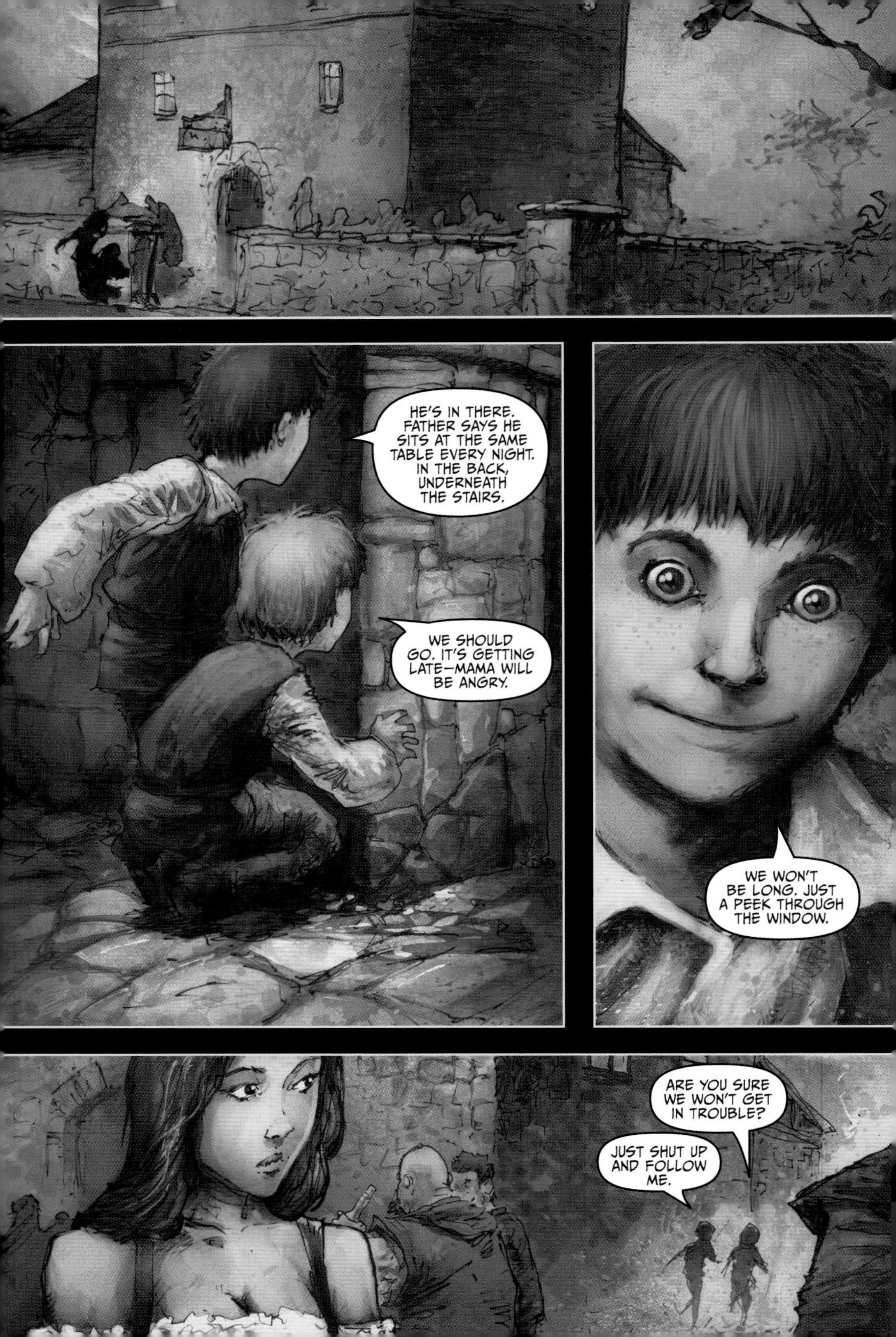
HE'S IN THERE. FATHER SAYS HE SITS AT THE SAME TABLE EVERY NIGHT. IN THE BACK, UNDERNEATH THE STAIRS.
WE SHOULD GO. IT'S GETTING LATE—MAMA WILL BE ANGRY.
WE WON'T BE LONG. JUST A PEEK THROUGH THE WINDOW.
ARE YOU SURE WE WON'T GET IN TROUBLE?
JUST SHUT UP AND FOLLOW ME.

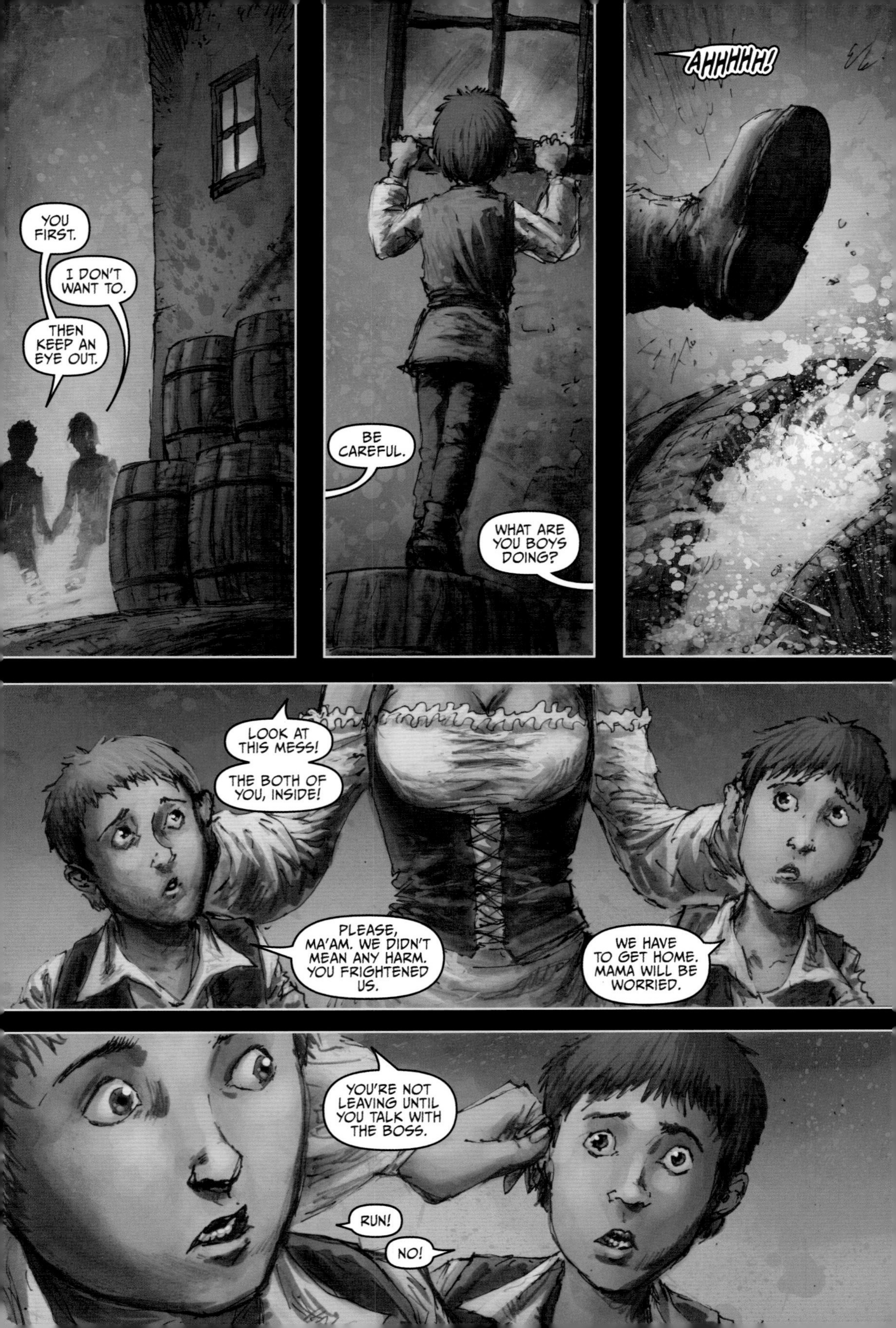
YOU FIRST.
I DON'T WANT TO.
THEN KEEP AN EYE OUT.
BE CAREFUL.
WHAT ARE YOU BOYS DOING?
AHHHHH!
LOOK AT THIS MESS!
THE BOTH OF YOU, INSIDE!
PLEASE, MA'AM. WE DIDN'T MEAN ANY HARM. YOU FRIGHTENED US.
WE HAVE TO GET HOME. MAMA WILL BE WORRIED.
YOU'RE NOT LEAVING UNTIL YOU TALK WITH THE BOSS.
RUN!
NO!

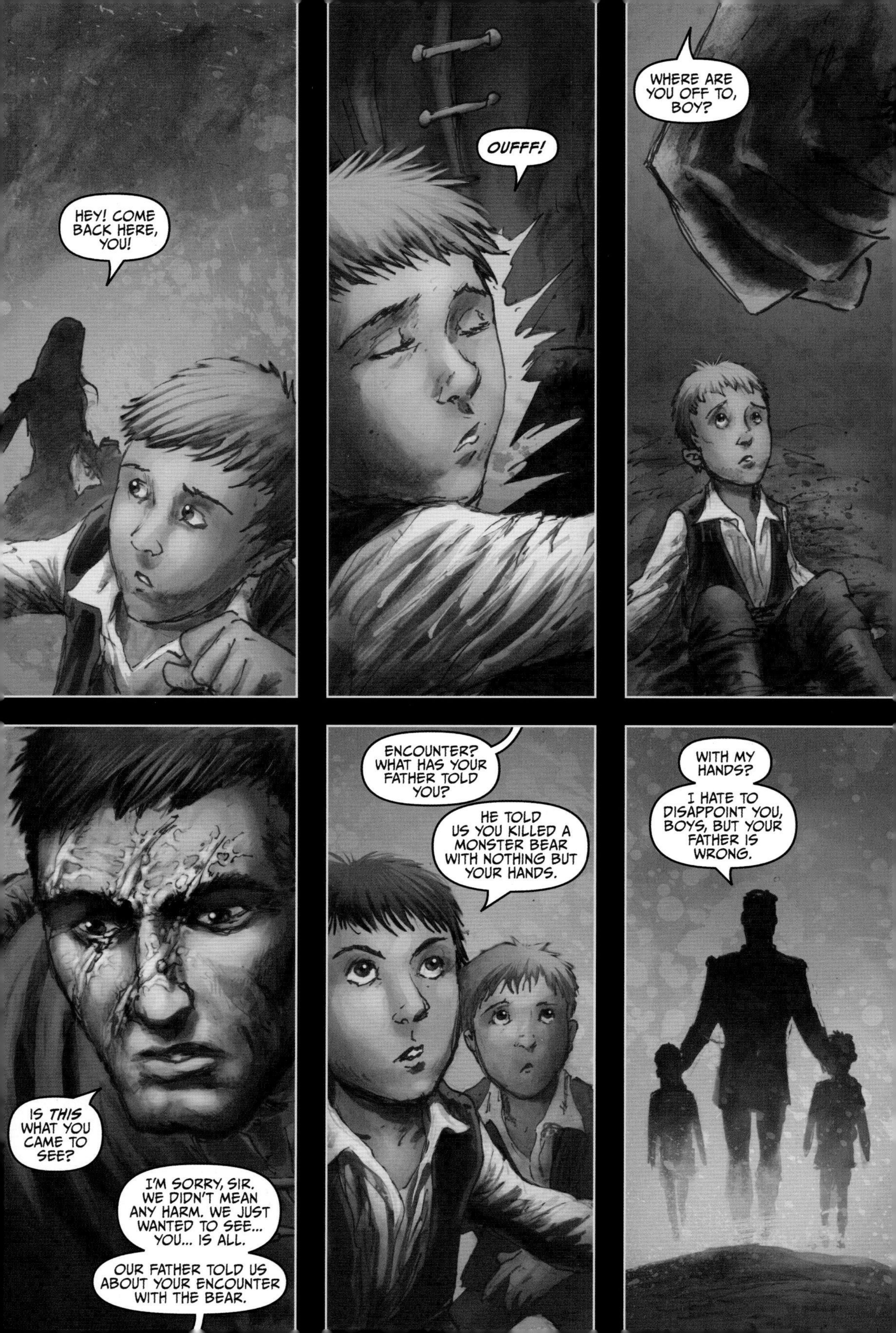
HEY! COME BACK HERE, YOU!
OUFFF!
WHERE ARE YOU OFF TO, BOY?
IS *THIS* WHAT YOU CAME TO SEE?
I'M SORRY, SIR. WE DIDN'T MEAN ANY HARM. WE JUST WANTED TO SEE... YOU... IS ALL.
OUR FATHER TOLD US ABOUT YOUR ENCOUNTER WITH THE BEAR.
ENCOUNTER? WHAT HAS YOUR FATHER TOLD YOU?
HE TOLD US YOU KILLED A MONSTER BEAR WITH NOTHING BUT YOUR HANDS.
WITH MY HANDS?
I HATE TO DISAPPOINT YOU, BOYS, BUT YOUR FATHER IS WRONG.

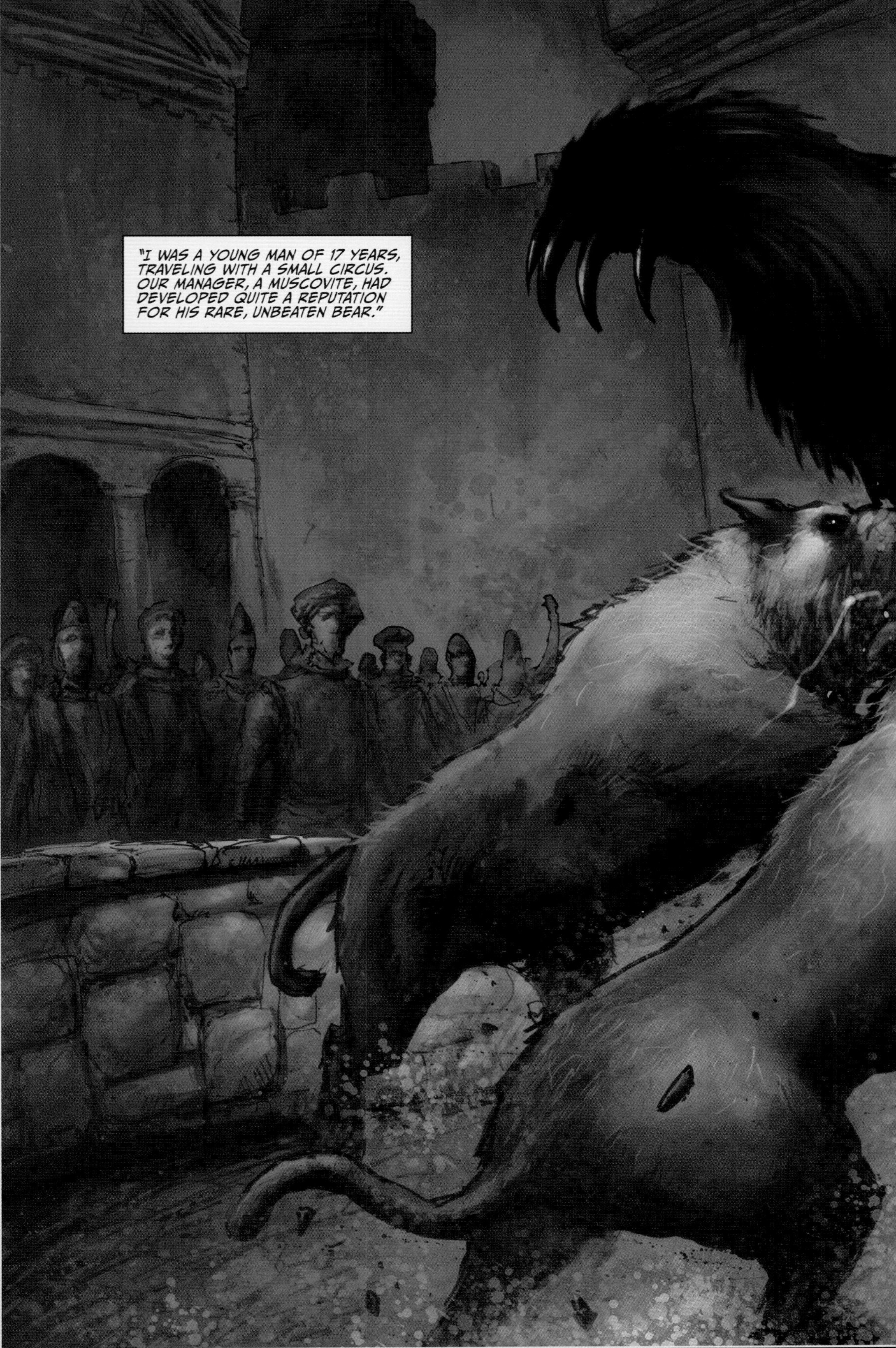
"I WAS A YOUNG MAN OF 17 YEARS, TRAVELING WITH A SMALL CIRCUS. OUR MANAGER, A MUSCOVITE, HAD DEVELOPED QUITE A REPUTATION FOR HIS RARE, UNBEATEN BEAR."

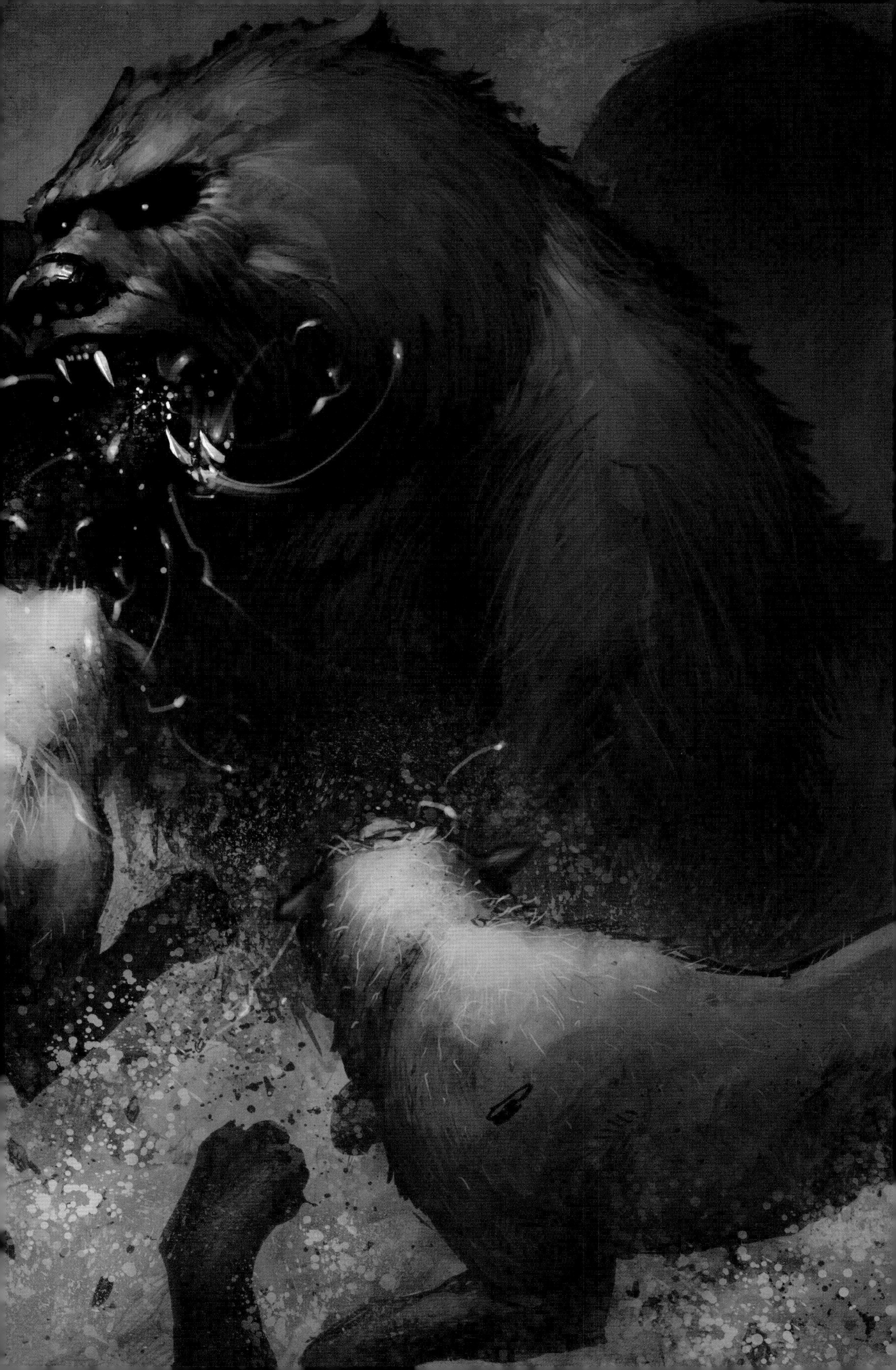

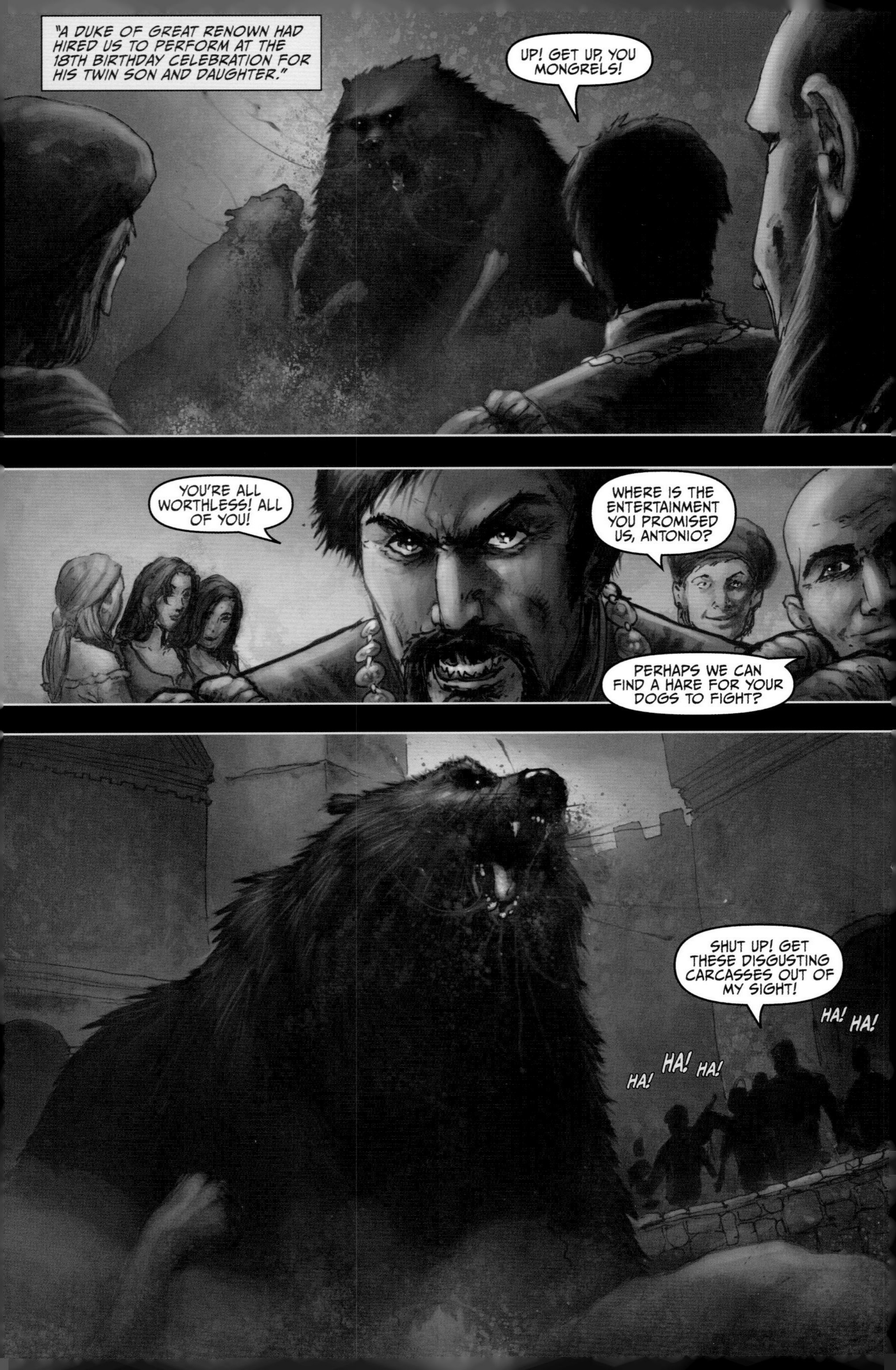
"A DUKE OF GREAT RENOWN HAD HIRED US TO PERFORM AT THE 18TH BIRTHDAY CELEBRATION FOR HIS TWIN SON AND DAUGHTER."
UP! GET UP, YOU MONGRELS!
YOU'RE ALL WORTHLESS! ALL OF YOU!
WHERE IS THE ENTERTAINMENT YOU PROMISED US, ANTONIO?
PERHAPS WE CAN FIND A HARE FOR YOUR DOGS TO FIGHT?
SHUT UP! GET THESE DISGUSTING CARCASSES OUT OF MY SIGHT!
HA! HA!
HA! HA! HA!

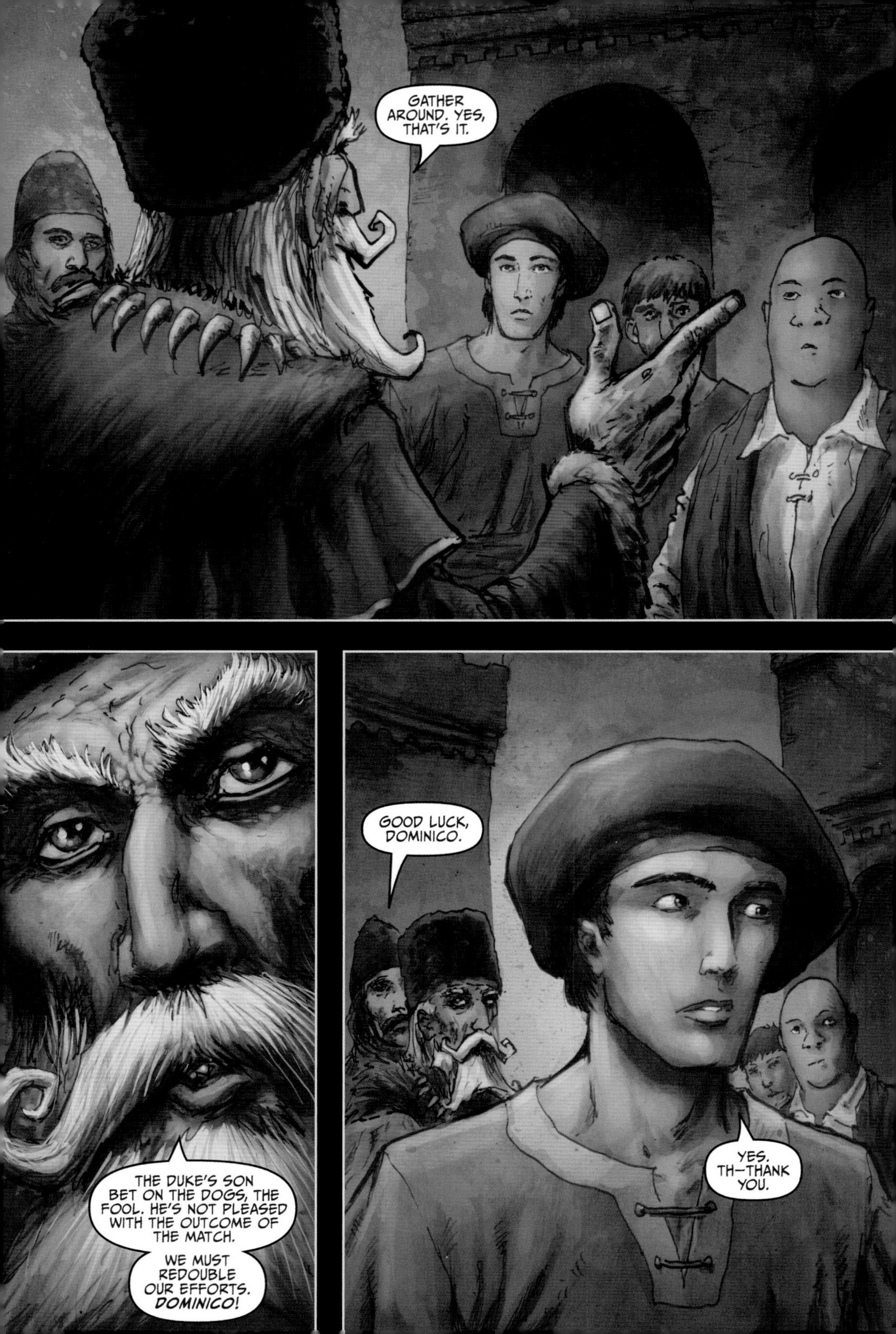
GATHER AROUND. YES, THAT'S IT.
THE DUKE'S SON BET ON THE DOGS, THE FOOL. HE'S NOT PLEASED WITH THE OUTCOME OF THE MATCH.
WE MUST REDOUBLE OUR EFFORTS. DOMINICO!
GOOD LUCK, DOMINICO.
YES. TH—THANK YOU.

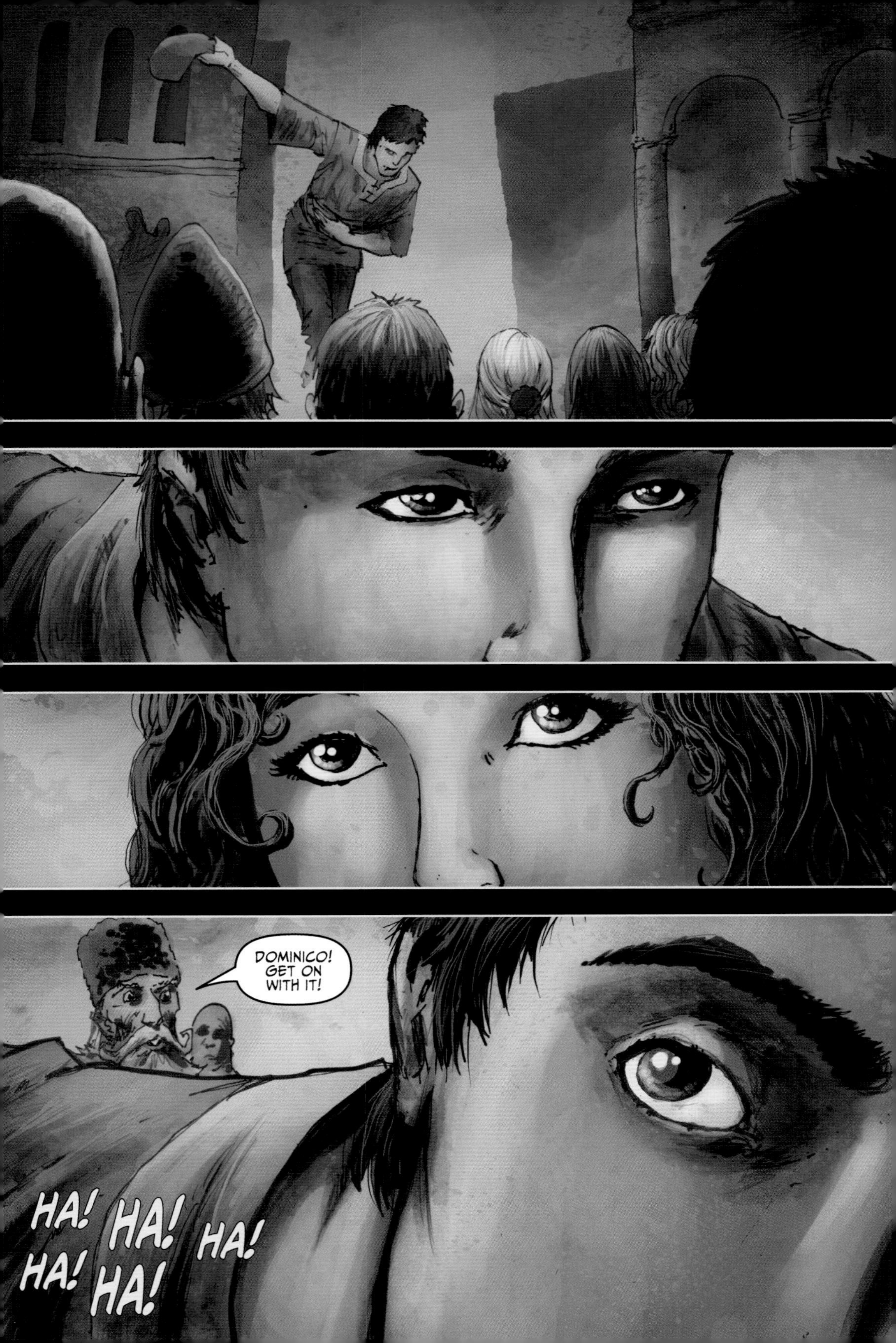
DOMINICO! GET ON WITH IT!
HA! HA! HA! HA! HA!

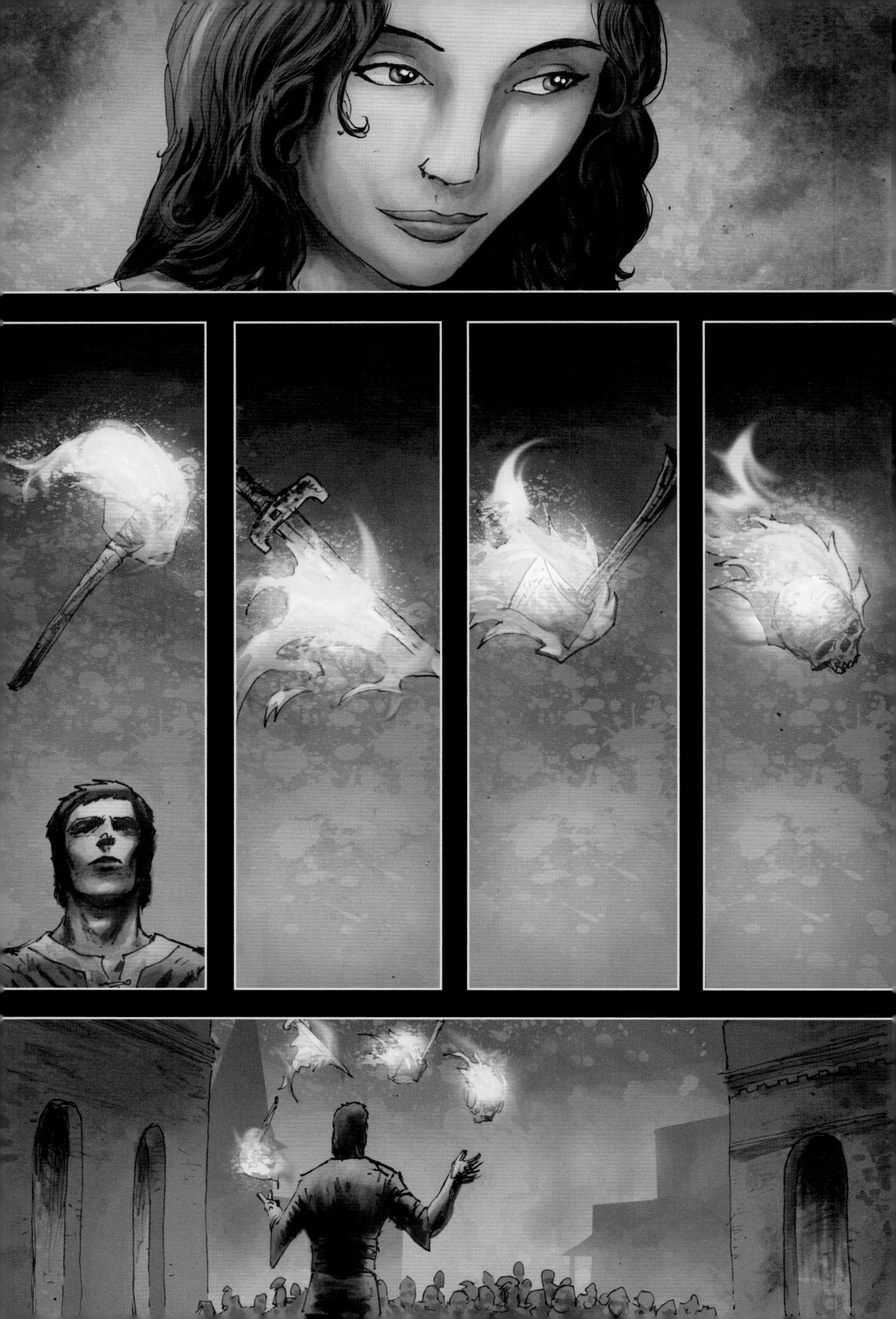

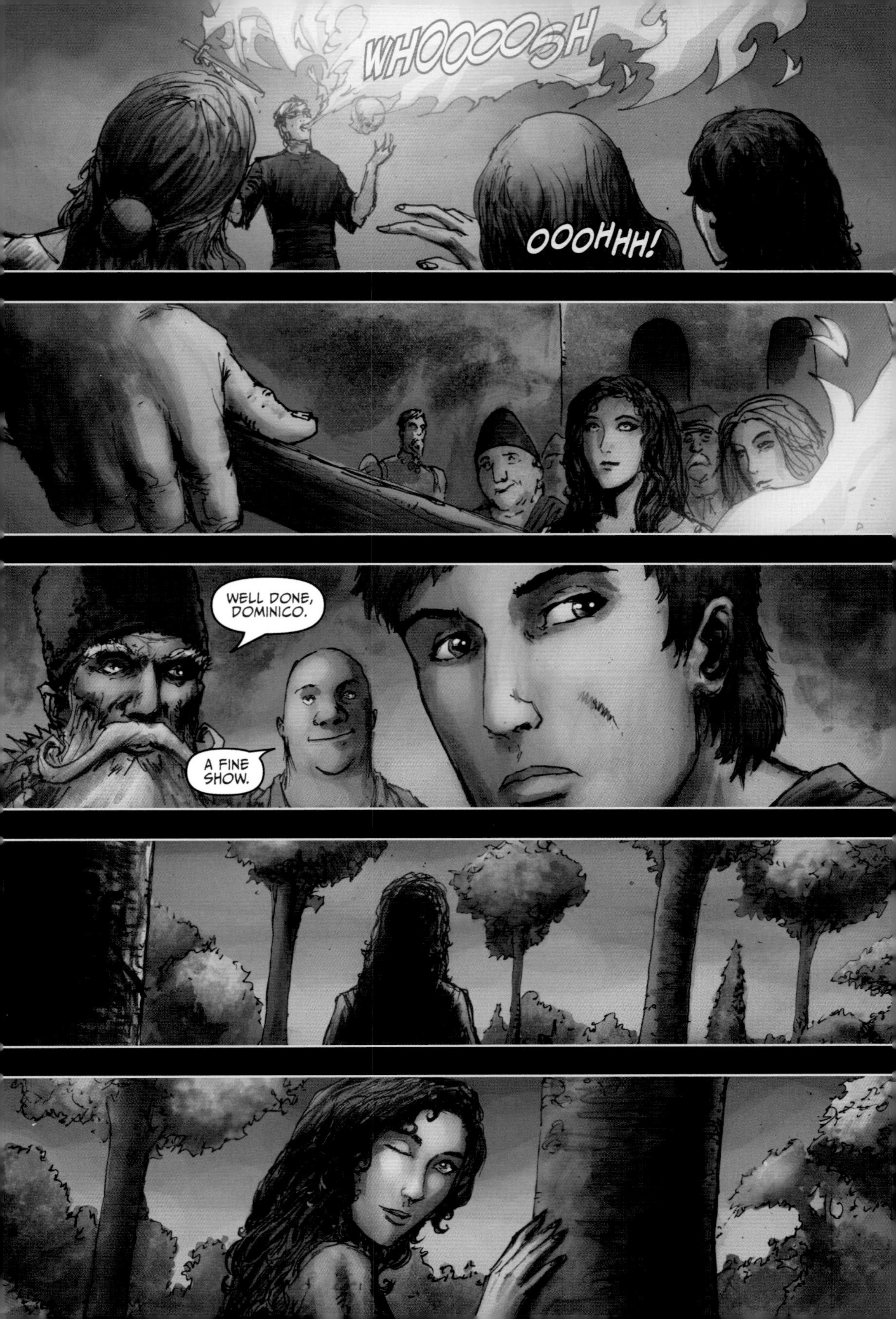
WHOOOOOSH
OOOHHH!
WELL DONE, DOMINICO.
A FINE SHOW.

DOMINICO! WE'RE ON AGAIN SHORTLY!

WHAT IS YOUR NAME, SIR?

DOM- DOMINICO.

SIT WITH ME, DOMINICO.

I SHOULDN'T.

PLEASE.

MY NAME IS...

ANTONIA, YES, I KNOW.

DO I MAKE YOU NERVOUS?

A LITTLE, YES.

THAT SOUNDS STRANGE COMING FROM A BOY WHO SPENDS HIS DAYS THROWING AROUND FLAMING AXES.

HOW DID YOU LEARN TO DO SUCH A THING?

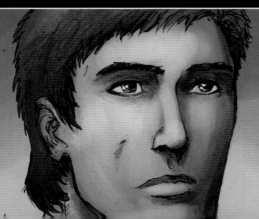

WHEN I WAS A YOUNG BOY, MY MOTHER TOOK ME TO SEE A GROUP OF PERFORMERS, MUCH LIKE OURS.

A FIRE HANDLER ASKED FOR A VOLUNTEER FROM THE AUDIENCE, AND PULLED ME ON STAGE TO SKIP A BURNING ROPE. I DID NOT KNOW THAT I WOULD BE VOLUNTEERING FOR THE NEXT TEN YEARS.

I JUST KNEW I PREFERRED LEAPING FLAMES TO CLEANING MY MOTHER'S STABLES.

SINCE THEN, HARDLY A DAY HAS GONE BY WHEN I DIDN'T HAVE SOME FLAMING OBJECT FLYING OVER MY HEAD.

WILL YOU TELL ME HOW YOU BREATHE FIRE?

IT'S AGAINST THE RULES TO TELL OUR SECRETS TO THE AUDIENCE.

YOU HAVE TO TELL ME. IT'S MY BIRTHDAY, AND THERE ARE NO RULES ON MY BIRTHDAY.

PLEASE.

BEFORE I TAKE THE STAGE, I STUFF MY CHEEK WITH LAMP OIL.

WHEN THE TIME IS RIGHT, I SPIT THE OIL THROUGH THE FLAMING WEAPONS, AND IT PRODUCES THE FIREBALL.

IT'S SIMPLE, REALLY.

MY GOD, THAT MUST TASTE AWFUL.

NO. NOT AT ALL. THE OIL HAS A SLIGHT HONEY FLAVOR.

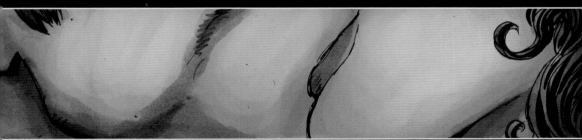

MMMM... MORE LIKE CHAMOMILE THAN HONEY.

GET YOUR HANDS OFF MY SISTER, DOG!

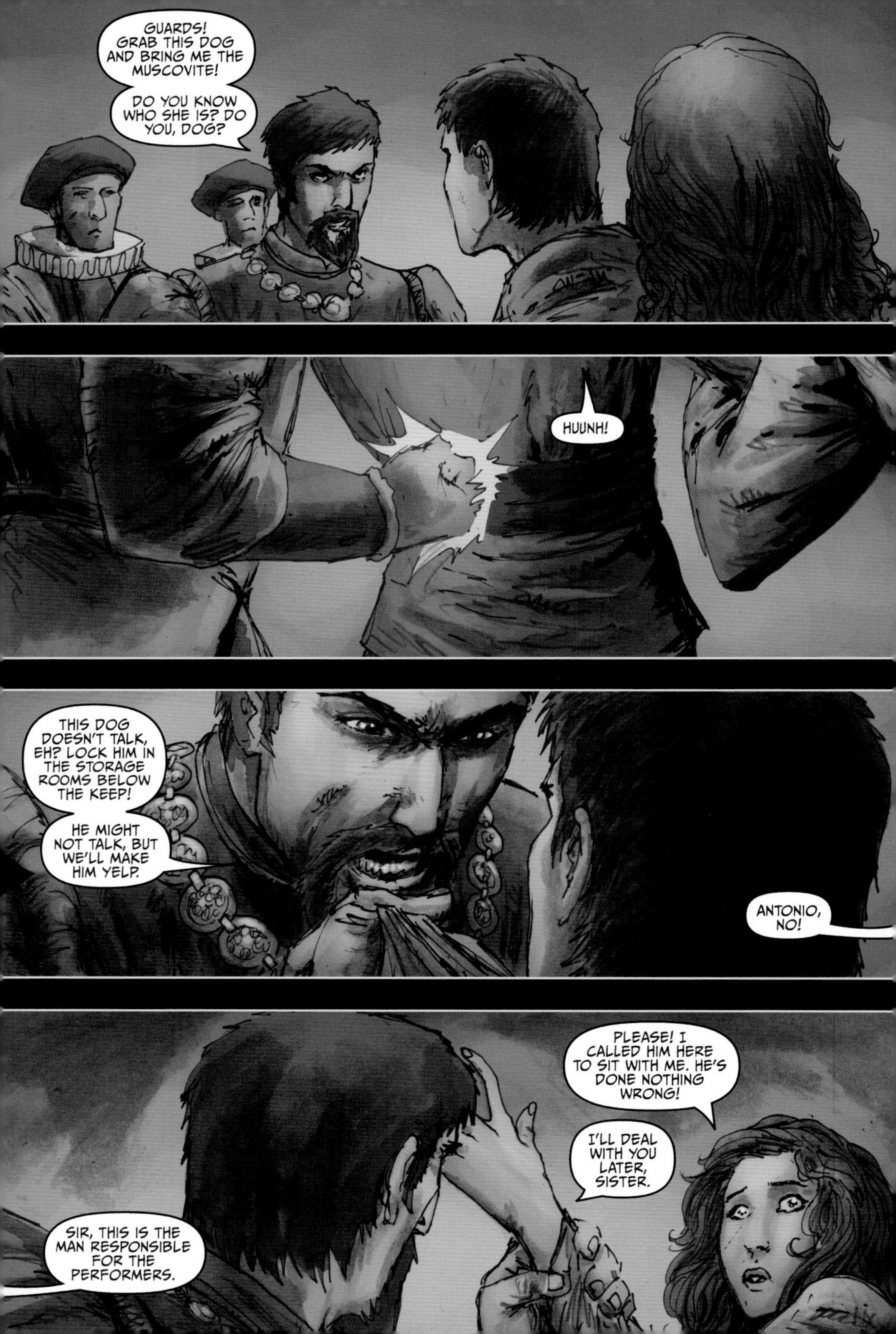
GUARDS! GRAB THIS DOG AND BRING ME THE MUSCOVITE!
DO YOU KNOW WHO SHE IS? DO YOU, DOG?
HUUNH!
THIS DOG DOESN'T TALK, EH? LOCK HIM IN THE STORAGE ROOMS BELOW THE KEEP!
HE MIGHT NOT TALK, BUT WE'LL MAKE HIM YELP.
ANTONIO, NO!
PLEASE! I CALLED HIM HERE TO SIT WITH ME. HE'S DONE NOTHING WRONG!
I'LL DEAL WITH YOU LATER, SISTER.
SIR, THIS IS THE MAN RESPONSIBLE FOR THE PERFORMERS.

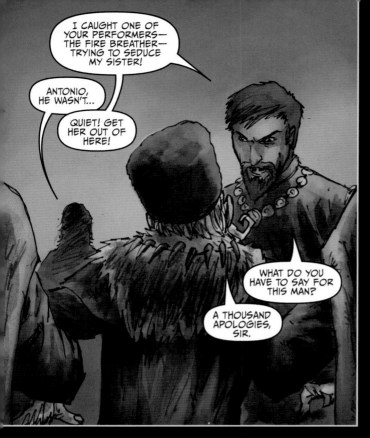

I CAUGHT ONE OF YOUR PERFORMERS—THE FIRE BREATHER—TRYING TO SEDUCE MY SISTER!

ANTONIO, HE WASN'T...

QUIET! GET HER OUT OF HERE!

WHAT DO YOU HAVE TO SAY FOR THIS MAN?

A THOUSAND APOLOGIES, SIR.

A THOUSAND IS NOT ENOUGH! THROW HIM IN THE STORAGE ROOM WITH THE DOG.

WHY WONT YOU LISTEN TO ME? THESE MEN HAVE DONE NOTHING WRONG.

WE'RE HEADING SOUTH, TO THE WINTER PALACE TONIGHT. YOU HAVE NO CHOICE BUT TO LET THEM GO, SO WHY BE SO CRUEL?

YOU'RE RIGHT, SISTER. I KNOW I CAN'T HOLD THEM LONG. I JUST WANT TO FRIGHTEN THEM. TO LET THEM KNOW THAT THIS KIND OF BEHAVIOR WON'T BE TOLERATED.

I WILL UNLOCK THE DOOR TO THE CELLAR AND LET THEM LEAVE AS SOON AS WE ARE ON OUR WAY.

YOU HAVE MY WORD.

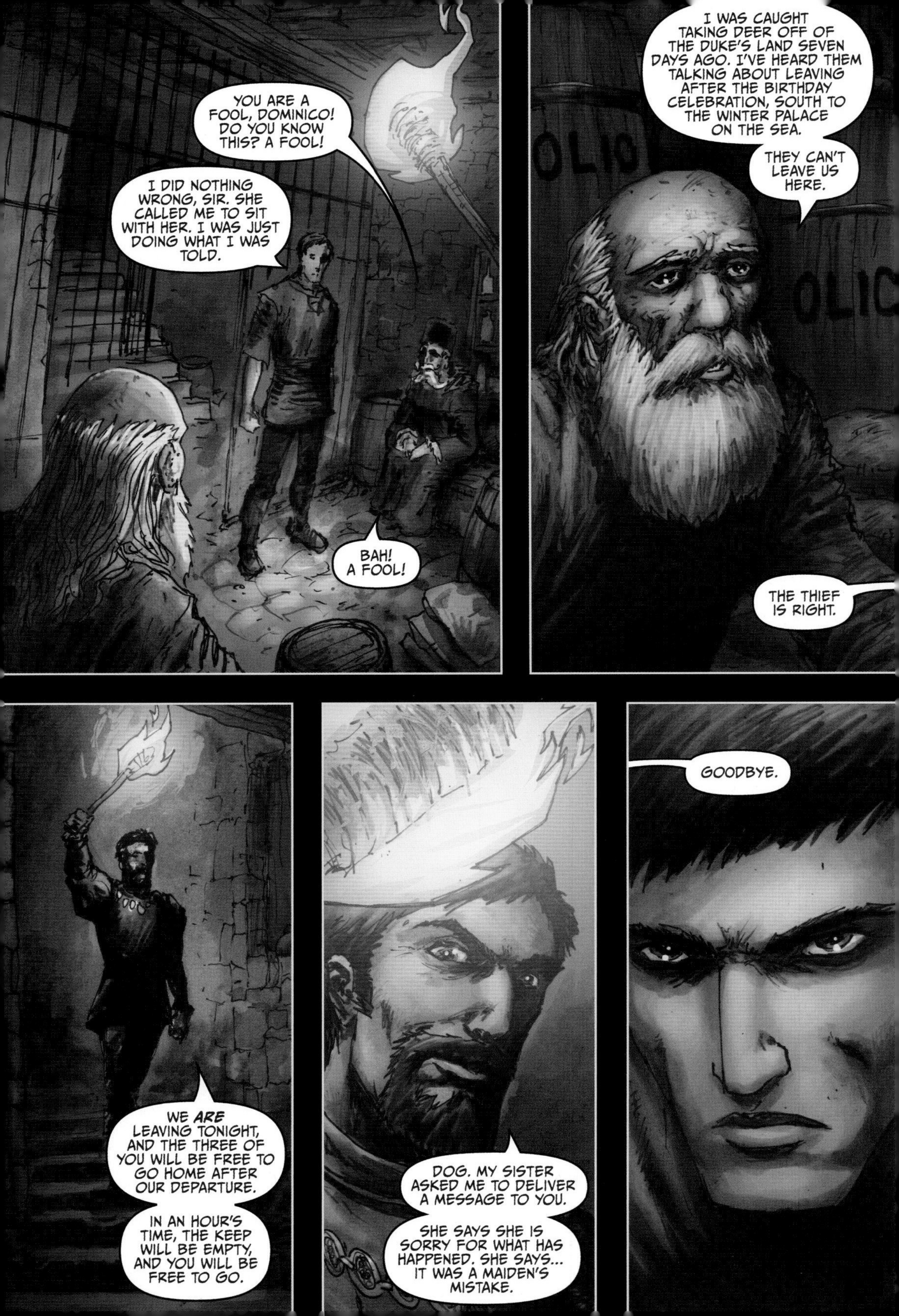
YOU ARE A FOOL, DOMINICO! DO YOU KNOW THIS? A FOOL!
I DID NOTHING WRONG, SIR. SHE CALLED ME TO SIT WITH HER. I WAS JUST DOING WHAT I WAS TOLD.
BAH! A FOOL!
I WAS CAUGHT TAKING DEER OFF OF THE DUKE'S LAND SEVEN DAYS AGO. I'VE HEARD THEM TALKING ABOUT LEAVING AFTER THE BIRTHDAY CELEBRATION, SOUTH TO THE WINTER PALACE ON THE SEA.
THEY CAN'T LEAVE US HERE.
OLIO
OLIC
THE THIEF IS RIGHT.
WE *ARE* LEAVING TONIGHT, AND THE THREE OF YOU WILL BE FREE TO GO HOME AFTER OUR DEPARTURE.
IN AN HOUR'S TIME, THE KEEP WILL BE EMPTY, AND YOU WILL BE FREE TO GO.
DOG. MY SISTER ASKED ME TO DELIVER A MESSAGE TO YOU.
SHE SAYS SHE IS SORRY FOR WHAT HAS HAPPENED. SHE SAYS... IT WAS A MAIDEN'S MISTAKE.
GOODBYE.

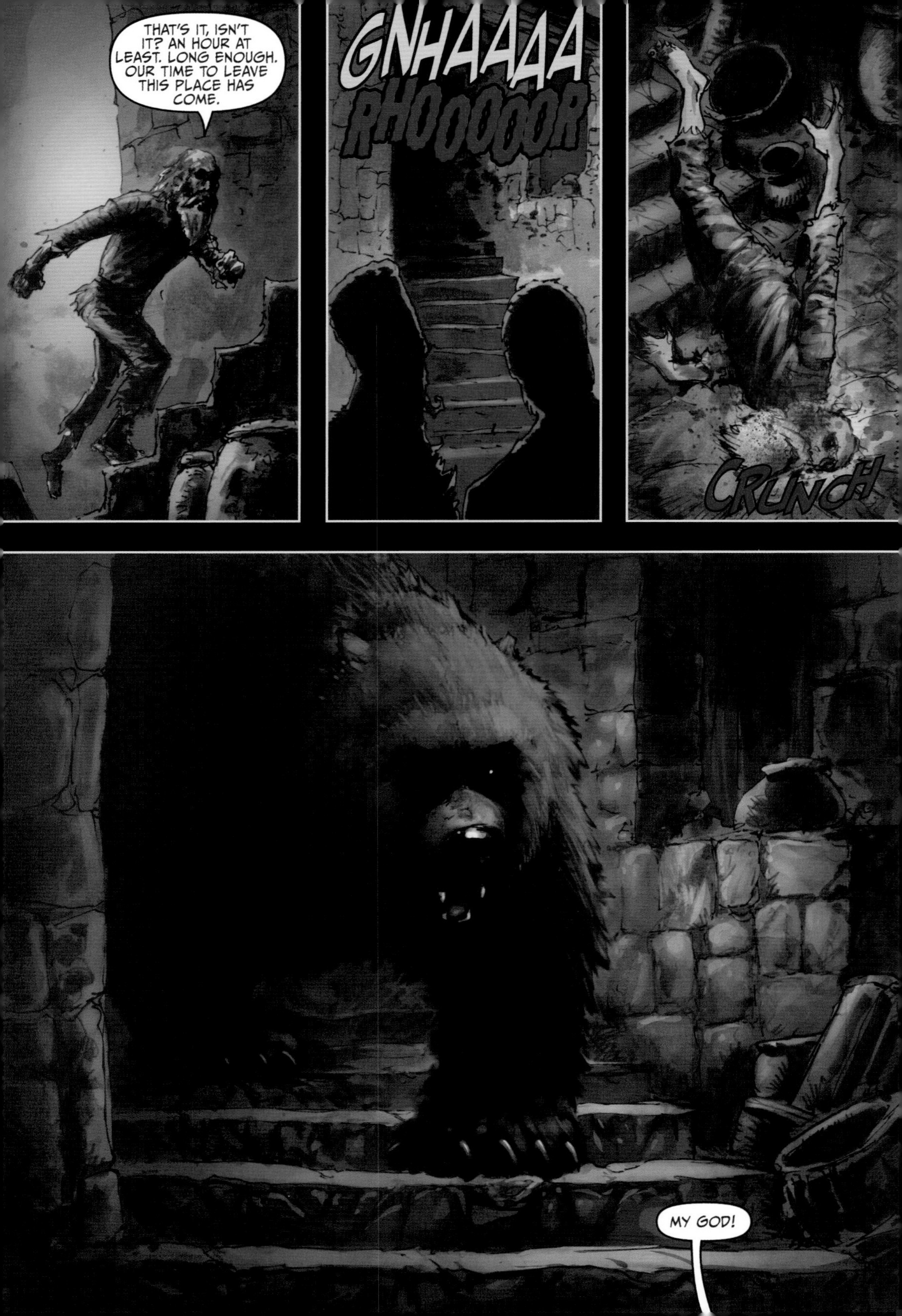
THAT'S IT, ISN'T IT? AN HOUR AT LEAST. LONG ENOUGH. OUR TIME TO LEAVE THIS PLACE HAS COME.
GNHAAAA
RHOOOOOR
CRUNCH
MY GOD!

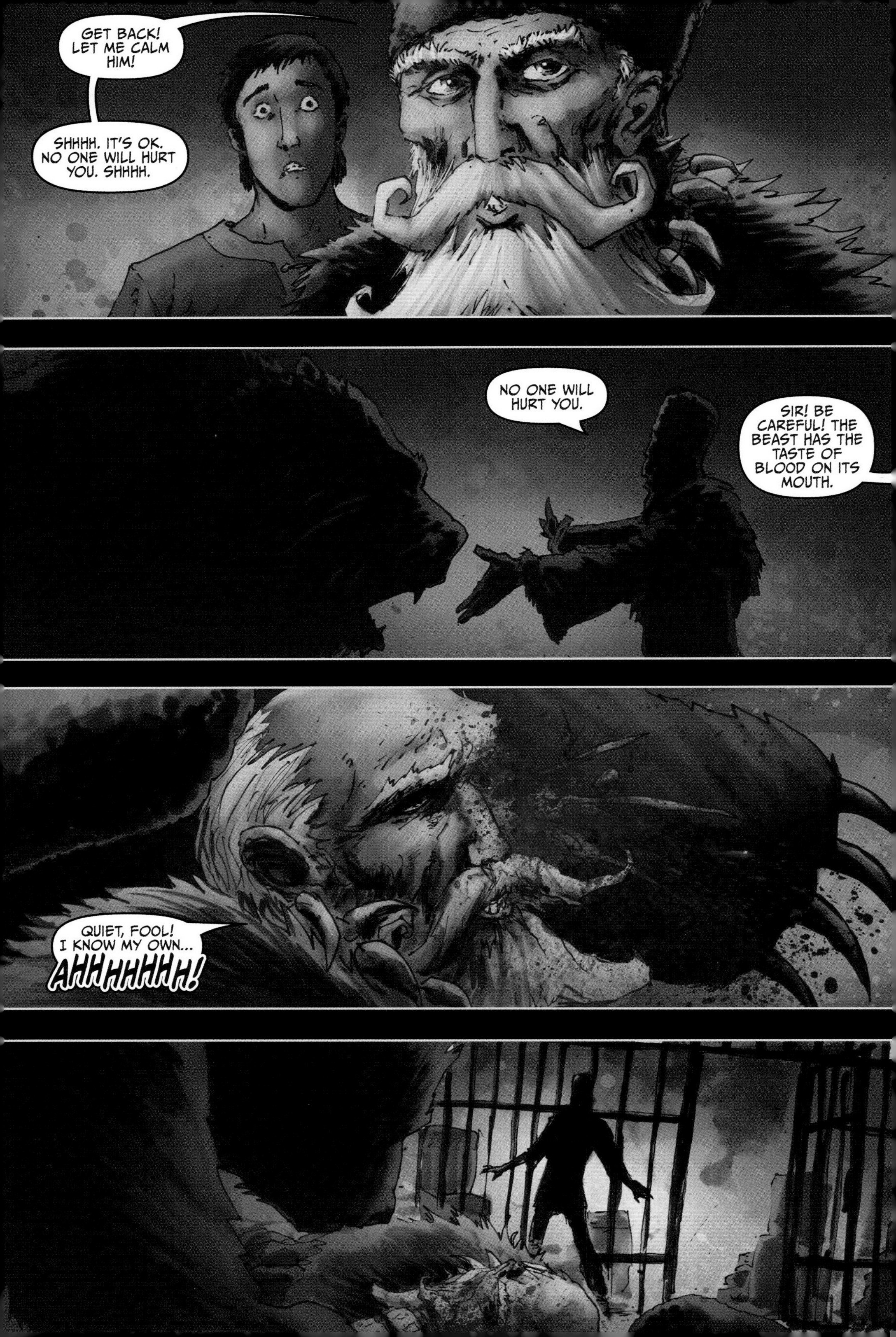
GET BACK! LET ME CALM HIM!
SHHHH. IT'S OK. NO ONE WILL HURT YOU. SHHHH.
NO ONE WILL HURT YOU.
SIR! BE CAREFUL! THE BEAST HAS THE TASTE OF BLOOD ON ITS MOUTH.
QUIET, FOOL! I KNOW MY OWN...
AHHHHHHH!

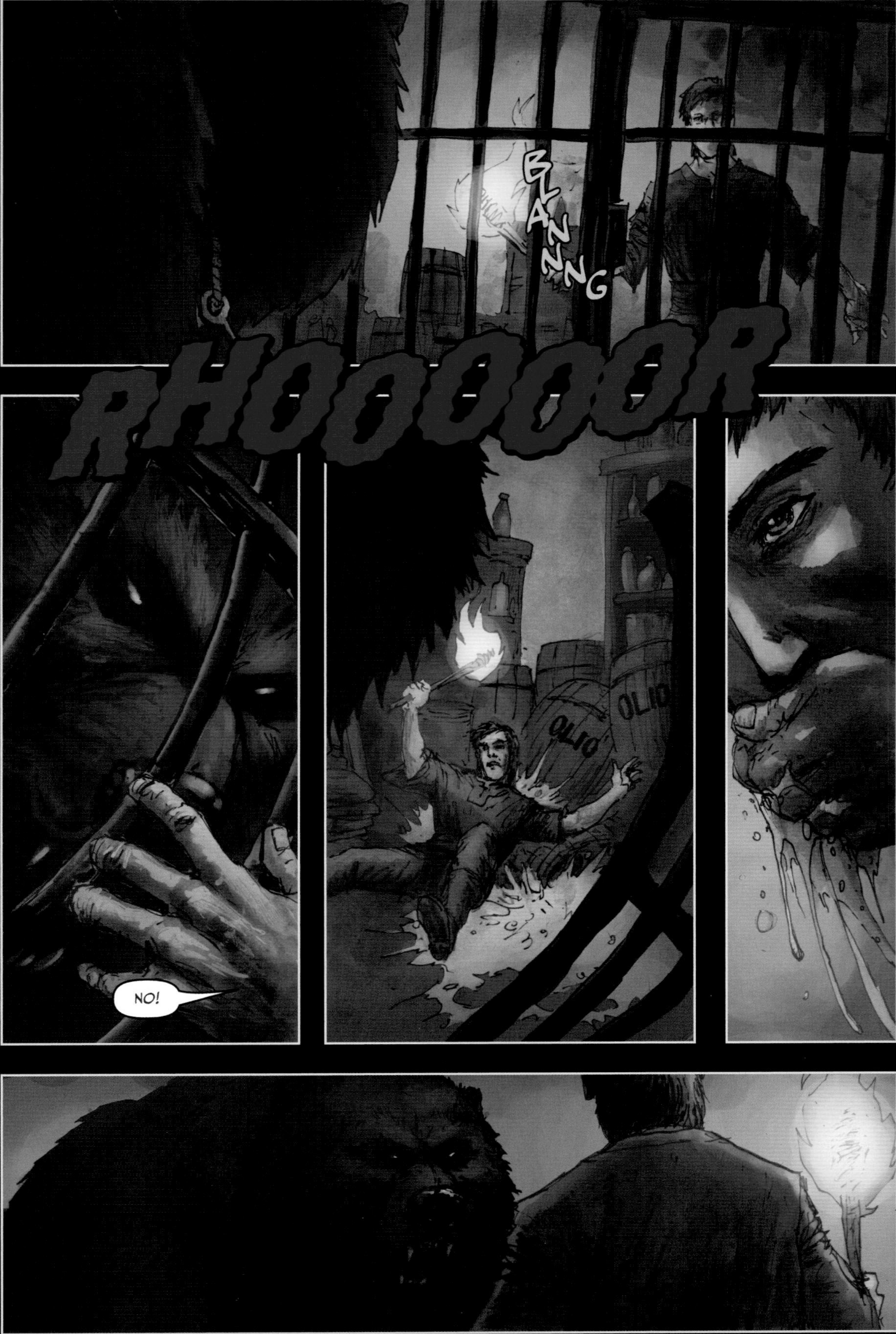
BLANNNG
RHOOOOR
NO!
OLIO
OLIO

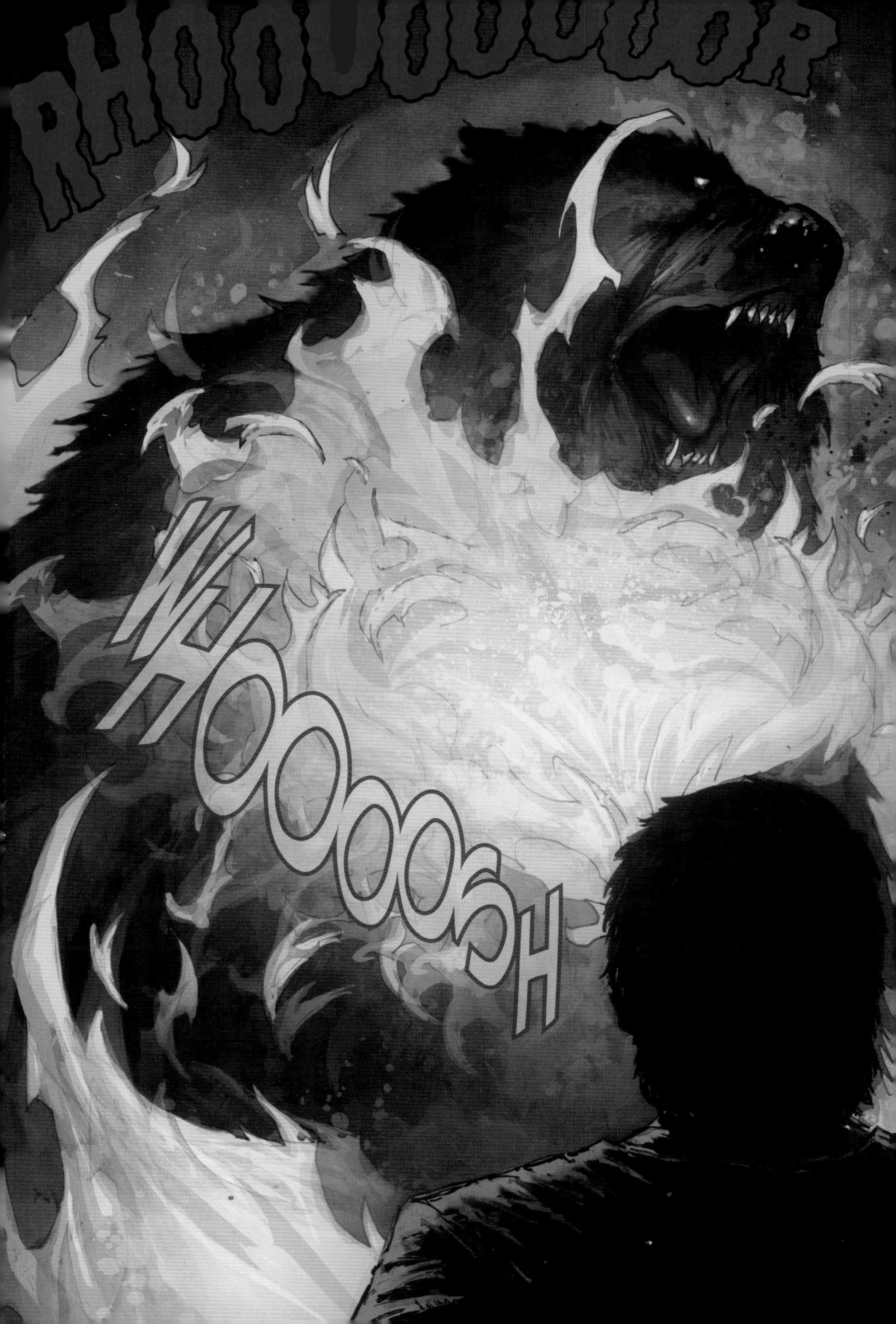
RHOOUUUUOR
WHOOOOOSH

RHOOOOOR
RHOOOOOR

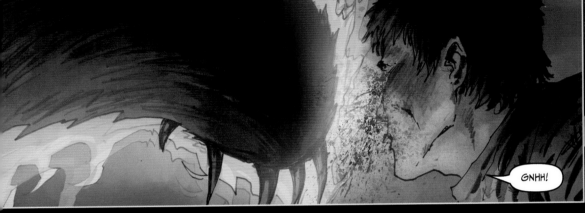

GNHH!

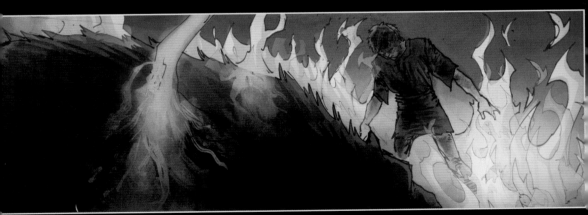

"THAT WAS THE DUKE'S SON FOR YOU..."

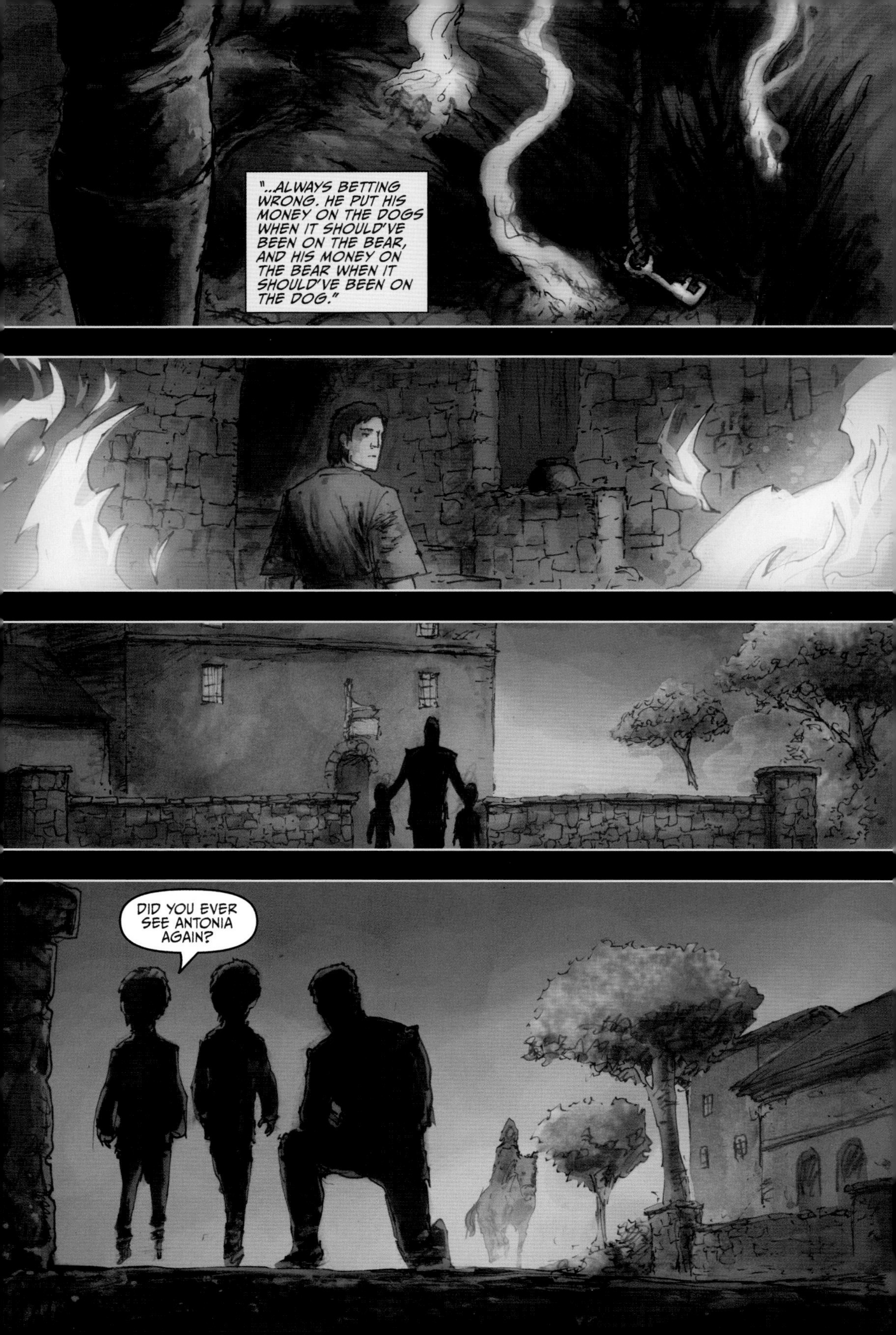
"...ALWAYS BETTING WRONG. HE PUT HIS MONEY ON THE DOGS WHEN IT SHOULD'VE BEEN ON THE BEAR, AND HIS MONEY ON THE BEAR WHEN IT SHOULD'VE BEEN ON THE DOG."
DID YOU EVER SEE ANTONIA AGAIN?

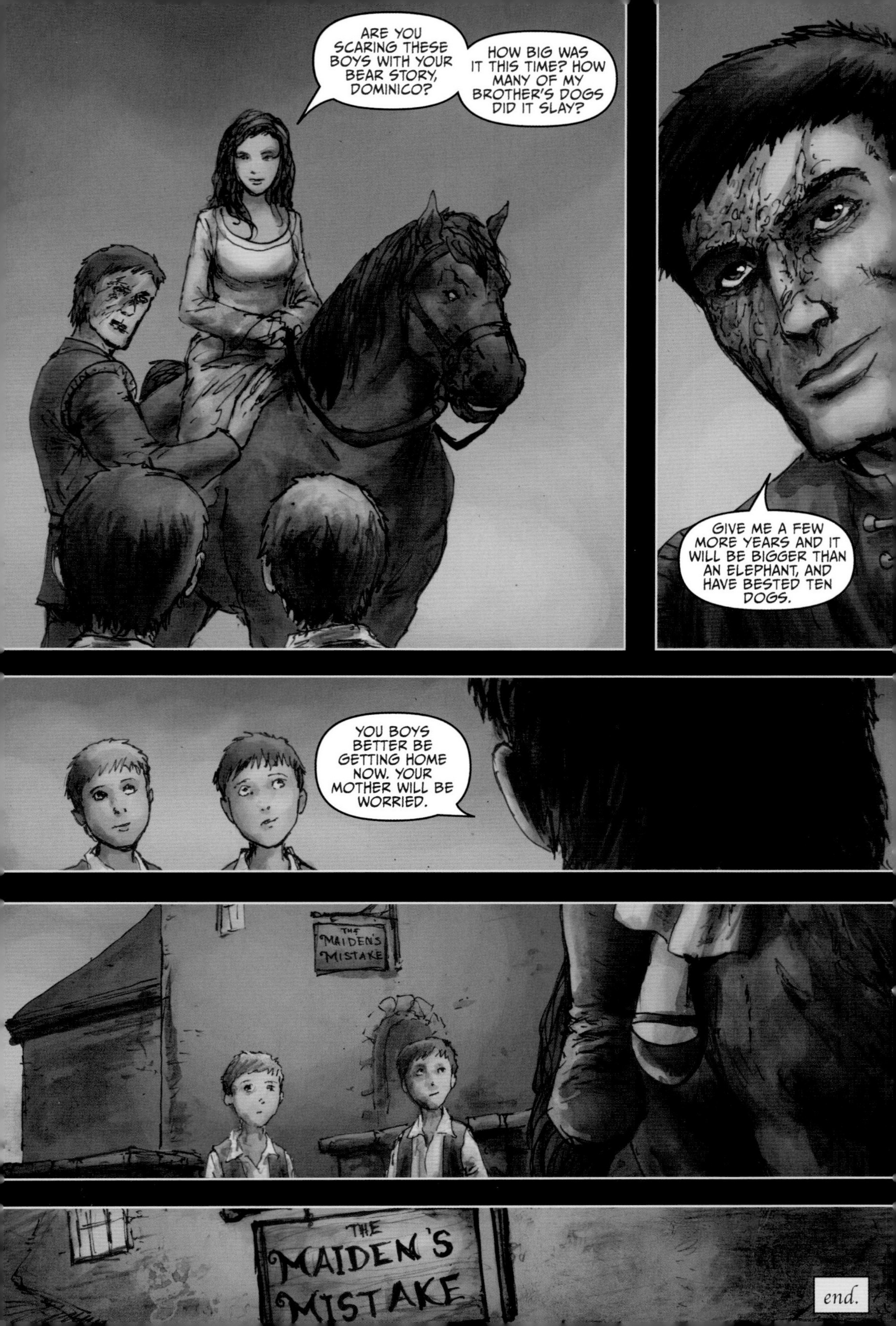
ARE YOU SCARING THESE BOYS WITH YOUR BEAR STORY, DOMINICO?
HOW BIG WAS IT THIS TIME? HOW MANY OF MY BROTHER'S DOGS DID IT SLAY?
GIVE ME A FEW MORE YEARS AND IT WILL BE BIGGER THAN AN ELEPHANT, AND HAVE BESTED TEN DOGS.
YOU BOYS BETTER BE GETTING HOME NOW. YOUR MOTHER WILL BE WORRIED.
THE MAIDEN'S MISTAKE
THE MAIDEN'S MISTAKE
end.